I0720102

LIANI

WENDELYN VEGA

Copyright © 2023 by Wendelyn Vega

All rights reserved.

No part of this book may be reproduced in any form or by any electronic or mechanical means, including information storage and retrieval systems, without written permission from the author, except for the use of brief quotations in a book review.

For permission requests, contact:

info@wendelynvega.com

Visit the author's website at WendelynVega.com.

Cover by Wendelyn Vega.

This is a work of fiction. Names, characters, places, and incidents are the products of the author's imagination or are used fictitiously. Any resemblance to actual persons, living or dead, businesses, companies, events, or locales is entirely coincidental.

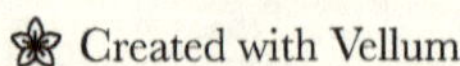 Created with Vellum

To my brothers. Your big sister is always here for you!
-WV

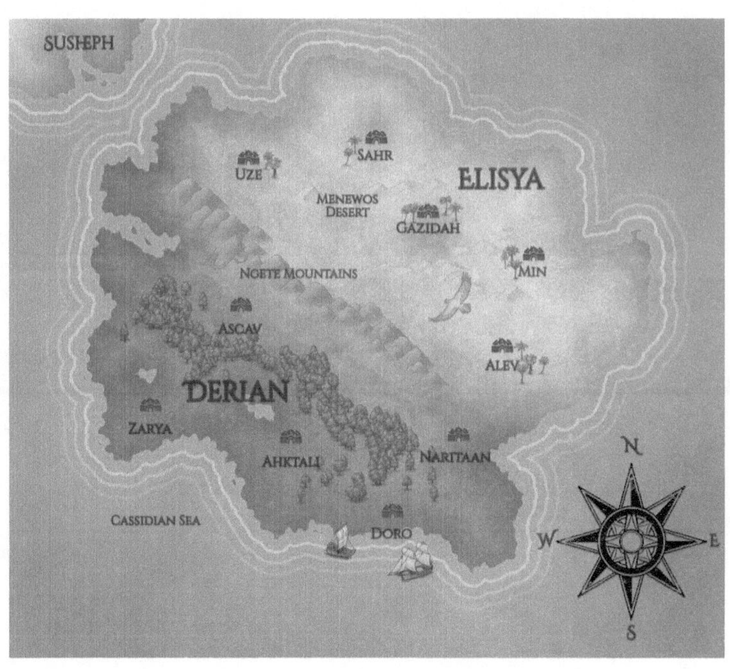

SUSHEPH
ELISYA
SAHR
UZE
MENEWOS
DESERT
GAZIDAH
MIN
NGETE MOUNTAINS
ASCAV
ALEV
DERIAN
ZARYA
NARITAAN
AHKTALI
CASSIDIAN SEA
DORO
N
W
E
S

GLOSSARY

- Aba: Elisyan word for father
- Datu: crown prince
- Derian: the country to the south of Elisya, also the common language spoken there
- Diyan: crown princess
- Enipae: a Derian nobleman
- Hara: a high princess, daughter or granddaughter of an emperor
- Ima: Elisyan word for mother
- Malik: ruler of a kingdom
- Menewos: a large desert in central Elisya
- Obipae: a Derian noblewoman
- Paidashar: a town in northern Ragien
- Paidashar Fadir: Satrap Paykhan's winter home
- Ragien: a province of Uze
- Ragienige: the capital of Ragien
- Ranat: the currency of Elisya
- Sali: noble princess, a princess of lower rank
- Satrap: ruler of a province
- Satrapha: a satrap's wife

- Suan: noble prince, a prince of lower rank
- Shaha: empress
- Uze: a kingdom in Elisya
- Uzepige: the capital of Uze

CHAPTER 1

Lia

My earliest memory isn't one of fire and falling, of pain and fear and sorrow too great for a child. That's what people believe it is. That's what I tell them it is when Aba has me speak to small, trusted bands of slaves to encourage them. But that's a lie. It's one of my memories—a strong one that weaves itself into my nightmares, forcing me awake drenched in sweat and tears. But when I soothe myself back to sleep, I remember my earliest memory is actually of sitting on my ima's lap, dangling a flower in front of my baby brother's face while she sings us a lullaby.

I hum that lullaby while I braid ribbon to decorate my charges' hair, my legs splayed out in front of me in the grass outside the satrap's winter house. An early summer breeze catches the grass and grazes my legs, drawing my attention outward to where two children play in the sunshine. My schedule is consistent, and every day, when I finish my morning household chores, I keep watch over the youngest children of the noble family we serve. Nalkendi and Khanda have no work to do, and if they're not taking their lessons, they're in everyone else's way. So it's my job to keep them occupied.

"Stop!" Nalkendi screeches at her younger brother, who has been pulling his sister's braids and running away for the past ten minutes. Often, Nalkendi will play along, but today she's being sensitive. She turns to me. "Lia, make him stop!"

I beckon to Khanda. "Let's put on your crown."

Khanda runs back over and kneels in front of me, suddenly solemn. I wrap the braided ribbon around his head and tie it at the back. When I've finished, Khanda stands and wags a finger at Nalkendi. "Now I am the malik, and you can't challenge me."

Nalkendi runs over and kneels in front of me, gesturing for me to crown her with a ribbon, too. "We'll see about that!"

The two of them chase each other around the outer yard of their parent's winter home until their mother's handmaiden comes for them.

"It's time to prepare for dinner," she tells them.

It will take a couple of hours to get them clean and dressed appropriately, but that's not my responsibility. I stand slowly and brush the dirt from my tunic. I need to wash up myself before I go to work in the kitchen. My left leg is aching today— usually a sign that bad weather is approaching. I survey the horizon, but no dark clouds catch my attention. The sky is clear blue, with only wisps of white obscuring it. Still, summer storms come up quickly, and my body doesn't lie.

I walk over to the well and clean my hands, arms, and face, letting them dry in the sun. My mother doesn't abide dirtiness in her kitchen, and taking care of the satrap's children is no excuse. I favor my aching leg a bit as I walk—not enough to slow me so much I'd get punished, but enough that walking doesn't do any extra damage. For a long time, Aba would insist that eventually, when I got older, I'd be able to run and play like other children, but when I reached adulthood, he stopped claiming that would be the case. Still, I don't have much need to run, and it's considered undignified for an adult, anyway.

The kitchen is in the east wing of the house, and the door sits open since the air is getting warmer and the kitchen no longer needs to help heat the wing. The aroma of stewed spices meets me before my eyes adjust to the dimmer light. Ima is inside leaning over a roast, testing to be sure it's been cooked through. This is her kitchen, and she lets nothing less than perfect leave it. When I enter, she waves me over without looking.

"Lia, set the table. The satrap is having a guest, and we only have three hours to be sure everything is ready."

A guest? A herald had arrived earlier this morning and spoken to Satrap Paykhan. That must have been what he was reporting. A guest means extra place settings, and it also means we'll use the finer serving dishes and linens. I pull the silver dishes from the cupboards where they're stored, and one of Ima's kitchen maids helps me carry them into the dining hall. Filled with gratitude, I smile at her. I've been doing this work most of my life, but I still haven't managed the grace it takes to carry armfuls of dishes across the wing without dropping half of them.

The table is long and low, formed from one piece of wood and surrounded by comfortable stools. Together, we set the table and make sure it's beautiful, draping the linens gracefully, placing a platter at each place at the table, and filling any gaps with flowers and lamps. We don't talk. Only the thudding of metal and ceramic against wood breaks the silence. Ima will inspect it all when we're done. Then Satrap Paykhan's chief steward will inspect it after her. Since there's a guest, everything must be in place early.

When we're finished, I help Ima plate all the dishes that will be served. We put three stews into bowls, place two roasts on platters, and stack tray after tray with piping-hot flatbread.

An assortment of spiced fruit and vegetables and several carafes of wine finish the meal. Chief Steward Goran enters the room just as Ima places the last dish—candied oranges from Susheph—onto the table.

We wait against the dining room wall to give him space to complete his inspection. Ima is closest to the entrance, and I wedge myself between her and her head kitchen maid, hoping to avoid being seen. Chief Steward Goran has never liked me, and he's never happy when I've been involved in a table setting. He says I make everything broken just like I am. Aba has cursed him many times under his breath for saying things like that.

"You may be clumsy, Lia, but you aren't broken," he always tells me. "You just weren't born for this life."

Chief Steward Goran crosses to the other side of the room and catches my eye. He frowns, and I try to sink into the wall. Ima moves closer to me and raises her head proudly. If anyone can stand up to the chief steward, it's the head cook, and they both know it. Goran's frown deepens, but he says nothing. Instead, he leans over a silver tray of vegetables, running his finger across its edge as if searching for cracks or dents. He won't find any, though. I didn't drop anything today. He moves on.

The inspection drags on, and Ima taps her foot. When Goran is close to the end of the table, she says, "The evening is chilly. Would the satrap prefer the curtains to be drawn?"

The curtains are already drawn, but we all know what she's really saying is that Goran should hurry before the food gets cold.

He purses his lips in disapproval, but after a moment, he nods. "This is an adequate arrangement for the satrap and his guests. Please take your places." He gives me a pointed look. "And put Lia in the furthest corner. The satrap and the imperial inspector will arrive shortly."

My breath catches in my throat at the guest's identity, and I steal a glance at Ima. I need to stay here? Can't someone else do it? Ima's face is inscrutable, but she meets my eyes and shakes her head slightly. I choke down a protest. Slaves do what they're told. But the imperial inspector is here. I can't be seen by him. Not yet.

Goran leaves the room, and each of the servants moves to take up their position around the room, but I can't bring myself to move.

"Isn't there someone else?" I ask, my voice barely more than a whisper.

Ima grabs my wrist, pulling me gently behind her. She positions me in the far right corner, in the shadow of a tall potted plant. I let her move me around. When the others are far enough away, she touches my face. Her expression calms my racing heart.

"You'll be fine."

That's all she says before she goes back into the kitchen to keep the rest of the food warm in case anything needs to be replaced, leaving me to face a man I pray won't recognize me.

CHAPTER 2

As soon as Ima is out of sight, my pulse picks up speed again. I've lived here at Paidashar Fadir, the winter house of Satrap Paykhan Nehim, most of my life, and he has never had a guest with a rank higher than his brother's—the disgraced malik. But the imperial inspector…

What if he recognizes me? Aba says he saw my father a few times—my birth father. He says I resemble him. What if I resemble him too much? Suppose the imperial inspector enters the dining room and discovers the face of the old datu, the former crown prince, lurking in the shadows of a plant? What if he tries to remove my slave's cuffs? Would the satrap be able to stop him from taking me away before I could act on Aba's plan? Would he even try?

As soon as I think of my cuffs, my wrists burn. I know it's just my mind playing cruel tricks, but I imagine the golden tattoos beneath my cuffs turning into fire. It's a painful irony that the institution that ruins my family's life saved mine.

I only see the tattoos once a year when Aba removes my cuffs to resize them. He always does it in private, just in case. There are few laws that everyone knows, but one of those few is that golden tattoos are illegal except for the imperial family. If someone saw them, the authorities would arrest me, and if they were fake, they would cut off my hands. But if someone authenticated them—as I know they would—I would probably be killed before anyone found out. I'm the only person from the old emperor's family who is still alive. Everyone else was killed twelve years ago, before the civil war.

A commotion in the hallway is a signal that the noble family is approaching. Khanda bounds into the room first, halting abruptly as his oldest sister Vroni enters behind him. At eighteen, she's several years into adulthood, and she frowns at her youngest brother, signaling that he should slow down. Normally she wouldn't care, but since they have a guest as important as the imperial inspector, I'm sure she wants Khanda to be more careful.

Khanda sighs and plods to his assigned place at the table, on the far corner near me, where he remains standing. He gives me a grin, and I twirl my finger to show that he should turn around. He frowns, disappointed. Vroni places herself at her own seat, and she too stands behind it. No one will sit until the satrap and the imperial inspector do.

Enra enters the room behind Vroni. He notices me almost immediately, as usual. Enra is only a year older than me. Vroni is not that much older than me, either. In a different life, we might have been friends. I would have been their equal, their superior, even. Aba says I still am. Sometimes, in my most foolish moments, I wish I could be close to them. Enra especially. He's always been kind to me, despite my station and obvious physical imperfections. For a while, when I was a silly child, I imagined what it would be like if I were still a princess. Enra was my prince in my dreams. He and Vroni used to play with Jorra, Atar, and me when we were younger, but when we became adults, that changed quickly, and I put my foolish imaginings aside. Still, Enra gives me a genuine smile as if he's greeting me, saying, "You're here today?"

I bend into a bow as politely as I can, trying not to let on that anything is wrong. But I must fail, because he gives me a quizzical eyebrow-raise before he turns his back to me at his seat. Since there's a guest, he doesn't ask me anything. For a moment, I worry that if Enra can tell something is wrong, the imperial inspector will tell too. But Enra has known me much of my life. If Juae is smiling on me today, this imperial inspector may never have seen me or the old datu before.

Nalkendi and her mother, Satrapha Edab, glide into the room. Nalkendi is beaming and holding her mother's hand. A necklace that is only slightly too big for her graces her neck. Satrapha Edab must have let her wear it for the occasion. Behind them, seven noblemen of varying ranks enter the dining room. They all know where they should go. The last people to come into the room are Satrap Paykhan and the imperial inspector, side by side and deep in conversation, and Chief Steward Goran, who takes his place at the room's entrance.

My breath catches in my throat, and I attempt to sink even further into the shadow of the plant.

Satrap Paykhan is wearing a frown, the kind he has when he's deep in thought. We've all seen him wander the halls of his home with that expression. It isn't cruel, but it lets us know not to disturb him. The imperial inspector seems unconcerned as he continues with whatever subject he'd been discussing. When they reach their seats, though, he says, "Let us continue this conversation later. I look forward to enjoying the meal you've prepared for us."

Satrap Paykhan's pensive expression changes to a pleasant smile faster than I've ever seen. "Yes, of course."

The satrap takes the head of the table and the inspector sits at the highest place of honor to his right, allowing the rest of the household and guests to take their seats. After the Satrap asks the inspector's traveling priest to pray, they begin their meal.

The conversation is lively, but I don't pay attention to its contents. Instead, I study the faces of the inspector's retinue from the relative safety of my plant. None of them are familiar, but I stare at each of them just in case, being sure to turn my eyes away before they notice.

I don't remember much of my life in the palace, but then, I've seen no one from there in all the years I've been gone. What would I do if any of them were familiar? I would have been four years old the last time any of them might have seen me. And after the fire and my fall, they shouldn't be able to recognize me, anyway. I don't know why that's not reassuring.

I study the imperial inspector last. He too is unfamiliar, but I recognize the air of importance he carries. While everyone converses, they keep one ear and one eye trained to his seat, waiting for any sign that they need to turn their full attention to him. I have few memories of the datu, my birth father, but one thing I remember is that air, the draw that his influence has and its power over everyone in a room. I remember when he visited the nursery—nothing I did could draw my nurses' or my mother's attention from him. And nothing I did could draw his attention to me. The contrast between him and Aba is sharp. I don't have to fight Aba for his own attention.

The imperial inspector glances in my direction, and I pull my eyes away, but not fast enough. I feel his eyes linger on me for a moment before their weight goes away. When it does, I turn my attention to the conversation. He won't ask about me, right?

He doesn't. Instead, I hear the end of his sentence directed at Satrap Paykhan. "The emperor will reward your loyalty. He looks forward to joining his family with yours."

The inspector's eyes drift to Vroni, who stiffens. His gaze

must be palpable to everyone else, too. Vroni is engaged to the emperor's grandson. Everyone in this household knows it was a show of support, a way for Satrap Paykhan to secure his position and save his family's life. Emperor Pakel was scouring the empire of anyone loyal to the old emperor, and Satrap Paykhan's own brother, Malik Tusun, fled the empire rather than submit. So the satrap had to do something drastic, several drastic things, as Aba explains it, and betrothing his daughter to the emperor's family was one of those things.

While Malik Tusun had three daughters, two are already married, and the third is young. And anyway, why would the emperor trust the malik enough to bring his youngest daughter into the palace? He already knows where Malik Tusun's loyalties lie. But Satrap Paykhan ensured that his loyalty could be compromised, ultimately saving himself, his family, and his brother.

It saved us—saved me, though none of them know it. When the malik returned, the emperor spared his life, though he took the malik's power and gave it to the imperial inspector. This imperial inspector. The malik is a prisoner in his palace, but his family still holds his right to rule. They will transfer it to Enra when Malik Tusun is gone. Satrap Paykhan was blessed to have two sons—one to succeed him and one to succeed his brother.

Both boys turn their attention to the inspector as he speaks to Vroni. "The prince is eager to meet you. I am glad to report that his excitement is justified. He is a blessed man indeed. You must be overjoyed."

It sounds like a command. Vroni blushes, and the hairs on Enra's neck bristle.

Satrap Paykhan replies in Vroni's stead. "I'm sure she is. She's just absorbing the news. When did you learn—"

"The day I departed," the inspector answers. "It's my honor to bring your invitation myself."

My breath catches in my throat as I follow the conversation. Invitation to what?

"We are honored, of course," the satrap says, "But it is little notice."

The inspector shrugs. "Well, instead of transitioning to your summer home, you can transition to Gazidah." He dabs his face with a handkerchief. "I wish I could attend. It will be a festival for the ages."

A festival for the ages. The satrap and his family are going to Gazidah.

We knew this would happen. Aba has been talking about it since the last maliks fighting the civil war in the south surrendered. It would only be a matter of time until the emperor consolidated his power through either a show of force or a show of peace. Aba had wished it would be a show of force—that would give people more of a reason to retaliate. But a festival is a show of peace. What does that mean to him? What does it mean for us?

The conversation shifts, and I want to run to the smithy, to see Aba, to ask him what a peaceful festival means. But I can't leave.

Several gazes move toward me, and I stiffen in the shadow of my plant. I return to the conversation in time to hear Satrapha Edab say, "—your mother."

What had she said to me? Enra glances toward the kitchen. They want me to get Ima. My hands are still behind me, against the wall, and I have to force myself away from the shadows. I lower my head as I cross the room, to keep the inspector and his people from seeing me as much as to show respect to the household. When I cross the threshold into the hall, I hurry to the kitchen. My leg still aches, and I rub it when I arrive.

Ima leans over a pot of warm spiced wine that will be served after the meal, its sugary sweetness overpowering every other scent in the kitchen, but she turns when she hears me. My face must betray me because she asks. "Lia, is something wrong?"

"They've asked for you."

She nods and steps back, an attendant taking her place at the pot. She puts an arm around my shoulders and turns me toward the entrance to take me back to the dining room with her. "Is that all?"

I shake my head quickly. We're already in the hall. I have to tell her before she goes inside, before they can hear us. "The emperor is holding a festival."

Ima is about to say something, but we've arrived at the dining room, so she quickly makes her face impassive.

When we go inside, I shuffle back to my place in the corner, and Ima steps to the side of the entrance, opposite Chief Steward Goran. "You sent for me, your highness?"

Satrap Paykhan nods. "Yes, Tasilla. Inspector Nesone has brought us wonderful news, and I thought to share it with you and Goran so you may prepare."

Ima is respectful yet appropriately interested, and the Satrap seems satisfied. "Emperor Pakel is hosting a festival for visiting dignitaries, and all his maliks and satraps will be in attendance. My dear Vroni—" he gestures to his daughter, "will be married during the festival as well."

The satrap pauses, so Ima says. "Many blessings, your highness. That is wonderful news."

Satrap Paykhan nods. "Yes. We will be in Gazidah for a longer season, so we'll leave the winter palace early. Set the house's affairs in order. We leave in two weeks."

Ima bows. "Yes, your highness."

She meets my eyes before she leaves as if to reassure me, to let me know everything will be fine. The satrap and his family leave every year for the summer. Going to Gazidah this time makes no difference. I can almost hear her speaking. But the knowledge isn't reassuring. I sink even further into the shadow of my giant fern and count the seconds until the end of the meal.

CHAPTER 3

Enra

Dinner lasted far too long. Inspector Nesone is a brute and a bore, and it took all my strength to keep from throwing my food at him when he started ogling Vroni. His men are no different. Why are each of Emperor Pakel's subordinates the worst type of person? They have no semblance of anything approaching decorum.

Lia's anxiety was palpable. She was almost more noticeable hiding herself away in the shadows, but Inspector Nesone had no eyes for anything other than the meal and my sister. Lia had nothing to worry about.

As we leave the dining room, I slow my stride to keep pace with Vroni. Once we're in the hall, Aba and the inspector retire to Aba's study, and the inspector's retinue return to the guest common room. When they're out of sight, I turn to Vroni, pausing under a decorative archway and blocking her way.

"Are you all right?"

She has her hands clasped in front of her, but she loosens her grip and relaxes her shoulders. "We knew this was coming."

I shake my head. "That doesn't answer my question."

I may be her younger brother, but I'm the oldest son. My family is as much my responsibility as it is my father's. Vroni shrugs. "I hope Emperor Pakel's grandson is more of a… nobleman than the inspector."

I have my doubts, but I don't want to worry Vroni with them. Instead, I accompany her to her room. To get to the women's wing, we have to pass the inspector's suite, and Vroni shouldn't have to pass there alone. Nothing is likely to happen, but I'll go with her just in case.

The walk isn't long since we take a shortcut across the courtyard garden in the center of the house. The doors to the guest suite are open, and raucous laughter spills out into the garden. Vroni and I are silent, though. The laughter lightens as we pass, and several people are watching us, but they return to their entertainment when we're out of sight.

Vroni sighs. "Sometimes I wonder what life was like before."

I know what she means, and I nod. "I do too, but Aba says it wasn't much different."

"We weren't under as much scrutiny."

"We weren't paying as much attention, either."

That was the problem. No one was paying attention as some maliks grew unhappy. No one was paying attention when the politicians started speaking under their breaths. And no one was paying attention when the soldiers disguised as party-goers' slaves slipped into the palace and killed the royal family. Only one person survived because my father saw to it. And she doesn't know that I know who she is.

Aba told me the truth three years ago, when I reached adulthood on my fourteenth birthday. We were at our summer home, a sprawling palace in the south that makes our winter home seem like a hovel. I like it better here, though. Before we went to my celebratory dinner, Aba called me into his study. I held my head high as I passed through the corridors, receiving congratulations from all our guests as I went. The halls were bright and full of people, but when I opened Aba's study door, a dark chasm greeted me. A sense of foreboding stalled me in the doorway, but Aba beckoned me in. I entered and shut the door behind me, shutting out the light and noise of celebration.

Several alcoves in the study's walls were lit with candles, and dancing light bounced off the tile in the alcoves and the floor, but it didn't do much to brighten the room. Instead, it made the room feel eerie and magical. I held my breath as I approached. Aba sat at a table near a window. I straightened my back and strode toward him. I was becoming a man that day, so Aba wouldn't see me acting like a child.

When I reached his side, he didn't greet me. He didn't even look at me. Instead, he focused on a sealed scroll on the table. The silence was unbearable, so I broke it first.

"You called for me, Aba?"

He nodded, finally facing me. "I must share some things with you today. It is time for you to learn to bear the weight of my mantle."

"Your mantle?"

I thought he had to be confused. I was—and still am—the heir to my uncle's throne. Uncle Tusun is a malik, the king of our territory of Uze. He has no sons, so he chose me to succeed him. It was his mantle of leadership I would take, not my father's. My younger brother Khanda is his heir.

But Aba nodded again. "Your brother is heir to my title, but you must be heir to my secrets. These cannot fall to him."

I stared at him in silence, my heart pounding in my throat. Aba was entrusting me with something important, and even though I didn't know what it was yet, I wasn't sure I was ready for it.

Aba tapped a finger against the scroll on the table. "We

have been under Emperor Pakel's rule for most of your life. But there was another emperor before him. What do you know of what became of him?"

"He was overthrown," I answered. "None of his lineage remains."

Aba shook his head. "None but one." His voice was so low I could barely hear it. "And it is my charge to protect her."

"Her?" My thoughts raced. A princess. Who was still alive, and where was Aba hiding her? How did she escape the attack?

Aba's hand fell on my shoulder, and he pulled me closer to him. "Hara Liani lives in our midst, in the lowest ranks of our household, where we can keep her safe from all scrutiny."

"Hara Liani..." I whispered as I put the truth together. "Lia—"

I glanced sharply at Aba, who gave me a terse nod. Lia, with whom I'd spent my winters chasing frogs. Lia, who took care of my younger siblings at our winter home. Lia, whose joints ached and whose hands and face carried the marks of fire. I knew Lia. She'd been my playmate as a child. We'd been close, at least, as close as a prince and a slave could be. How could she be the hara?

But Aba's nod confirmed it. So many questions swirled in my head, but I could only ask one. "Why?"

"There is power in knowing what others don't and even more in having what they don't," Aba answered. "As long as we have such a safeguard, we too will be safe, no matter what happens in Gazidah."

How was Lia a safeguard? She was a girl, the crown prince's daughter, and the crown prince's son was dead. Besides, she didn't even know who she was. Or did she?

"Does she—"

Aba silenced me with a gesture. "Yes, but we will discuss this more later."

A knock sounded on the door, and Aba called for the person to enter. It was the steward.

"Your highness, the celebration is prepared."

Aba put a hand on my shoulder. "Come, my son. We must not keep your guests waiting."

After that first conversation, he gave me the truth in waves. Over the years, Aba taught me how he kept his position as satrap after Uncle Tusun's dethroning, how he promised his firstborn daughter to the emperor, how he discovered Lia was the princess, and the steps he took to keep her safe all these years. And I learned why Aba kept Lia from knowing we knew the truth, and why I had to do the same. What I still don't quite understand is how she's a safeguard for us.

Vroni and I arrive at the entrance of the women's wing. I haven't been allowed inside since my coming of age, so Vroni opens the door.

She smiles at me. "Thank you, En."

"Of course." I smile back, but it feels hollow. When we return here from Gazidah, Vroni won't be with us. "Rest well."

When Vroni is safe inside, I start back to my rooms on the other side of the house. On a whim, I take the route through the outer courtyard, so I don't have to pass the guest wing again.

The outer courtyard is dimly lit by the light coming through the house's windows, and a shadowy figure crosses ahead of me. It's leaving the smithy, and I recognize the gait.

"Lia!" I call out.

She stops mid-step and turns toward me, her eyes fixed on the ground. "Yes, Suan?"

"Delivering your father's meal?"

Lia nods, still studying the dirt walkway. "One of the inspector's horses needed to be re-shoed."

I miss when she used to meet my eyes freely, but that was

when we were still children. I tilt my head at her. "He's a frightening man, isn't he?"

Lia glances at me. "Were you frightened, Suan?"

I take a step back in mock offense. "Me? Frightened? Of course not. But I couldn't help but notice you hiding in the shadows."

Her feet shuffle in the dirt, but I catch a hint of a smile on her face. "That's where Chief Steward Goran placed me."

I nod. "I see."

It seems Goran unwittingly did us a favor. I've never seen the old emperor or his family—other than Lia—but she might bear some resemblance, and the inspector might have known them. There's no need for Inspector Nesone to get curious.

Lia studies the dirt below our feet, and I resist the urge to tell her to raise her head. Royalty shouldn't cower, no matter their situation. But that would give me away. So instead of raising her head, I lower mine, bowing at the waist, forcing her to meet my eyes.

"You have nothing to fear from him. Aba and I protect you. All of you," I amend.

Lia nods. "Of course, Suan."

Satisfied at having received her affirmation, I leave. It's late, and preparations for our journey to Gazidah begin tomorrow under the inspector's prying eyes. I'll have to be up early to meet with Aba. I'm sure he has something he'll need me to do.

CHAPTER 4

Lia

The rumble of low voices seeps through the cracks around my house's door. I pause outside before entering, the wind chilling my legs. There are too many voices for it to just be my family. But no one said anything about a meeting tonight, and Aba is still at the smithy.

Aba doesn't bring me to every meeting. He doesn't even let us know about most of them. For a long time, I never understood why, but as I got older, I realized he's trying to protect us all. If we don't always know what's going on, we don't have to lie if someone asks. And the fewer people that know who I am, the better. Anyone could be a spy, and even if they aren't, I couldn't even blame someone for trading my secret for money or their own freedom.

I take a deep breath, push the door open, and step into a room lit by firelight. Ima stands near the door, and she pulls me in quickly, shutting the door behind me. Five other people occupy the room—my younger siblings Atar and Jorra, and three other slaves from the satrap's household. There are two men and one woman. I recognize them from

Aba's meetings. They're among those he trusts with my secret.

"It's certain, then?" the man sitting near the fire asks.

Ima nods. "Steward Goran informed me after dinner. We leave in a week's time."

I turn sharply. "We leave? Where are we going?"

Ima stares into the fire. "To Gazidah."

The name makes my heart race, and I can't catch my breath. My younger sister Jorra steps forward and takes me by the shoulders. She leads me to a seat on the floor.

Atar folds his arms. "The emperor has ordered that the satraps bring their full winter households to serve in the palace during the celebration."

My head spins. "What does this mean?" I whisper.

Ima frowns. "It means our plans have changed."

The man who's been silent so far glances at the door. "Should we call a meeting?"

Ima shakes her head. "We'll meet at our usual time. Goran may notice if we change our patterns right now. We should all be preparing to leave."

Our three guests file out of the house and into the darkness, scattering to their own homes in the slave quarters. When they're gone, Ima hands Jorra, Atar, and I our evening meals— bean stew with bread. Jorra tears her bread and dips it into her stew absentmindedly, and Atar drinks his broth. The room is quiet except for the crackling fire. I can't bring myself to touch my food.

"Why does he want the entire household?" My heart pounds as I wait for Ima's response.

"A show of loyalty and also a display of power," she says. "We'll have to wait until the meeting to learn more." She touches my shoulder. "Don't worry. You'll all be safe."

Her voice is firm, reassuring me for a moment. Ima will do everything she can to keep us safe. She's kept me alive this long, and she's the one who rescued me from the burning palace. I know I can trust her, but what is the determination of an Uze slave woman against the power of the emperor? This time, I can't rely on my parents to keep me safe. It'll be up to me to be the protection for them. I just hope I can handle the task.

Aba and Ima have been my shelter for the past twelve years. When my family was killed, Ima found me wailing in a pile of burning rubble. How she heard the cries of a child over all that commotion is still a mystery to me. She was fleeing death herself but took the time to put out the fire, pick me up in her skirts, and carry me to where Aba was waiting for her in a panic. All this with Atar and Jorra on her back. Ima is my hero.

Aba recognized me immediately, not by my broken body but by the golden tattoos he found on my wrists. Instead of leaving the city to save their lives, instead of leaving me to die, they hid in a smithy outside of town, where Aba worked all night to forge slave cuffs from abandoned gold so they could pass me off as their own and spare my life. He didn't take time to think about adopting me—he didn't have the time to think —he just claimed me and chose to worry about the conse-quences later.

My memory of that is vague. I can recall pain and cold and a woman who wasn't my mother but would be forcing me to drink broth. I remember being held in Aba's arms as they sold our family to Satrap Paykhan. The emperor allowed us to be sold together as a reward for not fleeing the city as many other slaves did, but sometimes—as I watch my family toil, as I work alongside them—I wonder if they wouldn't have been better off leaving the city. If they hadn't stopped for me, stopped to save me, they might be free now.

That was the last time we were in Gazidah. It was little

more than ruins then, and I still see it in my nightmares. But now, the emperor is forcing us back.

The door swings open, and Aba comes into the house carrying a pile of sacks on his shoulder. He drops them onto the ground. "Our allotment to pack our things."

"I didn't think it would happen so soon," Ima admits.

"What will we do?" Jorra asks.

Atar stares into the fire. "We have to be ready to fight."

His voice is a whisper.

Aba doesn't contradict him. "We are ready."

I don't feel ready, but I have to be.

AFTER ABA and Ima retire into their sleeping chamber—a curtained-off corner of our one room home—I roll onto the bed next to Jorra. She, Atar, and I sleep on pallets on the floor. We blow out our candle, and my eyes adjust to the darkness. Before long, I can make out the stars through the window.

Jorra tosses and turns for a while.

"Can't sleep?"

"Do you think we'll be safe?" she asks.

Her voice is quiet, but it carries in the room. I glance over at Aba and Ima's space, but there's no movement. I don't know what to tell Jorra. Knowing I'm terrified won't be much help to her.

Atar answers for me. "It doesn't matter if we're safe. We're trying to be dangerous, remember?"

I can almost hear Jorra frown. "Just because you want to run headfirst into catastrophe—"

I attempt to distract them before they argue. "We'll be… Ima and Aba will keep us safe."

Atar groans. "We don't need to be safe. We need to be free."

"Don't say that so loud," Jorra hisses.

"You think the emperor can hear us out here?"

"Maybe," Jorra says. She turns over under the blanket. "People say he can even control magic."

The thought of the emperor with magic sends a shiver down my back. "Maybe so. But either way, we need to sleep."

Jorra and Atar grumble, but they both settle in and quickly fall asleep. I toss and turn for a while longer before focusing on the stars. We left the curtains open tonight to let the breezes in, so they shine brightly into the house. I imagine they can hear my thoughts and tell them all my worries as I fall asleep.

CHAPTER 5

I ma is the first to stir in the morning, as she usually is. She taps each of our shoulders to wake us and hand us a quick breakfast of flatbread before we leave. Sometimes we talk in the morning, but this morning, we're each lost in our own thoughts.

Atar follows Aba to the smithy, and Jorra and I accompany Ima to the kitchen. It's chilly outside, since the sun has yet to rise, and when Jorra shivers, I wish I had a shawl to give her.

The kitchen is already warm—the chambermaids started the fire—and a fisherman drops off a couple of fish for the morning meal. Jorra and another slave girl clean them, and Ima points me to the mortar and pestle next to a stool.

"Peppercorns, cardamom, and ginger," she says.

"Yes, Ima."

She hasn't let me clean a fish since the last time I cut my hand open. I pull each spice from their shelves in the nearby storage room and bring them over to the stool. The ginger nearly falls from my hands as I bend to put the jars of cardamom and peppercorn on the ground, and I catch it just in time. A chorus of clicking noises behind me lets me know the other women in the kitchen noticed.

"Lia, Juae must have omitted your balance when he wove you together," Ima's second-in-command Kenan says with a chuckle.

Ima shakes her head. "She has her strengths."

She doesn't need to say grace isn't one of them.

I smile sheepishly. "At least I caught it this time."

"Certainly," Kenan agrees. "We won't have to fish dirt out of the spices today."

I sit on the stool and kick the peppercorns over.

Kenan laughs, and the other women in the kitchen join her. "I spoke too soon."

My face warms, but I bend to pick the peppercorns off the floor, blowing them off as best I can and setting them aside. Ima can use them for our meals later.

As I grind spices, I listen to the household gossip in the kitchen. If there is any news to be had in Paidashar Fadir, this is where to find it. The chambermaids trade bits of information as they pick up morning meals, and the cooks speculate on it all.

Usually there's a wealth of news from the house and the town, but today, all anyone is talking about is going to Gazidah. It makes sense, but every time someone mentions the city, I feel like I'm going to be sick.

"I hear the emperor doesn't have enough people to serve all the guests he invited," one chambermaid tells us. "So he's stealing slaves from his maliks."

Kenan shakes her head. "More likely he just wants to appear more impressive. The bigger the ego, the smaller the man."

A nearby cook laughs knowingly, and Jorra and I exchange a glance. She giggles, and I shake my head, holding back a smile.

"Either way, it means more work for us," Ima notes as she

hands off a platter meant for the inspector. "We'll have to close the house for the first time in years."

"And cross the Menewos Desert," another chambermaid adds, joining the conversation as she enters the kitchen.

She shudders as she says the desert's name. Menewos is legendary in Elisya, even among those who have never seen it. It covers much of southern Uze and Sahr and northern Gazidah territory. The last time we crossed it, I was a child, and I remember none of the trip, but I've heard stories.

It's an unspoken truth that this land was once full of magic, though it's long gone now. Legend also says it was once green and full of life, but that was before Elisya was even founded over four hundred years ago.

While Menewos bears no resemblance to the landscape story-tellers claim it once was, it holds remnants of the magic—huge scars of blackened earth, massive craters, ruins of cities and towns, animals too large and fast to be normal, and places where the air itself is hostile. Most who travel through it can't wait to leave, and anyone who can avoid it does, taking longer routes through the Min or Sahr kingdoms. But we have to get to Gazidah in time for this festival, which means taking the fastest route.

"I had to cross it once years ago," Kenan says, her voice low and conspiratorial. "During the day it was like any other journey, but at night, I could hear voices—shouting, fighting, and music, all calling to me. It felt like my spirit would leave my body. I was afraid to sleep. That was the longest week of my life."

The hair on my arms stands up as Kenan speaks, and Jorra stares at her wide-eyed.

Ima clears her throat. "I have crossed that desert too, Kenan, and no such specters called to me."

Kenan laughs. "That's because your spirit is much too stubborn to leave you."

Ima shakes her head and chuckles. "Perhaps. But merchants cross Menewos often as well. No one has anything to worry about. We'll each arrive in Gazidah with our spirits intact."

The conversation shifts to what Gazidah is like, but my head spins a bit at the mention of the city again. I keep shifting wildly between determination and fear. Maybe it would be better if Menewos took my spirit. How will I face Gazidah again?

⸻

Enra

Khanda and I sit on pillows in Aba's office across from him and listen as he goes through our agenda for the coming trip. He's been talking for a half hour, and I've been taking mental notes while Khanda has grown more and more restless.

"The foreign minister of Susheph will want to meet with us in particular," Aba says, "Given our proximity to their borders. It will be an excellent opportunity to revisit our trade agreements with them."

"Is there anything that needs urgent addressing?" I ask, trying to take part so Aba knows I'm paying attention.

"They were concerned when your cousin's ship passed into their waters without prior notice, so I'd imagine they want to discuss that."

I nod with a small smile. One of Uncle Tusun's daughters married a pirate, and like all pirates, he's unconcerned with national borders. But he has to be more careful with a princess on board, even if she is disgraced.

Before Aba can speak again, Khanda groans. "Can I go back to the nursery?"

I hold back a chuckle. "Is it that bad?"

He lowers his head. "I don't even know what you all are talking about."

Aba leans forward and pats Khanda's knee. "You'll learn. And this is how you learn. By being here. By taking part. This is how you'll know what to do when you are the satrap one day."

Khanda pouts at Aba. "Can't you always be satrap?"

Aba shakes his head. "You know I can't."

He turns to me hopefully, and I give him a regretful smile.

"And I can't because—"

"You'll be malik. I know." Khanda sighs.

Aba coughs and stands. "That's enough for today. You may go, Khanda. Enra, stay for a moment."

Khanda springs up happily before remembering himself and bowing. "Thank you, Aba."

He holds his back straight as he marches slowly to the door, but once he's out of view, footsteps patter away.

I laugh. He couldn't get away from here fast enough.

When the sound of footsteps has fully disappeared, Aba shakes his head.

I try to stand up for Khanda. "He'll grow accustomed to it. The only lessons he's used to are those with Nalkendi and their nurse."

Aba nods but doesn't respond, and my face warms. He doesn't need me to tell him that Khanda will learn. He's already been through the process once with me.

"Will Lia—" I start, but Aba cuts me off.

"Her father will take care of her as we travel. We will see what happens when we arrive."

"Yes," I reply, though I don't fully understand. Is Aba expecting something to happen?

Aba puts his hands behind his back. "There will be much activity in Gazidah, but don't act hastily. You are a man now, but you're still inexperienced."

I wince. When will my father start to truly trust me?

"I know," I assure him. "I can do this."

He nods and turns away. "We will have more to discuss in the coming days, but now, will you accompany the inspector into the village? He would like to take a tour."

I stifle the desire to groan like Khanda would.

"Yes, Aba. Of course."

I just told Aba he could trust me. Now I have to prove it.

CHAPTER 6

Lia

I am a ghost over the next few days, going through the motions of my duties, absent from reality. My mind is in the future and in the past at the same time. Gazidah almost killed me once. It probably won't fail again, but now I have a plan, though I'm not sure how prepared I am to execute it.

When the holy day arrives—the day of the week when no one works and we all go to the temple to pray and contemplate how we can better serve Juae—I wake before the sunrise. The temple horns have yet to sound, but I wouldn't be able to hear them over my heart pounding in my ears, anyway. Today, Aba's having a meeting—one I'm going to attend.

Aba doesn't often have us attend his meetings for our safety, but when he wants to prove that the plan can work, he invites me. I know what he wants me to do, what he wants me to tell our fellow slaves I'll do when I face the emperor. He wants me to ask for recognition, for a title, and for the end of slavery as recompense for my dead relatives and the ruined dynasty. It's a massive request, even as far as restitution for lives is concerned, but given who I am—and who it was that the emperor took from me—it has a high chance of being granted. So when Aba needs proof to inspire hope, he uses me.

We prepared the household meals yesterday—no one works on a holy day, not even slaves—so it's the perfect time, the only time, for slaves to meet in peace and private. We won't be missed as long as we're within the house's walls when the satrap and his family come back from the temple.

I slide from beneath my blanket, careful not to wake Jorra, and creep past Atar toward the door. It creaks as I open it, and I glance behind me. But no one stirs.

The sky is the dim gray of early morning, and no one is within sight in the slave quarters. I make my way to the fountain we all share. It's easier to use it earlier, when you don't have to vie for a place in line with everyone else as they rush to prepare for the day.

I approach the fountain situated under a tree, pump water into my hand to drink, and then wash my face and hands. The water I spill is quickly soaked up by the dirt, disappearing like it was never there. The land of Elisya is always thirsty. For a long time, its people were too, but that was before my ancestors began their campaigns. At least, that's how the stories go. Not that people remember my ancestors fondly. Few people take kindly to being conquered, even when the conquest was generations ago.

The temple horns sound as I finish, and on the ninth or tenth sound, candlelight flickers alive in the windows. Rays of sunlight burst over the horizon as if summoned by the candles, turning the sky pink.

"Lia!" Ima calls.

It's time to leave.

Paidashar is a small city, and most people walk to the temple. It isn't far from the satrap's mansion, so he leaves when the rest of us do—he and his family ride before us on horseback. I link arms with Ima and Jorra as we walk behind Aba and Atar. The conversation around us swells as we reach the road outside the mansion—groups from other homes meld into the satrap's party of guests, servants, and slaves. Most of the discussion is about the additional horses at the front with the satrap. The inspector and his retinue are joining us for our parade to the temple. It isn't a surprise that they would, but I'm glad to be far behind him. As slaves, my family and I stand near the back of the group.

The walk to the temple is slow to maintain an air of peace —no one can enter Juae's house in agitation. It's a simple journey to reach the temple. It's on the same road as the mansion, so no one can get lost, and while most of the buildings in Paidashar are low slung with flat roofs, the temple soars three stories tall with a spire at each of its octagonal corners. They are painted white with golden tips, a sign of the temple's wealth and supposedly of Paidashar's devotion to Juae.

We reach the temple's gates just as the priests sound their final horns. The satrap, his family, and the inspector dismount their horses, and the temple's pages take them away. They also swing open the massive doors, allowing dozens of people to enter and leave at a time. Those who reached the temple earlier than us part to let the satrap through. His place inside the temple is reserved. Once inside the doors, the men turn to the right and the women to the left, parting at a barrier built of stone.

On the women's side, the din of conversation brings the air to life. The sun isn't high enough to reach over the temple's walls yet, but light streams in from the windows close to the ceiling. Nearer to the ground, large lanterns heat the room and provide us with dim light to see each other. I hold tight to Jorra and Ima to avoid separation. I've lost them a few times here, and every time I do, I have to wait at the back wall until they find me again. Ahead of us, the crowd of women parts and closes as the wealthiest and most powerful women of Paidashar make their way to the front. Satrapha Edab and her daughters are up there somewhere. But my family will remain here in the back. As we shuffle around other groups searching for places where we can kneel and pray, someone brushes against Ima. She stiffens and stops moving as a voice from over our shoulders whispers, "This afternoon?"

Ima gives a terse nod.

We take a few more steps, then a woman bumps into Jorra. Jorra's eyes widen, and she tilts her head slightly toward Ima. "In the glen," Ima says.

The information will make its way to the correct people, I know. But I recognize neither of those women. It's rare that there's more than one stranger. My breath catches in my throat. When Aba lets new people meet me, he usually makes me give a speech. That's difficult for me on a normal day—I stumble on my words, and people tell me to speak louder—but we're going to Gazidah soon. I don't think I'll be able to force a word past my lips.

We find an empty corner near the temple wall, and I finally let go of Jorra and Ima, kneeling between them to bow in prayer. I let my forehead touch the floor as the voice of a priest rings out over the din of ours. He recites the morning prayer for the day of worship and presents his passage of scripture for the day. After he finishes, we lift our heads to thank him and then bow them again to thank Juae. From then, we may spend anything from a few minutes to several hours here in prayer. If we're not inclined to pray, we may give our offerings to the temple pages—those who have offerings to give—or spend time in nature to contemplate divine power and majesty. Voices once again fill the air, the sounds of women in prayer. I feel Ima stand to leave. She'll be going to the glen to prepare. Slowly, others will follow suit. I give Juae a silent prayer of my own. "Juae all powerful, mighty in battle and full of mercy, please…" I pause. I want to pray for safety, for my family's deliverance, for us to somehow not have to go to Gazidah, to stay here. Instead, I pray, "Please help me say the right thing."

Jorra touches my elbow, and I raise my head. We both stand and link arms as we tiptoe around praying women to leave the temple. As we leave, the pages don't hold their baskets out for offerings, as our cuffs reveal us as slaves.

As we step outside, the sun warms my face, and I pause on the stairs. The sky above us is bright, but clouds loom on the horizon. Jorra waits patiently, giving me a moment, but then she tugs my arm.

"Are you ready?"

I shrug. "Yes. Let's go."

The glen is a short distance away from the temple, about fifteen minutes away. It's one of a few patches of trees in Ragienige, a bit of green and dusty gray breaking up the beige of dry grass and sand. A few figures move around in its shadow, but I'm sure more wait within it.

Jorra must see them, too, because she tries to distract me. "We should go to the sea later, with Ima and Aba."

"If we have time," I reply. "This meeting may last long."

Jorra shakes her head. "Aba won't want us to gather for too long. It's—"

She trails off, but I know what she means. It's too dangerous. Most don't mind slaves gathering on a holy day. As long as you include food, prayers, and songs in your gathering, any casual observer will conclude that you're worshipping or socializing. But today, the inspector is here, and we're all preparing to travel. People will be more aware, and some observers may be more than casual.

"Well, you ask our parents," I say. "They'll be more likely to say yes to you."

"They'll say yes. Who knows when we'll see the sea again."

I glance at Jorra, and she lowers her head like she wishes she hadn't spoken. "I'm sorry."

"Don't be. We'll come back."

I try my best "certain" voice, attempting to use it before I'll have to in the meeting. It's not convincing, though Jorra is kind enough to give me a smile.

Thunder rumbles in the distance, warning us of rain.

"Let's hurry," I say. There's no need to get caught in a storm if we can avoid it.

When we reach the glen, we see a dozen people sitting on blankets or cloaks on the ground and eating their midday meals while they wait. A small group of men has congregated not far off in the shade of a tree. I recognize many faces, but at least four are new. Aba has trusted many new people with my secret, it would seem. That means the plan really has moved up. I'll find out how much at the same time as everyone else.

Atar waves us over to where he and Ima are sitting. Aba is probably at the center of that group of men. Ima has spread our modest meal out onto her cloak—flatbread and a bean spread. A large skein of water is enough for the five of us to share. Jorra and I sit down, and after Ima offers prayer, we each take a piece of the flatbread. I chew on mine but can't bring myself to swallow. While Jorra and Atar discuss which of their friends are here, I rehearse my story in my head. "You know me as Lia Benarvela, but I was born Asil Liani Hara Elisya. I know it's hard to believe…"

Ima touches my shoulder. "You'll be fine."

I nod like I believe her, but I'm not sure I can. It's one thing to be a nebulous hope that people can hold on to, but it's another thing entirely to have to fulfill the dream that's been promised, as much as I want to.

Aba has nurtured the plan in my mind since I was young. As soon as I was lucid enough to understand what had happened to my birth parents, Aba explained I had a duty to avenge them. When I was old enough, he and Ima told me how I could.

The Ajudakai Akori, the laws that govern Elisya, are old and contain the procedure for dealing with all kinds of conflicts. According to the law, the kin of a murderer's victim can—and in some interpretations, must—demand restitution for the lives of their family members.

The casualties of war don't count as murder victims, but the royal family wasn't killed in a war. They were killed in a coup on a day of celebration, which even the most generous interpreter of the law has to interpret as murder.

Lives are not of equal value in Elisya. The life of a slave is worth almost nothing, but the lives of nobles are precious. According to Aba, the first test of the law was centuries ago, when a satrap of Eutu assassinated a rival. He was executed in return as restitution. Since then, no aspiring murderer of nobility has made the same mistake. If they're going to kill one noble, they'll kill the whole family, so no one is left to claim restitution. I'm sure the current emperor thought that was what he'd done, but he failed.

It's Aba's understanding—and most of us are inclined to believe him—that the life of the former emperor alone would be worth a change in the law as restitution. As the former emperor's only living relative, I can demand the end of slavery instead of the emperor's life, and he would have to grant it.

They didn't have to work to convince me. I've lived the life of a slave with them. It's the only life I truly remember. Though I spent my first four years in the palace of Gazidah, I grew up in the back rooms and the hallways of the satrap's home. I know what this life is like, and I understand why it has to end. But that doesn't mean I'm not terrified at the idea of facing a man who did everything in his power to ensure I ended up dead. My family believes in me, so I want to believe in myself, but I just can't see myself the way they do.

After a half hour, Aba calls the meeting to order, and we turn toward the men beneath the tree.

"Those of you from the satrap's household know, and the rest may have already heard, but we have been called to Gazidah. We leave in three days."

A wave of whispers makes its way through the group. One voice near the back calls out, "What will we do?"

Aba nods as if he's been waiting for that question. "It may not look like it, but this is the opportunity we've been waiting for. For those of you who haven't met her yet, let me introduce to you my daughter Lia."

He reaches out for me to approach him.

My heartbeat speeds up, but I stand shakily and approach him. I try to keep my feet firm, but my steps are always less sure when I'm nervous. I hate to betray my stride in front of so many people. It feels like I'm giving myself up for judgement. But Aba's face glows with pride. When I'm close enough, he wraps an arm around me. "Lia, introduce yourself."

"You know—" I start, but my voice sounds like a whisper. I clear my throat and start again. "I am Lia Benarvela, but I was born…" I pause, pushing back the fear that always comes from saying the next part out loud. "Asil Liani Hara Elisya."

The four words that make up my birth name ripple through the crowd. Those who don't know turn to those who do as if to ask, "Is this true? Can she prove it?"

When the whispers die down, I continue reciting the words I've rehearsed with Aba countless times. "I was born the first child of the crown prince, Asil Nahan Datu Elisya, and I have a blood right to the restitution for his life."

Someone in the crowd blurts out the inevitable statement that is always made at meetings like this. "Asil Liani is dead. How can you claim to be her?"

Aba enjoys answering that question, so I leave it to him. Instead of speaking to the man who'd called out, Aba reaches into his cloak and pulls a tiny key from it. It's one of two keys. One is in the hands of the satrap because only he can free his slaves, and one is in the hands of my father because he fixes and resizes our cuffs. Aba unlocks both of mine and raises my hands to the crowd so they can see my wrists.

There is a collective gasp. There always is. Most people have never seen a golden tattoo. They're illegal for anyone outside the royal family. Emperor Asil, my grandfather, made getting or giving one without imperial permission punishable by death. That punishment was probably too harsh because only one person could give such a tattoo, one of a few men with magic in Elisya, and he died during the coup. So mine are the only ones left.

They glow in the dim light of the glen, and when Aba releases my hands, I pull them into myself, hiding the tattoos from the world.

Aba extends his arms as if to embrace the crowd. "We will go to the judges to face the emperor, and we will win. No one can deny Lia's claim."

"What will you do if he denies it anyway?" a man calls out. "He is the emperor."

And the emperor can do whatever he wants. Until he's dethroned. I shudder as a breeze bringing the looming storm courses through the glen.

Aba's expression darkens. "If he denies us, we will take action. There will be a new sunrise in Elisya."

Several people in the crowd nod. They're ready to fight for their freedom if they have to. I'm here so they don't have to. I don't want to think about what may happen if I fail.

CHAPTER 7

Enra

It's late evening when I retire to my room in the men's wing. Candles have already been lit, and I cross the room to close the curtains before I let myself get comfortable. Most of my belongings are already packed, ready to be returned to their places in Ragienige.

I'm well accustomed to closing Paidashar Fadir to return to Ragienige. We've been a family of noble migratory birds since before I was born, as all the satraps and maliks are, traveling from mansion to mansion and palace to palace. Typically, my family only goes in two directions—from the mansion in Ragienige to the mansion in Paidashar and back. But tomorrow, we're being called further to Gazidah, as are all Emperor Pakel's rulers. He's mandated that we leave our inspectors in charge to attend a festival in Elisya's honor—in his honor—to celebrate the end of the civil war.

It's a test of loyalty. I know it, as does everyone else in my family. When we get there, we'll have to marry Vroni off as a show of our fealty. I don't know what the other rulers will have to do.

We leave tomorrow morning. It will be several weeks to Ragienige, and then another couple to Uzepige where we'll stay and refresh with my uncle. Though he's a disgraced and distrusted malik, the emperor has yet to harm him. Instead, the emperor appointed the imperial inspector as the de facto leader of Uze, and my uncle Tusun is just a figurehead. A bargain with Derian saved his life several years ago. I don't know what it was, but Emperor Pakel has been trying to build ties with Derian's queen—an empress in her own right—ever since. It's been difficult; no one is eager to ally with a nation at war. But with the war over, I won't be surprised if a delegation from Derian is present at this festival.

I'm Uncle Tusun's heir, but I don't want to be another figurehead for the emperor to use. If I'm going to rule, I want to truly rule, not become a placeholder for whomever Emperor Pakel wants to do his bidding.

A knock sounds at my door, and when I answer, Goran enters. "The satrap has sent for you, Suan."

I follow him to my father's study. The walk through the dark hallways reminds me of when Aba called me to his study on my birthday years ago. A sense of foreboding grows in my chest. What kinds of secrets will he spring on me now?

Aba waits until Goran has left before he speaks. "Are you ready?"

I know he's not asking if I'm packed. I nod, but I have to speak up for my sister at least once. "It doesn't seem right, sacrificing Vroni like this."

Aba's face is solemn. "She understands her duty."

"But that doesn't mean we can shirk ours."

Aba waits for me to continue, not betraying his emotions.

"It feels cowardly, saving ourselves by using her as a shield. We should fight."

"With what power?" Aba asks me. "How could we fight

more than the defeated maliks in the south did? Can we afford the price they paid?"

The rebellious maliks in the south of Elisya paid with their lives and their legacies. Their titles were taken, and they were replaced. I shuffle my feet as my will deflates. "Still…"

"This is not a battle to be won with swords."

"That's how Emperor Pakel did it," I note.

"Pakel should have failed." Aba shakes his head. "His success is still beyond my comprehension. But whether he won the crown by coincidence or by holy blessing, his victory cannot be repeated."

My shoulders fall. "Then we do nothing?"

Aba nods. "Change will happen without us, and that will be our time to act."

"What do you mean?"

"A shift is coming," he says. "I don't know which direction it will turn, but that will be our sign."

I think back to what I've heard Aba and his allies whisper about in private.

"The Ajudakai Akori?" I ask. No one has invoked the founding words of the first emperor in centuries, but that record on several hundred stone tablets provides for how the empire is to be run for the foreseeable future. Although my family isn't happy with Emperor Pakel, no one is unhappy enough to risk challenging him. At least, not yet.

Aba shakes his head and turns his attention outside.

The shuffling of men packing carts with household items comes through Aba's window. They're working well into the night. The voice of our best blacksmith, Benar, carries over the rest. He calls directions to the men checking that the carts will last through the journey.

"Lia?" I venture.

Aba nods. "I'm sure they'll make an attempt. Now is the time."

"An attempt at what?" My voice is barely above a whisper, but Aba hears me.

"Freedom. It's what Benar wants—what many of them want—and Lia can give it to them."

My mind races, putting what I know together with what I've just learned. Lia will attempt to end slavery by herself? That would mean revealing who she is, and then everyone will know where she was and who it was that rescued her. Aba expects that, and he's ready for it.

"What do I need to do?" My hands itch for activity. I want to take part in Aba's plans, not just watch them.

Aba shakes his head. "Nothing. Not yet."

I frown. "Why not?"

"You will act when the time is right."

"Why did you call me here?"

Aba puts a hand on my shoulder. "You are a man now, my son, so you need to be ready."

"Ready for what?"

"Anything. Keep your eyes and ears open. When we arrive in Gazidah, be friendly, but be careful not to trust. No one in that city is our ally, and we must protect ourselves."

I know all that. He says I'm a man now, but Aba still treats me like a boy. "Why not just say outright who we can't trust? We're in private here."

Aba smiles. "You'll know all things in time."

"Why not now?"

"The time is coming when your ignorance will be your blessing."

I sigh, frustrated, and then regret it. "You're speaking in riddles, Aba."

Aba pats my shoulder. "As all old men do from time to time."

"You're hardly old."

He laughs. "That is subjective, but don't deny me my wisdom, my son."

Then his expression turns somber. "I called you here to tell you we will… I will rely on you much on this journey. I trust you to act when you know you must, even if the task is unsavory. Can you promise me you'll do that?"

My stomach turns a bit in worry. We may be disgraced, but we're still noblemen. Others do the unsavory tasks. But when I meet Aba's eyes, I can tell there's more he isn't telling me. Still, he's finally said he trusts me, and I won't let him down.

I nod as resolutely as I can. "I promise, Aba."

"For your mother, for your siblings, for all of us."

My worry grows deeper, but I nod again. "I will. You can trust me, Aba. I know my responsibility to them and to you."

At this, Aba seems satisfied. "Good." He pats me on the shoulder again. "Rest. Tomorrow will be an early day."

Lia

When I wake, the first thing I do is lift the curtain blocking our window. The curtain will be my bag and hold what little belongings I have, and also, I want to check the weather.

It's a good day for traveling. The wind is cool, the sky is clear, and the sun is warm. I'm tempted to curse them all. I would have wished for a terrible thunderstorm to keep us here at least one more day, but my wishes don't often come true. Ima, Jorra, and I spent much of yesterday evening sewing whatever extra padding we could find into the bottoms of our shoes. The journey will be rough, Ima assures us, no matter what the sky foretells. Elisya's terrain is dry at best and rocky in its worst regions, and crossing the Menewos desert is treacherous.

I take the curtain from its nails and spread it out on the floor, and after filling it with my other dress, my undergarments, and cooking utensils, I tie it to a rope that can be slung across my back.

The rest of my family is awake and getting ready to leave. Aba and Atar are nailing wood planks to the outside of the windows to keep them covered while we're gone. Those in other houses are doing the same. Ima, Jorra, and I move around the little house in silence, so I can hear the rest of the satrap's household stirring. Horses whinny and donkeys bray, and men call out to one another. A knock sounds on our door.

"Benar?" a voice calls.

Aba strides past the door. "We're ready."

He and the man outside share a handshake, but it's no normal handshake of greeting. They're exchanging information. Instinctively, I turn away, and I know my siblings are doing the same. It's better if we don't actually "see" anything.

Fading footsteps in the dirt outside let us know the man is gone. "Come," Aba calls. "It's time."

I let out a ragged breath and steel myself as I watch my family file out of the door. I take one last look at the house, now empty of everything but the couple of chairs we're leaving behind. We carry everything else we have on our backs. It's a sad little room, and I have no love for it, but I can't shake the feeling that I'll never see it again.

Outside, I let my eyes adjust to the sun. The last of the slave and servant families are gathering in our common space, those who weren't needed to prepare the animals. We go to the main courtyard so we can be ready before the satrap and his family come outside. Atar and Jorra stay next to me.

Atar rolls his shoulders and grins at us. "Are you excited?"

"Excited?" Jorra rolls her eyes at him. "To walk for weeks?"

"Excited to see someplace other than here. To have a life." He drops his voice to a whisper. "To be free."

I almost choke on my breath. "Don't talk like that. You never know who's listening."

The main courtyard is crowded, and I know Aba hasn't won everyone over to his cause... our cause. As if to prove my point, Steward Goran crosses our path, giving us a disdainful glare. He walks to the center of the courtyard and rings a bell. The nobles are coming. We split into two groups on either side of the courtyard, clearing a path for the satrap and his family to reach their horses.

The doors to the house open, and the nobles enter the daylight sun. Even they make a grim procession to their horses, but at least they're able to ride. The visiting inspector and his entourage are first, followed by Enra and his father. Enra glances over as he passes, and I could promise he's looking at me. I push the thought from my mind. I have bigger things to worry about than his attention. When Satrap Paykhan's wife and children are safely in their carriage, we are officially ready to leave.

A priest from the temple who came to bless the journey steps forward, waving a burning bunch of herbs. He waves it in front of the horses, causing them to snort and filling the air with the scent of embers and earth.

"Juae bless you on your journey. May he keep your feet strong, your legs firm, and your head high. May he deliver you safely into the bosom of Gazidah, and may he guide you on your return."

The priest continues his litany of blessings, wishing nothing but good on the travelers. Well, not everyone. The priest noticeably omitted us, the household workers, but it's no surprise. No one blesses slaves.

A murmur of "May it be so," ripples through the crowd. Jorra and I echo it, but Atar is silent. I glance over at him, and his face is resolute as he stares defiantly ahead. I tug at his shirt.

"What?" he hisses.

"Stop. You'll draw attention."

He groans but averts his eyes. "I hate this."

Jorra takes his hand, and I nod.

"I know you hate it, but bear with it. We'll be traveling soon enough, and we won't even have to see them."

Atar grits his teeth in a cross between a grin and a sneer. "Soon enough, we won't have to deal with them at all."

I lightly slap his arm. "Will you please show some restraint?"

He rolls his eyes at me but doesn't say anything else. The nobles mount their horses, and the guards take their places at the front and back of the group. Then we begin our slow journey from safety into danger.

CHAPTER 8

The journey to Ragienige is an arduous march; we take a month to reach the city, and from there it's another week to Gazidah, through the Menewos desert. No one was excited to cross it, except perhaps Atar, but he's excited about anything new.

We travel during the day, stopping for food and rest in the heat of midday and setting up camp at night. When we camp near a town, the satrap and his family stay in the town master's house, but the rest of us sleep in tents. A few other satraps and the malik of Uze have aligned with our route, and accommodating them all has overwhelmed the town masters.

But now, we're a day's journey into the desert, and there won't be a town between here and Gazidah. We set up camp for the night among the satrap's slaves. The different households have arranged themselves like a gigantic wheel around several massive fires, and we all cook our food there. When the sun sets fully, it'll also serve as our light until we sleep.

We eat a quiet meal in the light of the summer sunset. Everyone is tired, so there's little conversation. People are lost in their own thoughts and nervous about sleeping for the first night in Menewos. Even for those who claim to not be superstitious, it's hard to deny that the region has an oppressively bleak air, bringing your worst moments to the forefront of your memory.

When we go to sleep, my family crowds into our tent with the entrance rolled up to let fresh air in. I wrap myself tightly in my shawl. Atar is the first to fall asleep—I can hear his low snores—and gradually the rest of my family drifts off as the fire outside dims, and darkness covers the camp.

The line between sleeping and waking blurs for me, and sounds of fighting in the distance ring in my ears. Flames of candlelight flicker on the walls of a lavish room. A woman arrayed in jewels and glittering cloth rushes into the room. She cries out, and another woman tries to help her block the door. I'm dreaming, I realize—I've had this dream many times before—but the realization doesn't make it any less horrifying.

My adult mind wants to stand and help them, but my child body stays rooted to the floor, not understanding why my mother and nurse are trying to close us into the nursery.

Get up, I will myself. Tell them to run. Do something, anything. But I never do. I can't.

The door bursts open. A baby cries, his voice overpowering all other noise until he is silenced. The color of blood blinds me. There are screams of terror, the grating twinge of metal against metal, and wails of grief that wrench my heart. The ground falls out beneath me, and fire surrounds me.

I awake with a gasp, my heart pounding and tears in my eyes. My hands are shaking. But it was just a dream, I tell myself. I count the members of my sleeping family. Everyone is here, safe.

So why do I still hear fighting?

I hold my breath, trying to listen over the sound of my heartbeat. It's still there. There's a battle outside. It's happening again. Bile rises in my throat, but I choke it down. I need to act.

I get on my hands and knees and crawl to Aba, shaking him awake.

"Aba! Aba, wake up!"

He groans and opens his eyes. "Lia? What is it?"

My voice shakes as I whisper. "We're under attack! We have to get to safety."

He blinks in confusion but sits up. "I'll check outside."

Jorra stirs, and Ima's eyes open.

"No, Aba, please! We need to escape. Don't you hear the fighting?"

Aba tilts his head at me. "Lia, I don't hear anything."

Tears pool in my eyes. "It's just like then… it's just like that night."

Aba sighs, and Ima sits up and wraps her arms around me.

"You're safe," she says. "You're safe."

As she rubs my back, my heart slows down, and the sounds of battle fade. Was it all my imagination? Or was the desert playing tricks on me?

"Look at me, Lia," Aba says, his voice stern but not cruel.

I blink my tears back. His expression is solemn, but he's not angry. Instead, I see pity. He makes me take a few deep breaths, and then he puts a hand on my cheek.

"Nothing like that night will ever happen to you again. You're strong enough to fight for yourself now."

I hang my head. "I don't think I am, Aba."

My words spill out instead of my tears. "I still have nightmares. It still hurts. I'm still afraid. Every step on this journey is terrifying. I—"

Aba shakes his head. "No. I know you can do this, Lia. You may not feel it, but you are strong enough. You just have to believe it. Now rest. We have another long day tomorrow."

He lays back down, signifying the conversation is over. He always refuses to listen any time I say I can't do something.

Ima rubs my back. "Go back to sleep. It will be better in the morning."

I take a few ragged breaths before laying back down and wrapping myself in my shawl again. The cacophony of battle is gone now, replaced by the songs of nocturnal animals and desert wind. Jorra pretends to be sleeping as I lay down, but I know she's awake. She always wakes up when I have nightmares.

As if to confirm my thoughts, she reaches out and squeezes my hand before curling up again.

I sleep fitfully throughout the night, waking often, but at least the nightmares don't return.

The next morning, my nerves are frayed. The typical noise of breaking camp puts me on edge, and laughs sound like screams. Any time I hear a baby cry in our camp, I'm tempted to burst into tears. My baby brother's name won't leave my mind. It's one thing I remember. Duin. Named for the first king of Gazidah, but there was nothing kingly about him. He was an infant, a sweet, chubby, gurgling baby. He was. If he were alive, he'd be a twelve-year-old boy now, running and playing with other children his age. If he were alive.

CHAPTER 9

Enra

The heat in the desert is oppressive, beating down on us without remorse. Of course, Emperor Pakel would make his subjects travel through the heat of summer to celebrate a victory he defeated us all to gain. We're two days away from Gazidah, and the days have become monotonous. Hour after hour, we pass mountains of rock and sand, all reflecting the sun back at us. In centuries past, travelers had to carve routes through the desert themselves, but the founding of the empire lead to roads through it. They make the journey much easier, but they do nothing about the sun. My mother, sisters, and the other women have been wearing headscarves to protect themselves from the heat for a week now, and over the last couple of days, the men have joined suit.

I'll be grateful when we arrive in the city only because of the change of scenery. I laugh to myself for a moment, but my amusement passes quickly, replaced by shame. We're trading Vroni for our honor. I shouldn't be looking forward to anything. I should be planning. Aba is surely planning.

My thoughts turn to Lia. She walks ahead of our caravan

with her family and the rest of our slaves and servants. Our staff and guards surround us to protect us. The slaves are sometimes ahead of us, sometimes behind, but they serve as a buffer of safety.

Lia has her head down. Sometimes she jumps when horses whinny or a person coughs. Whatever's going on, she's clearly nervous about it. If I asked, would she tell me?

It isn't foolish, I assure myself as I spur my horse forward. I'm only preparing, learning what I need to know to do what is necessary. When I get close, I hop down from the horse and approach her, leading the horse behind me.

People part in front of me, and as I approach, I realize I may not have thought this through. Her father is right there with her. It's not like she's going to tell me anything with him listening in. I berate myself, but it's too late to change my mind now. They've already noticed me.

"Suan," Tasilla says with a bow. If she's surprised to see me here, her face doesn't betray it. Her children however, are obviously confused, especially Lia. If I didn't know better, I'd say her expression is one of silent horror.

Benar gives me a deferring bow but doesn't speak.

"Can we help you?" Tasilla asks.

"Ah, yes… I was…" I flounder. "I require Lia for a moment."

The entire family wears masks of blank confusion. But I figure I might have a better chance of getting her to talk if we're a distance away.

Tasilla bows. "Of course, Suan."

She pushes Lia forward a bit, and panic crosses Lia's face before she averts her eyes. I lead her a ways away, hopefully out of her family's hearing range.

When we're a distance away, I realize maybe we should move away from all the household staff. There's no need for them to overhear either.

So I lead Lia off to the side, where no one is close enough to listen in if we keep our voices low.

She walks in silence behind me.

"Lia," I scramble for a way to ask what I want to without making it obvious.

"Yes, Suan?"

"How has the trip been for you so far?"

Her eyes stay trained on the ground as we walk. "We have been fortunate to have a journey without incident."

"Yes… but…" I trail off. How am I so bad at this? "How has it been for you, in particular?"

Her face scrunches in confusion.

"I… have not suffered."

I decide to try a different approach.

"What are your thoughts about going to Gazidah?"

She gives me a sharp glance and then averts her eyes. "Gazidah, Suan?"

"Yes…" Perhaps I should have thought this through. "Do you have… anything you plan to do there?"

I could slap myself. What kind of question is that?

"I… will work, Suan," Lia answers.

Of course, she will work. What else would she possibly say to me?

"But do you—"

A man shouts in the distance, and the noise grows, traveling in waves toward us.

"Dust storm! Prepare yourselves!"

The skyline darkens as a wall of dust hurtles toward us. My heart sinks, and I grab Lia's hand and tighten my other hand around my horse's reigns, pulling us all toward the heart of the caravan.

"Aba! Ima!" Lia screams, but I hold tight to her. She won't make it back to them in time.

"Get down!" I yell.

Someone tosses me an old, rough blanket, and I wrap it around our heads, including my horse.

"Hold on to the blanket," I tell Lia, and she grabs onto the edges and pulls it tight.

The wind whips at my ankles, stinging them with bits of sand. Lia grimaces in the blanket's shadow, wincing as the sharp wind bites her legs, too.

"It won't last long," I assure her, though I don't know that for certain.

We stand huddled together in silence as the wind screams around us. I close my eyes, praying the storm away. And just as quickly as it came upon us, it disappears, leaving dust hanging in the air in its wake.

Lia lets the blanket down, her eyes wild as she searches the crowd. People around us are gathering themselves and regrouping. Many names are called out. I even hear my own, probably from my mother. Lia's hands shake, but she folds the blanket and places it on the back of my horse.

"Go," I tell her. "Find your family."

"Thank you, Suan." She bows and runs off toward the servants.

That was an utter failure. Not only did I not learn anything from talking to Lia, I got us caught in a dust storm. I brush sand and dirt from my tunic and set off to find my family. Hopefully, no one asks me where I went.

CHAPTER 10

Lia

Late that night, after the fires have been put out and everyone has gone to sleep, the tent moves as Aba stirs. Fabric rustles, and a burst of warm desert air swirls in as he leaves. I try to ignore it. He told us not to attend this meeting.

"Too many people," he'd said. "There's no need to risk lives unnecessarily."

He'll be safe, I assure myself. Aba's always been safe. I comfort myself with the thought as I drift to sleep, listening to Ima and my siblings breathing and ignoring the distant cries that have been tormenting me for nearly a week. But as my consciousness slips away, another burst of air enters the tent. I can still hear Jorra and Ima. But Atar's low snores are missing.

I squeeze my eyes shut. He's probably just gone to relieve himself. Why don't I believe that? Because I know Atar better than that. I groan inwardly and draw myself up as gently as I can to avoid waking anyone else, grabbing my threadbare shawl as much to hide my face as to protect me from the winds. I slip from the tent in time to see a slight figure dip toward the hills behind a tent.

The camp is quiet, and the hills aren't far. I know from Aba that the hills and mountains in Menewos are littered with caves. That would be the wisest place to meet. But he didn't tell us which one he'd be in. If I were Atar, what would be my guess?

I walk as carefully as I can to not disturb the rocks, sand, or lonely patches of grass—not to mention any animals that might live among them. When I reach the edge of the camp, something touches my shoulder, and I have to stifle a scream. I whirl around to see Atar grinning at me.

"What are you doing here?" I hiss at him.

He shrugs. "What are you doing here?"

"Stopping you. Aba said not to attend the meeting."

Atar frowns. "He's still treating us like children."

I roll my eyes. "We are his children. Come back to the tent."

"No. I know where they are, and I'm going to hear what they have to say."

I try to hide my surprise at his having that information. Instead, I try to appeal to his sense of boredom. "It's not going to be anything we've never heard. They'll just talk about how…" I pause, suddenly nervous. "I will free you all."

"If it's nothing new, why meet at all? And why not have you there?"

I have no response to those questions.

Atar is smug. "They're planning something else, and I want to know what it is."

"We can't always get what we want."

I know that for certain. I want so many things, so many simple, boring things, and yet, I have none of them.

"Well, I'm still going," Atar insists.

"They'll have lookouts. They'll catch you. Aba will be furious."

"I won't get caught if I know where the lookouts are."

I can't hide my surprise this time. "How could you possibly know that?"

Atar gives me an impish grin. "I pay attention."

I frown. "Well, I tried. I'm going back to the camp. When you get caught, your suffering will be on your own head."

Atar tilts his head and gestures around us. "You've come this far, so you might as well come with me."

I examine our surroundings for the first time. We're several hundred yards away from camp. Atar has been walking away this entire time, and I've been mindlessly following him. I kick myself mentally. I really need to pay more attention.

"I'm not coming with you. Aba may forgive you, but if I show up…"

Atar frowns. "I don't want you going back alone. We aren't at home, Lia. You don't know who might lurk around the camp at night."

I glare at him, but I know he's right. I sigh. "Fine."

"What woke you up?" Atar asks. "Usually, you're all sound asleep when Aba leaves."

"I haven't slept soundly since we entered this…" I stop mid-sentence. "What do you mean 'usually'?"

Atar shrugs. "I always follow Aba to his meetings. There are lots of people there, and it's dark, so he doesn't notice."

He falls silent, and for a while, the only sounds we hear are our own footsteps in the dirt and the cries of animals far away, probably warning that humans are in their territory. We approach the base of a tall hill, where a cave gapes open uninvitingly, and Atar says, "Keep an eye out for a guard. He'll have to let us in."

Sure enough, when we're barely thirty yards into the cave, someone calls to us from the dark. "Who goes there?"

"Only a friend," Atar answers.

A man steps from the shadow of a stone and into the moonlight, and I tighten my shawl around my face, praying he won't recognize me. He may be from a different household. There are many families here traveling with their servants and slaves. He frowns at us, preparing to ask us for the password, no doubt. My heart drops into my stomach at the thought of the password. I had forgotten. It changes at every meeting, and Aba didn't invite us to this one. We don't know it.

"What news does my friend bring?" the guard asks.

I glance at Atar, and he shrugs. Does he not know? But he said he follows Aba all the time.

The guard taps his foot. He puts a hand on his belt, no doubt ready to pull a weapon from it.

"A new sunrise," Atar says in Derian, my father's first language.

The guard's eyes narrow, and he fixes a glare at us as if trying to read our intent.

Atar matches the man's stare, but I look back out toward the camp. If we stay here too long, there's a chance of us getting caught by a camp guard. If they think we're trying to escape, the punishment will be worse than any Aba could give us.

After a long, painful moment, the man nods, letting us pass. We walk deeper into the cave. Below us, a small fire with several dozen shadows around it beckons us. Atar gives me a reassuring nod before we walk down toward the group.

The meeting is well-attended for a small gathering. There are fewer people than there were at the one meeting in Ragien-ige, but Aba said they're being cautious. Still, there are many unfamiliar faces. It makes sense. After all, the caravan contains most of the noble households of Uze, and there are certainly others who feel the way Aba does. I pull my shawl tighter around my head. If we run into anyone who recognizes us, Aba will know we're here within minutes.

The people here look like us, tired, dusty, wearing clothes that have seen better days, but their faces are alert. Some look bright and hopeful, others look jaded and worried, but they're all here for the same purpose—to make sure they don't leave Gazidah in the same condition they arrived.

There are few women, but enough to ensure I don't look out of place. Atar is drawn to the fire where several men are gathered, and I trail after him, keeping to the shadows. One of the men is handing out daggers small enough to be kept in belts.

Atar pumps his fists a bit.

"It's finally happening," he says to me in a low voice.

I nod, but I can't share his excitement. If only I could just be less afraid, then maybe I could be as happy and hopeful as he is. Maybe I could be the beacon they need me to be. But why are they sharing weapons? If I do my job correctly, they shouldn't need them. The transition is supposed to be peaceful. A knot of worry forms in my stomach. Aba has spoken of defending me, of the slaves standing with me, but he can't mean for this to become violent. Given the emperor's temperament, we would all be killed.

CHAPTER 11

I hear a few snippets of conversations as we pass by. They speak of news from different regions of the empire, the end of the conflict with the rebellious maliks, the injustices and atrocities committed by those in power, and the urgent need for change. One man shows his most recent scars to another—a relation, judging by the pain on his face. Nearby, two women—one pregnant—share a tearful embrace. I try not to think the worst, but as my eyes are drawn to the pregnant woman's abdomen, nightmarish scenarios fight their way to the forefront of my mind. Aba is right—we need freedom.

Atar strides forward, but I grab his arm and pull him back. "We shouldn't get too close."

"I want to listen in."

"But if someone sees us—"

Atar rolls his eyes. "Don't worry. We'll be fine. I do this all the time, remember?"

Atar moves deeper into the crowd, and I follow behind him, praying with every step that he'll deem us close enough and stop moving. But he's determined to get to the heart of whatever this meeting is. The man handing out daggers comes up to Atar, who takes one, and then to me. He holds it with its hilt out, and I reach out despite myself.

"What are these for?"

The man's eyes dance with the firelight and with his own hopeful excitement. "All extras are being given to the women. You must be able to fight too."

My hand trembles as I take the small weapon from him, and he gives me a knowing nod. "We'll do what we must."

"But isn't this going to be peaceful?" I ask, my voice shaking as much as my hands. I look down, suddenly afraid the man will recognize me, even though I've never seen him before.

But the man doesn't seem to notice. As he turns away from me and to the next woman who approaches, I hear him answer, "No revolution is ever peaceful."

Atar is further ahead of me now, and I trot to catch up with him, the knot in my stomach growing bigger. We get far too close to the council convening at the center.

They sit around a low fire on a variety of mats and pass a bowl of food around as they discuss the changes in the world. Someone steps aside, and I glimpse Aba sitting between two elders. I duck behind Atar, but Aba doesn't seem to notice any of the people milling around him. He and the others are deep in conversation.

"—Matter of time. We cannot afford to be cowardly."

"Cowardice is not a factor. Our very lives are at stake. Caution is the least that is warranted."

"We've already lost too much time to caution," Aba says. "It has its place, but we can't allow ourselves to keep waiting. We have been living—no, surviving like this for far too long. It's time, and we're ready. Everything is in place."

There are affirmations around the circle, but some faces still look apprehensive. I can't blame them. They express what I feel in my heart. Aba seems sure he'll succeed—I'll succeed

—but I can't avoid the fear that we're all walking into our doom.

After all, the emperor overthrew my entire birth family and took over an empire in a night. Yes, he has been fighting ever since, but that proves he's a man ready to quash an uprising at a moment's notice.

I look down at the dagger now in my hand. It's small and unadorned—meant for use more than decoration. I place it on a nearby rock, where no one will trip over it. Maybe Aba's confidence isn't in me at all. The horrifying thought that he could plan to take freedom by force fills my mind. He's spent my whole life telling me this was my purpose, my destiny. But it wouldn't be like him to rely on me alone.

I step back into the shadows, trying to get lost in the darkness as I get lost in my thoughts. Atar stays near the fire. I should take him back with me. When the meeting ends, Aba will certainly see us. We need to leave before that happens.

I take a step forward, but as I do, a cry stops me cold. This one is louder than the ones I've been hearing in the silence every night—louder and closer.

Someone dumps sand on the fire, and people run.

I hear one word, and bile rises in my throat. "Guards!"

In the darkness, people flee in every direction, jostling me as I stand frozen. I need to move. I have to go somewhere. Anywhere. To hide. But my body has stopped working.

There's screaming, so much screaming, and clanging metal in the dark. Am I dreaming? I must be dreaming.

A hand falls on my shoulder, pulling me back, and my voice gets caught behind my lips. But I can make out a few features in the darkness, and the face that looks at mine is familiar. Atar.

"Come on!" He grabs my hand and pulls me toward the cave entrance.

But something grabs the back of my tunic. I do scream then.

Atar whirls around, new dagger in hand, but his hand falls midair.

Does a guard have a knife to my back? I look over my shoulder and see not a guard but Aba. And even in the dark, I can tell he's furious, but he grabs hold of both of us and drags us back deeper into the cave. I don't fight him.

We hurry through twists and turns and cramped spaces—deeper and deeper into the cave.

We're going to get caught. The thought repeats in my mind. But after a while, the only sounds I hear are our own footsteps and breaths.

Aba doesn't let go of us, though, and being dragged along in silence is almost as terrifying as being taken by guards.

After what feels like hours but is probably only minutes, the first thing I notice is that we're walking uphill. Then a burst of fresh, dry air mixed with the earthy odor of sand fills my nose.

The star-filled sky bursts into view in front of us as we come out of the cave through a thin crack in the rock. The camp is in sight. But unlike the meeting, it looks peaceful—like no one there knows of the terror occurring in a cave not far away.

Aba pushes Atar and me down, showing we should duck without words. We do so, and he pushes us quickly through the brush and into camp. A few times, we splay ourselves in the dirt breathlessly to avoid being seen by guards.

My heart pounds in my ears, and I hold my breath as Aba keeps a hand on my head while one guard passes far too close. But he doesn't see us.

When we get back to our tent, Aba practically throws us inside. He whips the curtain shut and hunches near it, listening for a few moments. Ima and Jorra stir and then wake fully when they realize we're all already up.

Aba turns to Atar and I.

"What were you two thinking?" he hisses.

"What's wrong?" Ima's eyes are wide.

"These children," Aba answers, glowering at us, "Disobeyed my direct orders and attended the meeting."

"What?" Ima's voice is quiet, but it belies the fire in her eyes. "How could you?"

I look at Atar, but he avoids my gaze, trying not to reap any more of Aba's ire. At any rate, I'm the oldest, so I'm responsible.

I take a deep breath. "Aba, I'm sorry. It was—"

"And we were raided," Aba continues, more to Ima than to any of us. But Jorra gasps, covering her mouth and looking at us all in horror.

"Was anyone—" Ima starts.

Aba shakes his head. "I don't know. We can't discuss this."

"Aba, I—" I try again.

Aba cuts me off. "Not a word from either of you."

Ima slaps us both on our knees, but her face shows more than anger. She's scared. She has every reason to be.

"I—" I start, but a glance from Aba silences me.

I finally meet Atar's eyes, which glisten. I grimace. He was terrified, too.

People may die because of what happened tonight. Some may already be dead.

I should have stopped him. I don't know how I would have, what I could have done or said to convince him. But maybe something else would have made a difference. I shouldn't have gone along.

Or maybe, since I did, I should have protected everyone. That's what I'm supposed to do. But I froze as people around me—people who rely on me—were attacked. I'm no savior, no matter what anyone thinks. And Aba may already know that.

Aba sits near the entrance of the tent as Atar and I settle in next to Jorra and Ima, trying to look as though we've been here all night. I can still hear screams outside, but this time, I'm certain they're real.

CHAPTER 12

Enra

There was a situation last night. At least, that's what I've been told. Guards found slaves outside the camp—in a nearby cave—having a meeting of some sort. We don't know what they discussed, but the captain of the guard believes it was dangerous enough to break up. So that's what he did. A few got away, but they captured several without killing them.

The captain detained the errant slaves they'd captured until this morning, so now Aba and the other nobles on this journey have to decide what to do with them.

I sit under a dim pavilion behind Aba and listen as the captain of the guard describes what happened last night, tuning out the noise from the rest of the camp. According to the captain, a guard noticed two figures walking out toward the hills. He followed them until they disappeared. After searching for a short time, he found the mouth of a cave. When he came back to report this discovery, the captain took control of the situation.

I'm trying to pay close attention, but it's only the morning, and it's already hot. The sun beats down on my back, and the heat is distracting. At least my face is in the shade.

Still, my mind is working as well as it can. A meeting of slaves? I wonder if Benar had anything to do with it. None of our slaves were among those captured, but that doesn't mean none were there. Aba has shown he has no intention of stopping Benar's plans, whatever they are. And yet, we can't not be here. I suppose it is possible all this has nothing to do with him or Lia, anyway.

"What is your recommendation, Captain?" a satrap from Sahr asks.

"They refuse to name their compatriots," the captain admits. "So I believe punishment is in order. We cannot risk danger to your majesties."

Another satrap nods, waving his ornate fan. "I agree. If they're willing to sacrifice themselves, let them."

But my uncle Comar, another Uze satrap like my father, balks at this idea. "Three slaves are mine," he notes. "I will not permit the murder of my investments."

"Would you rather your investments murder you?" the Sahr satrap asks.

Uncle Comar purses his lips. "I'm not saying they shouldn't be punished. But I will not accept their deaths."

"Then we make an example."

Everyone turns in our direction as Aba speaks for the first time. "Give them a thief's punishment. Do it in public."

I have to stop myself from gaping at Aba. The suggestion is unheard of. While people punish their servants and slaves all the time, they do it in private to preserve their honor, as required by the law. Only criminals receive public punishments, and then only if their deeds were so egregious as to warrant their humiliation.

Even Uncle Comar is aghast at Aba's proposal. "What will that accomplish?"

"They may be unwilling to betray their comrades, but that doesn't mean we can't punish their comrades through them. They'll bear the weight of watching as others bear the pain and shame of their cowardice for them. We will show them all there's no honor in protecting the guilty."

There are murmurs of agreement around the circle.

"We have decided, then."

Aba turns to the captain of the guard. "Prepare whipping posts in the center of camp. Then gather all the slaves and servants. They must all bear witness."

The captain bows and leaves, and then the men in the circle begin to stand and go about their business. The guilty slaves need to be punished before the caravan can leave, but I suppose everyone has other things to attend to as well.

I stand as Aba does, and he studies my face. "You have thoughts?"

"It is... unconventional," I admit.

"Do you disagree?"

"I..."

Do I? I'm not sure. We don't even know what they were meeting about. It could have been something innocuous, not worth the price of the punishment. It could have been that they just wanted the freedom to converse in private. But then, it could be something dangerous, as the captain said.

Aba nods as if he'd expected my hesitation. He puts a hand on my shoulder. "Often we must do harsh things for the greater good. Appearances are important."

I purse my lips. Of course, he has to keep up appearances. If anyone thinks he's harboring a potential uprising and doing nothing about it, it would be our own heads in danger.

Still, something about all this doesn't sit well with me.

. . .

I'M OBVIOUSLY out of place here. In a gathering of slaves, servants, and guards, any nobles who turn up will look like a tree among wheat. I'm not the only one, which is why I felt secure enough to even come see the punishment. Some are curious, and others may just be morbid onlookers. I'm not sure which I am. When I heard they were gathering, I just came out. I still don't know why.

I've never seen a servant, a slave, or even a criminal whipped. The most I've ever seen is a caning or two in Ragien as punishment for unruliness. Perhaps Aba has sheltered me too much.

I stand at the back of the crowd among the other nobles who came. Some brought daises, seats, and pavilions to see past the crowd. A few stand, like me. But they're all talking, discussing politics, fashion, food, anything but the ordeal we're all about to witness.

The slaves and servants are silent. They all stand in front of us, facing seven wooden pillars in the sand. There is a bit of nervous movement, but there's no conversation, not even whispers. Most people stare at the ground or straight ahead, not even daring to look at each other. There's a palpable weight in the air.

The weight gets heavier as the guards lead their prisoners to the posts. There are five men and two women, and they all look like they've been beaten halfway to death. Their tunics are torn and bloodied, and their faces are swollen so badly I can see it from here. Some of them limp as they are dragged behind the guards. All that to determine who they were meeting with?

One by one, guards tie them to the posts, and then the captain comes into the opening to declare the reason for punishment.

"These prisoners have harbored and protected suspected criminals. Under the law regarding betrayal and insurgence, they will each be punished with 20 lashes in the presence of the public." He turns to the guards standing behind the beaten slaves. "You may begin."

In unison, the guards whip each prisoner, slashing at their backs and arms. Several of them cry out in pain, but one man and one woman remain silent, bearing the punishment while making no noise.

I wince each time the whips crack and the people cry out. None of them say any words, no names, no apologies. They know why they're being punished, and they're accepting it without bending.

Blood spatters in the sand with each crack of the whip. I close my eyes. My stomach is too weak. Guilty or not, there can't be anyone who deserves this. Behind me, a noble laughs at a joke.

My blood boils. Do they not have the decency to at least stay quiet as their slaves are punished? Yes, they outrank them, but that doesn't give them the right to belittle their suffering.

The whips continue to crack. The screams break through the air.

I can't take more of this.

I walk through the nobles and back to my tent. While this punishment may have been necessary, it doesn't feel right.

CHAPTER 13

Lia

Gazidah looms over the horizon ahead of us, a manmade mountain among natural ones. Our pace has been slow since the city was in sight—no doubt soldiers are at the gates to inspect everyone entering the city for the festival. Part of me is grateful for the slow pace. The desert was a trial, made infinitely worse after the raid and the punishment. A rumor spread through camp that two people were spotted, and that's how we got caught. I can't shake the feeling that it was Atar and I.

We all kept quiet after that, but even with the pall hanging over the end of the journey, I'd like to spend as much time outside of Gazidah as possible. Still, there is a part of me that just wants to get it all over with.

Ima wraps an arm around my shoulders as if she can sense what I'm thinking. "Don't worry," she says. "You have nothing to be afraid of."

I nod. She sounds so certain, but I don't think I can believe her.

When we reach the northeast gate of Gazidah, the soldiers

have us stop on one side of the road. Soldiers inspect all our horses, wagons, and satchels while smaller parties pass us. They even inspect the satrap's gifts for the emperor. The satrap doesn't complain, though. I'm sure he expected this.

It's not surprising that the emperor would be cautious. My parents tell me that my grandfather was overthrown because no one inspected the gifts brought for the prince's birthday. The current emperor smuggled weapons and fighters into the city under the guise of coming to honor his future ruler. Of course, he'd be afraid someone would attempt something similar against him.

After inspecting the satrap's belongings, about a dozen soldiers make their way through our ranks. When they reach our family, one man stares at me, an older soldier who was certainly alive during the coup. I lower my eyes to the ground and resist the urge to pull my shawl across my face. Any action like that will look even more suspicious than doing nothing would. After a few painful moments, he moves on. I breathe a sigh of relief when he turns to the next family instead of calling the other soldiers to examine me.

When we've all been inspected and approved, we're allowed to cross the threshold of the gate into Gazidah. The city shows few signs of having been rubble twelve years ago, its towers and walls destroyed. While the poorer areas of the city still exhibit signs of wear, and new walls have been erected beside the crumbling old ones, the affluent regions are pristine. The homes of the wealthy are gated with rich, oiled wood, the roofs of their houses painted with pitch instead of the thatch and straw of the poorer homes.

When we reach the palace, I stifle a gasp. It looks nothing like the tangle of ruin and ash Aba and Ima have described. All I remember is my nursery and fire. But Ima says that the palace was unrecognizable by the next morning. Now, it towers over us in deep red clay, jewel encrusted windows peeking over the stone walls. Emperor Pakel must have had extra resources to rebuild even as he was fighting rebels in the south. The satrap leads us all into the courtyard so that he can go in and pay his respects and his taxes. Those of us not needed to carry the gifts will stay here.

Steward Goran walks over to us while other servants unload the gifts. He talks to Ima and Aba for a moment, and they nod, but they look upset as they glance at us. Steward Goran walks around them and waves to us. "Lia, Jorra, follow me."

"Yes?" Jorra says as I say, "Sir?"

Goran rolls his eyes. "The satrap needs two girls to escort Vroni to the throne room."

My heart falls into my stomach. Those two girls are us?

Goran beckons for us to follow him, and Jorra and I exchange a nervous glance before we do. We walk through the crowd of our people organizing the satrap's gifts and come to the front of the group, where Vroni and Satrapha Edab are waiting inside their litter.

Around us, Satrap Paykhan's servants arrange themselves into a sort of parade of gifts, of which Vroni will be last. My hands shake, and Jorra takes one of them.

"We'll be alright," she whispers.

But I don't believe her. Vroni and Satrapha Edab step out of their litter and into the group at the back. Jorra and I take our places behind them, each of us picking up a corner of Vroni's train so it doesn't get trampled or snagged anywhere. I take a ragged breath, and Satrapha Edab turns around to look at me curiously but says nothing as we start our procession into the building.

The walk to the throne room is long, and I have to remind myself to breathe the whole way. I imagine flames around every corner, and I hear screams echoing down each hall. By the time we stop in front of the doors to the emperor's court,

I'm fighting back tears. The doors are carved with ornate flowers and birds, displaying the luxury of the palace. I wonder if they're new or if they survived the attack.

A page announces us. "Paykhan Nehim, Satrap of Ragien."

Then the doors open, and we walk forward into the most beautiful space I've ever seen. The soaring walls are covered in white plaster with what looks like gold filigree pressed into it at intervals. Every few steps, a brazier burns with the rich spice of incense. The room is massive, but we're surrounded. At least two dozen pillars the size of tree trunks hold the ceiling up above our heads, and below them, several hundred people—either local nobles or visiting rulers—mill around inside seeking an audience with the emperor. They part to let us through, and ahead of us, there is a wide dais with several figures on it. I can't distinguish their faces though.

Satrap Paykhan reaches the front first. He bows and steps to the side, and one by one, his servants lay gifts at the emperor's feet. We are the last gift to enter the room, and while the glittery baubles in the chests distract many, others are eager to see the human gift at the back.

Waves of whispers follow us. The fleeting thought that someone has recognized me passes through my mind, but I dismiss it. Jorra and I are slaves presenting a beautiful bride to join the emperor's family. In several years, she will be their empress consort. No one is looking at us.

Just to be sure, I glance at a few courtiers as we pass them. They are entirely enchanted by Vroni and Satrapha Edab, who is a renowned beauty in her own right. In fact, few in the receiving audience could compare to them. No wonder the emperor was so amenable to marriage, even if he isn't doing the marrying himself. Beauty is a currency for women in Elisya, especially in the courts. Noble women can use it to their advantage, but for slave women, it's a dangerous currency to have.

Jorra is pretty, but not anywhere near the level of the nobility whose train we're carrying, and I'm not beautiful by any stretch, so we warrant no attention. My lack of a pretty face has occasionally caused me grief, but not today. Today I give thanks to Juae for making me plain.

When we reach the center of the room, the figures on the dais become more distinguishable. To the right of the throne, a small cluster of people stands watching us. An older man sits beside a young man who gapes as we walk, his eyes following our every movement. This must be Vroni's betrothed, Emperor Pakel's oldest grandson. And the couple behind him are certainly his parents, the new datu and diyan, the titles my parents used to hold. The bejeweled circlet on the older man's head assures me. I'd only seen the circlet once—my father wore it for special occasions.

To the left of the throne, a group of priests watches us impassively. They will perform the betrothal ceremony, I'm sure, but they can't mean for that to happen now. Certainly, the emperor will want Vroni to rest and look her best for that.

A smaller chair sits next to the throne, and the woman in it makes herself as small as possible. One of her hands crosses against her body to rest in her lap, and her posture is relaxed so that she almost sinks into the chair given to her, making her look even more diminutive than she actually is, which is fairly small to begin with. Even though I've never seen her, I feel like I recognize Empress Saretha. Next to her, the emperor looms larger than life itself. She is the picture of deference to her husband, but her fingers strum against the arm of her chair as she appraises the satrap's tribute. She has her own manner of power here.

I've been stalling, but I finally bring myself to look at the throne. An older man with a scowl of perpetual disapproval sits on it. Emperor Pakel. His eyes meet mine as they graze over us all, and I focus on the floor, my heart pounding. When Satrapha Edab and Vroni reach the foot of the dais, separated from the emperor by hills of treasures, we all bow low. Satrap Paykhan has been bowing all this time. Jorra and I are kneeling on the floor. We must stay this way until the emperor tells us we can stand.

The emperor seems content to let us all stay in a kneeling position. My knees hurt, and my left ankle aches. I glance at Jorra, who gives me a brief grimace. What is he waiting for?

After several long moments, the emperor says, "You may rise."

Jorra and I wait until Satrapha Edab and Vroni are standing before we follow suit. We display Vroni's train, splaying it out in the vast corridor of space the courtiers have provided for us, though many of them have crowded in behind to see and hear better.

When the train is in place, Jorra takes my hand, and we scramble off to the side, pressing our backs against the nearest pillar. We have to stay close to carry Vroni's train when they leave, but we know we have to stay out of the way. Courtiers stand in front of us, getting as close to the throne as they dare. I bless them for being obstacles between me and the emperor.

"Your gracious majesty," Satrap Paykhan says over the din, "May I present my wife, Satrapha Edab, and my daughter, Vroni."

A herald strikes his staff against the stone floor twice, and the whispers fall silent. The emperor is going to speak.

"Welcome, my sons. Welcome, my daughters," he declares. "It is a joy to welcome you here and to celebrate the union of our two families. We delight that the beauty of marriage will be the culmination of our celebration of peace."

"We are honored, your excellency," Satrap Paykhan answers.

Emperor Pakel nods toward his grandson. "Mandla, greet your bride."

The besotted young man on the dais steps down and around the plethora of tribute gifts to take Vroni's hand. He says something to her, and they both bow in greeting. Vroni's bow is lower than Mandla's.

Mandla is grinning when he looks back up at his grandfather, who gives the first nod of approval I've seen him make since we walked in. He surveys the crowd, and his eyes rest on me for a moment. My breath catches in my throat. Does he recognize me?

But his eyes keep moving and eventually rest on his wife. Some kind of silent communication passes between them, and Emperor Pakel nods. "The betrothal ceremony will take place at sunset. Until then, let the women retire to prepare. The satrap and I have matters to discuss. You are dismissed."

The emperor stands and takes his wife's hand, and they exit the room from a door that I hadn't noticed behind the throne. The family, and then the priests, exit after them. Prince Mandla is the only one who looks reluctant to go.

When they've left, the herald strikes his staff against the floor again. This must signal that people are now free to do what they please because conversations strike up all around us as people choose where they will spend the rest of their day until the betrothal ceremony. Jorra and I rush forward to take Vroni's train so she and Satrapha Edab can retreat. A servant girl steps from the crowd and bows.

"Allow me to show your highnesses to your suites."

Satrapha Edab nods, and the girl directs us through the crowd and out the doors. Only after I hear the heavy thud of the throne room doors closing behind us do I feel like I can breathe again.

CHAPTER 14

Enra

After he strikes his staff to indicate the end of audiences with the emperor, the herald turns to Aba. "You may follow me to the emperor's private receiving rooms."

Nalkendi and Khanda's nurse steps forward to take them, but I look at Aba. "May I come with you?"

Aba glances at the herald, who doesn't indicate whether the emperor would approve. After a moment, Aba nods. "It's appropriate."

I hold myself a little higher at his acknowledgement.

The herald leads us out through a side door near the throne—not the one the emperor left through—and into a wide hallway. As we walk, I focus on stifling my distaste for Emperor Pakel and the entire display of extorted presents, including my sister, in the throne room. Emperor Pakel must be certain we're on his side. That's the only way Ragien, and all Uze really, is safe.

The emperor's private receiving rooms are a lavishly appointed suite on the far side of a small garden. We pass through a wide archway and beside a trickling stone fountain surrounded by flowers. The summery blooms fill the air with a refreshing fragrance, but it offers no comfort. The herald opens a door for us across from the archway and bows, showing that we should step inside. When we do, we find the emperor, his son, and his grandson already relaxing on cushions by a low table, waiting for us.

Emperor Pakel nods. "Enter. Be seated."

I bristle but try to remain calm. I suppose we get no further words of greeting outside of the court. Aba bows and sits across from the emperor with his legs crossed beneath his tunic. I do the same. We don't have the luxury of reclining on cushions before the emperor.

When we're seated, the emperor speaks again. "Ideally, we would have liked to settle this much earlier, but now we must address the bride price and dowry for our families."

It's unusual to settle the exchange of resources for a marriage a few weeks before the wedding. Typically, people do that at the betrothal. But the political upheaval made an early in-person betrothal impossible. With the coup, and the subsequent war, it makes sense that Emperor Pakel wouldn't have wanted to travel to Ragien to settle things. But he could have sent his son, a brother, or even a nephew. Any adult male members of the bride or groom's family may attend betrothal negotiations. Given who he is, though, he probably wouldn't have wanted to risk letting an heir out of his sight. People are always afraid that what they've done to others will be done to them.

I glance at Aba, but his face is passive. He will make no note of the unusual circumstances, and I'll keep my thoughts to myself. If the emperor has any honor at all, the bride price his family pays will show the care they intend to provide for Vroni, but I wonder what he'll ask from us as a dowry. We're already his subordinates—everything we have to give is his. Aba and I wait in silence.

"First, the matter of the bride price." The emperor gestures to a wall where a servant waits like part of the room's decor. "We are pleased with our new daughter's presentation. She is lovely… quite a treasure. Her grace is obvious, and her decorum is appropriate to one of her position. Her training has been excellent. We are prepared to be generous in our gifts for her."

My skin crawls at his description of Vroni's "presentation", but Emperor Pakel looks at us like we're supposed to be grateful. Aba smiles and nods, giving the emperor what he wants. The servant steps forward and sets a ledger on the table in front of us. Emperor Pakel opens it and turns it so we can read it. It starts with the typical wording of an imperial declaration and outlines the things we'll receive when Vroni is married. There are many gifts indeed. Extra food for Ragien's storehouses, a lower rate of taxation for five years, jewels for Ima and Nalkendi, six horses for Khanda and me, a herd of a hundred hills of cattle. It goes on and on. Vroni truly impressed him. I try not to frown as I read what we're trading for my sister's life. The emperor hasn't told us what he wants in return yet.

When we finish reading, Emperor Pakel looks at us expectantly. Aba bows, and I follow suit. "You are incredibly generous, your excellency," Aba says.

The emperor smiles, the first smile I've seen from him. "Much better than the days of Niotek, no doubt."

I stifle a gasp at his use of the previous emperor's given name. He may have killed the man, but he clearly has no respect for him in death, either.

But Aba doesn't even flinch. "We are all prospering, excellency."

Emperor Pakel nods. "As for the matter of the dowry, we expect little. You have already provided a bounty this afternoon. Is there anything else you wished to provide?"

I breathe a sigh of relief. He's leaving the dowry up to us instead of demanding something. We've been preparing a generous dowry just in case.

Aba nods and pulls a scroll I didn't know he had from his sleeve. He presents it to the emperor with both hands. "We have prepared a winter palace for you and your family in Ragien. It sits on the coast where you may enjoy the mild northern weather. In addition, we have provided for Vroni to have an income of a million ranat per year from the management of the palace's ranch and farm."

While it may not be much to Emperor Pakel, a million ranat is a substantial amount of money, especially for a satrap's daughter. I gauge the imperial family's reactions. Prince Mandla doesn't seem to be paying much attention, but his father's ears perk up at the mention of income from a property in Ragien.

Emperor Pakel's expression is inscrutable, but he nods. "We will enjoy the use of the palace in the winter."

He pauses, and I think he's about to approve the betrothal and end the meeting, but then he holds up his hand to his servant again, who brings him a scroll instead of a ledger this time.

"There is one more thing we need from you," he says. "A trifle, really."

My heartbeat picks up speed, but Aba nods. "Anything, your excellency."

"We will have many guests over the next few months for the festival, so we will distribute the staff from Uze throughout the imperial palace. It is a small, temporary dowry gift. One that will not harm you to give."

He says it like an order, not a request, and it is an order. A punishment framed as a dowry. The emperor still doesn't trust us.

Aba takes the scroll from the emperor and unrolls it. It's a list of assignments for all our servants and slaves. The number of people we have with us is exact. He must have had spies watching us.

"We have heard," Emperor Pakel adds, "That there was trouble on the journey here."

He definitely had spies. He must be referring to the slave meeting the guards broke up. But we handled that on the journey. I start to say so, but Aba puts a hand on my knee, stopping me. He shakes his head once almost imperceptibly. I keep my mouth closed.

"The households dispersion will discourage any further… collusion," the emperor finishes.

Aba rolls the scroll back up and bows. "I will give this to my chief steward."

The emperor nods. "Then the betrothal is approved. You are dismissed. We will see you at sunset."

With the emperor's permission, Aba and I stand to go. The herald waits outside the room to lead us back to our party. Well, not ours anymore. The emperor is trapping us here in the palace, making sure we can't rely on any of our own people. It's not a mistake that he picked only the staff from Uze, and he's using a small gathering of only a few men as an excuse. As we walk back through the long hallway, I frown. The emperor doesn't need to trust us for us to get what we want.

CHAPTER 15

Lia

I carry a basket holding Satrapha Edab's belongings into the shadow of a doorway to be taken inside as the familiar voice of Steward Goran cuts into the din of activity.

"Household of Satrap Paykhan! Gather!"

I look around for my family and position myself with them as we all gather near a tree.

"You are being reassigned to new areas in the palace," Steward Goran says.

The group is quiet. I glance at Aba, whose mouth is pinched into a stiff line. The rest of the surrounding faces hold expressions of surprise, some better concealed than others. Even as Steward Goran informs us, he looks taken aback himself. We had expected to be directed into the service of particular members of the satrap's household. No one was expecting this.

Steward Goran reads our assignments to us while a delegation of imperial slaves looks on, waiting to direct us to our assigned locations. We're being dispersed all over the place, put to work in the emperor's house. I had expected to work here, but I thought I would at least be with my family.

Instead, my stomach falls as Steward Goran directs us. Aba and several other men are sent to the emperor's smithy at the palace's east wall. Ima and the kitchen maids go to the emperor's kitchens in the palace basement. Atar and three other young men are taken to the emperor's stables near the palace's outer wall. When Goran gets to me, my heart lightens to hear Jorra's and my names paired together at the end of a string of young women's names, seventeen in total.

"You are to report to the chief imperial steward's office for assignment." Goran nods, showing we should leave right away. Jorra and I glance at each other before walking toward the waiting imperial slaves. A woman holds her hand up for us and, after counting that she has the same number of people Goran read out, she leads us through a small door and into the palace.

"What does this mean?" Jorra whispers to me.

I shake my head. "I don't know. Nothing good."

These hallways are much smaller than the ones we walked to get to the throne room. These must be the servants' halls. A cluster of people with linens in their hands hurry past us, confirming my theory. After three sharp turns and a walk down a flight of stairs, the woman knocks on a door at the end of a hallway, and a male voice calls out, "Enter."

The servant opens the door and has us file into the room one by one. It's a tight space, with small windows near its ceiling to let in what little air and light the room can get. The only furniture is a desk, a shelf weighed down with records, and a table the chief imperial steward occupies. The chief imperial steward does not work in luxury. By the time all seventeen girls are in the room, Jorra and I are crowded in next to his desk.

He gives us all a cursory glance. "Is this everyone?"

The woman nods. "Yes, sir."

"Good. Listen carefully."

For a second, I think he's talking to us, but when the woman nods again, I realize his direction is for her.

"You, and… you," he points at two girls in the back, "to your mistress' chambers."

"You." He points to Jorra, and I expect him to point to me, since I'm standing right next to her, but he gestures to the girl behind Jorra. "To the prince's betrothed."

He continues like this, assigning us in pairs to different chambers for all the palace's visitors, but when he comes to the end of his list, there are no more pairs to make. There's just me. Wherever I'm going, I'm going alone. The thought makes my head pound.

The imperial steward's eyes fall on me. "You—"

A knock interrupts my assignment. "Enter!" the steward calls out, frustration in his voice. A man comes in with a letter and hands it to him.

"From Derian?" the steward asks.

The man nods and moves his lips, but his voice is so quiet that even standing next to the desk, I can't hear what he says.

"Finally." The steward continues his questioning. "Who did they send?"

The newcomer winces and whispers a name.

The steward's face falls. "What?"

He tears open the letter, a single piece of paper folded and sealed, his expression growing grimmer by the second as he reads. When he's finished, the steward crumples the letter then thinks better of it and smooths it back out, saying under his breath, "Of course, they would."

He looks at me again. "You'll go to the Derian delegate's chambers."

He says it like he means to say, "May Juae have mercy on your soul."

The man who brought the letter looks at me with pity. Just who did Derian send as their delegation, and why do I have to face them alone?

The imperial steward waves us away. "Take them."

The servant woman bows and leads us back out of the room, and soon I realize why he told her to listen carefully. In Ragien, servants use the same hallways as everyone else, but here in the palace, the servant's hallways are a maze. I don't think I'd be able to find my way back to the steward's office even if I asked directions, but the woman leaves each of us at the door to the place where we will work. We go up staircases, down staircases, through doorways, across courtyards, and occasionally we pass through a hallway meant for the nobles. Our group grows smaller as we go until finally, it's just me left. I feel compelled to break the silence, so I ask the woman. "Who do I report to?"

She glances at me for the first time and answers like it's a ridiculous question. "To the steward."

Which steward, I want to ask, how do I get there, and where do I go if I need something? But I hold my questions back, and the woman deposits me in front of a heavy wooden door. She hands me a key, nods, and then disappears back through the labyrinth of hallways to whatever her work is for the rest of the day. I unlock the door and pull it open. On the other side are three steps up and a heavy red tapestry, no doubt to hide the servant's door from the nobles. I scale the stairs and push the tapestry aside to enter the most lavish room I've ever seen.

The first things I notice are five doors, two to the right, one across from me, and two to the left, and candelabras scattered around the room. They're unlit, but there are plenty of them— no doubt I'll be lighting them later. I make a mental note to find flint. Near the candelabras, several low sofas piled high with bright, plush cushions provide plenty of places for the chamber's guests to lounge and talk.

A short table covered with a blanket is in the center of the room, but I can't imagine any ambassadors or diplomats dining in their rooms often. I turn around to find that the tapestry I've just passed through is flanked by two windows with cabinets beneath them—no doubt why there were stairs, so the servant's halls won't impede the nobles' views and fresh air. This room overlooks a peaceful courtyard, one that looks eerily familiar. A pang in my chest makes me turn away, and instead of studying the view, I search through the cabinets. It looks like they contain much of what I'll need to care for the rooms. I rejoice when I find flint and an oil lantern behind one of the cabinet doors.

I turn my attention to the doors next. The door across from the tapestry leads to the noble halls. I close it quickly. One that had been to my right houses a room for bathing. It too has lavish appointments, with a huge stone tub in its center. I'll have to find out how to draw water for it. The door next to it encloses a room with a small bed and table. It's the least impressive room I've seen in the suite, so it must be mine. The two other doors that had been to the left are bedrooms, where my temporary masters will be staying. They are already filled with trunks and baskets. The delegation from Derian is here. I remember the expression on the chief steward's face and shudder. Who could they possibly be? Someone abusive? Or perpetually unsatisfied? Someone so particular that they cause even the chief steward trouble? Whoever they are, I'm going to have to face them soon. I reach out for the handle of the last bedroom door when I hear a woman's voice behind me speaking in Derian.

"Well, it would seem we already have a guest, and she's curious."

I wince. Getting caught snooping through noble rooms is a

terrible way to make an impression. I turn in a bow. "Forgive me… mistress." I say in Elisyan, pausing before the word "mistress." Though the Derian language would seem to indicate I'm talking to someone from the Derian delegation, I can't be sure.

There's annoyance in the woman's voice when she answers in Elisyan. "Stop bowing and face me. And I'm not your 'mistress'."

Slowly, I raise my head, fully intent upon being as contrite as possible, but I freeze when I meet the most terrifying eyes I've ever seen. An almost luminescent green pierces into my mind, and I think I can feel my thoughts being read. I stifle my breath to avoid crying out.

There is movement behind the woman, and I gratefully tear my eyes away from hers. A tall, handsome man enters the room and puts a hand on the woman's shoulder. "Don't frighten the girl." There's a laugh in his voice, though his expression stays impassive. He turns to me and nods. "What is your name?"

The intimidating woman adds, "And what are you doing here?"

I scramble to introduce myself. "Suan and sali…" I don't know what to call them, so I default to Elisyan for "noble prince" and "noble princess". "Forgive me. My name is Lia. I am your chambermaid."

The man gestures to the woman as though that explains everything. "See? She's supposed to be here."

The woman huffs, but her shoulders relax. "Very well, Lia. We're not your 'prince and princess' either."

I start to bow again but think better of it. "Forgive me. How should I address you?"

It feels strange leaving off a formal title at the end of the question, but I think any other guesses will make the woman angry again.

"Obipae Kula and Enipae Gowan will be fine."

Obipae. It's a lower noble's title, though Aba says Derianites are more liberal with their titles than Elisyans are. Maybe she wasn't born into nobility. "Yes, Obipae Kula," I respond.

Enipae Gowan, the man, studies me, but his eyes aren't nearly as frightening as Obipae Kula's. They have a warmth in them. "Were you going through our belongings, Lia?"

I stumble over my words as I answer. "No! Certainly not, Enipae Gowan. I was familiarizing myself with the suite—"

Obipae Kula scrutinizes me. "Why does a chambermaid need to familiarize herself with the suite?"

I take a moment before I realize she expects an answer. None of the noble guests in Ragien ever spoke to me so much. "We arrived today, and I wanted to be ready before you came."

"You aren't from the palace?" Enipae Gowan asks.

"I am from Ragien, Enipae," I answer.

Enipae Gowan glances at Obipae Kula. "Ragien?"

Obipae Kula nods. "Further northwest."

They're speaking in Derian now, so I glance between them, trying not to show I understand what they're saying. If they learn they've been sent a chambermaid who speaks Derian, they may think I'm a spy.

"She got here just before we did," Enipae Gowan notes.

Obipae Kula's expression darkens. "This place just doesn't seem right. Are you a slave or a servant, Lia?"

The last sentence was in Elisyan, so I answer. "I am a slave, Obipae Kula."

Obipae Kula's frown deepens, and she and Enipae Gowan exchange a meaningful glance. "We must be careful," Enipae Gowan says in Derian.

This makes Obipae Kula smile. "You're always careful."

I feel like I'm intruding on a private conversation, so I go against my better judgement and bow. "I will unpack your things."

Obipae Kula scrutinizes me, and I struggle not to cower under her gaze. She must find whatever she's looking for, though, because she nods. "Thank you, Lia."

I retreat into the nearest guest room with Derian whispers at my back.

So far, the Derian delegation doesn't seem so bad. Obipae Kula must be enchanted—I think she can see into my soul—but I'm not on my way to the dungeons, so I consider it a blessing. I untie the trunks and baskets and shake the dust from the linens out the window, after checking below to make sure I didn't shower an unfortunate passerby with the spoils of travel. Once I've set the clothes out, I organize the trunks against the room's walls.

While I don't work as a chambermaid in the satrap's house, I'm well-acquainted with the duties. As I air out the last of the clothes, I wonder what my family is doing. How will I see them? I don't even know where to look.

The sun is getting lower, closing in on the palace's rooftop, so the enipae and obipae will probably want to prepare for Sali Vroni's betrothal ceremony and celebration banquet. I tiptoe back into the antechamber, where Enipae Gowan and Obipae Kula are still deep in hushed conversation. I try to determine who I should address first. From the way they are sitting—huddled close on a sofa, his leg brushing against her skirt—and the fact that they arrived here together and their belongings are all in one room, I assume they're married. Obipae Kula did most of the talking when they first arrived, but I don't want to offend Enipae Gowan by speaking to his wife instead of to him.

Juae must have mercy on me, because they look up, and Obipae Kula asks, "What is it, Lia?"

I try not to make my relief too obvious. "Would you like me to prepare your outfits for the evening?"

The couple exchanges a glance, presumably signaling the

end of their conversation, and Enipae Gowan smiles. "There's no need to prepare my outfit."

They both stand, and Obipae Kula adds, "You may help me, though."

The three of us go into their room, and Enipae Gowan collects his things to change in the next room while Obipae Kula pulls three wrap skirts from her collection—a deep red that's almost brown, a rich yellow, and a muted green. I make note of her preferences.

"Which one do you think?" she asks me.

I'm taken aback for a moment. No one has ever asked me my opinion on their clothing choices, and certainly no one noble. But Obipae Kula looks at me expectantly, so I weigh the benefits of each color. Red is the color of Derian, I know that much, but the darkness may be untoward for a betrothal. The green is lovely, but it is more suited for serious occasions, and whatever the couple's true feelings about one another, a betrothal should be joyous. I lift the yellow one. Obipae Kula frowns, but she nods. "You know your court."

I don't really know the court, but I know the culture of betrothals. I've seen enough of them at the temple. "Would you like to refresh in the washroom?" I ask.

Obipae Kula indicates she would, so I collect the rest of the items that pair well with the yellow skirt and lead her across the antechamber. Obipae Kula opts to use the small washbasin rather than the large tub, so I pick it up to leave the room. There must be a well or a pump somewhere nearby. I can't imagine anyone lugging buckets of water across the palace just to fill a washbasin.

But when I reach for the door, Obipae Kula laughs for the first time. It's a bright laugh, one that belies her intense stare. She comes over and takes the basin from me. "I think I'm more suited to be a chambermaid than you are."

She walks over to a spout in the far wall I hadn't noticed

before. There's a cork in it, so she removes the cork and places the basin beneath the spout. Then she uses her foot to press down repeatedly on a lever I also hadn't noticed. After a few seconds, water gushes out of the spout, filling the basin.

I must be gaping because she laughs again. "It surprised me my first time here, too. I still can't figure out how they pump the water so many stories from the ground, but it works."

After figuring out the water pump myself, I help Obipae Kula prepare without further incident. When she's ready, we meet Enipae Gowan in the antechamber as a knock sounds on their door.

"Enter," Obipae Kula calls, and a servant I don't recognize steps into the room. "Allow me to escort you to the betrothal."

Within moments, the obipae and enipae are gone, and the door is closed behind me. I'm left in the room alone as the sun disappears behind the roof of the palace, leaving the room dim. I could light the candles now, but it will be several hours before the betrothal ceremony and banquet are over. There's no need to waste candles. But there's also no reason for me to sit here in the dark until Obipae Kula and Enipae Gowan return. I look at the tapestry hiding the door to the servant's halls. No one told me I had to stay here, and I could look for my family now and be back before the banquet ends. Surely, someone can direct me back to the delegation's suite. And I need to find my way around here, anyway.

Before I even realize I've fully decided, my hand has drawn back the tapestry. I push the door open and lock it behind me, and then I step into the hall.

CHAPTER 16

Enra

The emperor's court is even more crowded this evening than it was this morning. All the nobles—and commoners with money—are clamoring to see the prince's betrothed and to connect with the emperor, no doubt. Many guests have lined up for an early audience with him before the ceremony starts. Others are taking the chance to coordinate and bargain with each other. The sun is settling near the horizon, so people are getting in as much conversation as they can.

Things are much more open here than I'd imagined. I've heard several agreements made since we arrived, people trading favors and gifts alongside news and gossip. Three older men in traditional robes huddle together and discuss a transition of power in the south.

"… Wasn't given to the new malik in time," one man says.

Another clicks his tongue. "No wonder he didn't dare show his face. It'll take years for him to escape the shame."

Nearby, a woman laughs behind her veil while listening to two men in what looks like garb from Susheph.

The throne hall was transformed while we arranged for my

sister to be traded away, so now the floors are covered in rugs with low tables. Plush pillows show where guests can sit. After the ceremony, the food will be served here. As the bride's family, I have a seat near the front. I choose a pillow near the wall, stand near it, and attempt to look happy as people recognize who I am and congratulate me. Becoming part of the emperor's family is enviable, at least from the outside, and many guests are glad to let me know that.

I see a face I recognize and smile. Uncle Tusun beckons me over and puts a hand on my shoulder.

"This is my heir," he informs the man he's talking to—a man about my father's age in a luxurious tunic and a gold-embroidered hat.

"Enra," Uncle Tusun continues, "This is Malik Beckeer of Sahr kingdom."

I bow at the waist. "It is an honor."

Sahr is Uze's neighbor, but this is my first time meeting the malik. While my uncle is friendly and open, Malik Beckeer seems closed-off and distant. I can feel him scrutinizing me before he returns my bow, though his is not as deep.

"I hope we will be steady allies," he says.

"As do I, your majesty," I reply.

Uncle Tusun claps me on the back. "I'm glad you've finally met. I was Beckeer's mentor for several years before he took his father's throne."

Malik Beckeer smiles, but it doesn't quite reach his eyes. "You were an apt teacher."

Uncle Tusun's smile is genuine, but he continues talking to me. "I've discussed sending you to other courts with your father, so you may learn as others have. Malik Beckeer's realm would be a good place to start."

The malik nods. "I would be honored to instruct him in the ways of leadership, since you cannot."

I stiffen at this insult of my uncle. Everyone knows why he

can't instruct me in leadership. His ability to lead was taken away because he stood up for his beliefs and didn't join forces with the emperor.

My father was here in Gazidah, as was Uncle Tusun, for the former datu's birthday. Neither of them knew what was coming, but they both survived. They survived because Aba and his siblings swore fealty to the new ruler as he rode triumphant into the city. They promised him their loyalty and renounced the old emperor, but Uncle Tusun wouldn't. Emperor Asil had been his ally, and his honor would not let him renounce him, even as his siblings did.

I don't blame my father. If it weren't for him, it's possible that none of us would be alive right now. But I have to admire Uncle Tusun for his bravery and his loyalty. He wouldn't join the new emperor, but he didn't fight against him, as those in the south did, either. Instead, he left, taking his family to safety in Derian before returning to negotiate for Uze's neutrality. I need to defend him against this malik, at least.

"Malik Tusun has already taught me much about honor," I say. "I would be grateful to learn what I can from you as well."

Malik Beckeer frowns, but Uncle Tusun squeezes my shoulder and smiles.

Temple bells ringing through the city let us know the ceremony is about to begin and we should take our seats. Khanda and Nalkendi settle into seats next to me wearing some of their finest clothes. I don't think I've ever seen either of them look so put together—Nalkendi in a patterned purple wrap dress with an elaborate bow at the back and Khanda in a classic woven tunic that obviously makes him uncomfortable. They glance at me nervously, and I give them what I hope is a reassuring smile. Aba sits at the head of the table, on my right, where he has a good view of the ceremony and access to the dais for when he must proclaim his acceptance of the emperor's marriage terms. A couple of my uncles sit across from me with their wives and children, around Uncle Tusun. They give me a nod of acknowledgement before turning their attention to the dais.

Conversation in the room dies down to a low hum as the emperor and his family enter from behind dais and take their positions. The emperor's throne has been replaced with a long table where he and his family will sit. The emperor and his wife take their seats at the center, flanked by the prince's mother—I recognize her from earlier—and Emperor Pakel's other children. At opposite ends of the table are two women who hadn't attended before, but their seats at the table and the way they preside over the emperor's children show they are his consorts.

Consorts aren't uncommon in the higher echelons of Elisyan society, but the temple officially frowns upon it. However, those with enough money only receive a disapproving look from the priest as their punishment. I wonder if Vroni will end up having to share Prince Mandla with consorts in the future. Aba didn't discuss it in the marriage negotiations, but I know he despises the practice. He wouldn't want Vroni to have to live in such a situation, no matter how high up her station would be. I glance at him, but his face is impassive.

The rumble of an indecipherable chant sounds from the back of the room. The ceremony is starting. I turn to get a better look at Vroni coming down the aisle. The procession starts at the back of the hall, as it did this morning, but this time, a half dozen priests holding candles and chanting precede Ima and Vroni. Their words become clearer as they near the center of the aisle, where they stop to wait for Prince Mandla and his father.

For the honor of Juae,
May He bless this union.

They repeat the phrase over and over, a common betrothal passage from the sacred book, *Guidance for the Union of Lives.* I'm grateful they chose that text instead of the ones about love or fertility. They're probably saving those for the actual wedding.

From where I'm seated, I can barely see the top of Vroni's veiled head between the priest's swaying shoulders. More male voices join the chant from the direction of the throne, and soon another half dozen priests are leading Prince Mandla and his father, Datu Pachul, to meet Ima and Vroni.

When the two groups of priests are facing each other in two complete columns, their chant becomes one sustained note, and they part so Vroni and Mandla can meet between them. The two of them bow between the wall of priests. Mandla says something to Vroni, and she bows and replies, but she doesn't smile. My heart twists, and my hands ball into fists before I can stop them. Nalkendi notices and takes one of my hands. Her little hand is trembling, but she holds mine firm, giving it a reassuring squeeze. My anger dissipates, replaced by resolve. I may not be able to rescue Vroni, but I can fight to keep Nalkendi from the same fate.

Vroni and Mandla turn and walk side by side toward the dais, Datu Pachul in front of them and Ima behind them. They come to a stop in a row before the emperor's table, and the priests stay in their columns behind them. The chief priest comes out from behind the dais carrying a small golden bowl full of fragrant oil.

"Under the power of Juae's glory, this couple has united to be bound in marriage forever. On this day, they make their promise. Do they receive their fathers' blessings?"

Datu Pachul steps forward and bows to the priest. "They receive my blessing. May they prosper."

The priest nods his acknowledgement as Aba stands. Aba strides to the dais to face the priest. "They receive my blessing. May their descendants flourish."

The priest steps forward in between Vroni and Mandla. "Under the blessings of their fathers and the blessing of their father Juae, I bind these two in holy betrothal until the day they become one."

The priest dips his hand in the oil and touches Mandla's head. The oil seeps from his hand into the prince's hair and onto his face. Prince Mandla winces as oil drips into his eyes, and Khanda giggles. A look from Aba silences him quickly, though. The priest repeats the motion for Vroni, and the oil skims her veil and pools on the floor, leaving dark streaks in its wake. Mandla and Vroni clasp hands, and the priest proclaims. "Let this promise never be broken."

And just like that, their betrothal is sealed. There are cheers in the audience, and I force myself to shout twice, to lend to the appearance of happiness.

As the priests retreat, servants with trays full of food sweep into the room. Several stewed meats, spiced potatoes, fried pastries, seasoned vegetable mashes, desserts of nuts and honey, and mountains of flatbread are distributed to every table. The aromas are intoxicating, and even though I know it's an obvious display of Emperor Pakel's success, I can't help but look forward to eating, especially as my favorite dishes are set in front of me.

Vroni and her betrothed sit with the emperor at his table, but Ima comes to sit between Aba and me. I scoot over to make room for her.

"It is done," Aba says to her.

She nods as she breaks the flatbread brought to our table, handing it first to Aba, then to me and my siblings, her expression solemn, not at all like a woman joyfully giving her daughter away in marriage.

My uncle Comar—sitting across from me—leans in. "You expect improvement then?"

I glance at him sharply. What does he mean?

Aba shakes his head slightly. "Not here."

He glances toward the emperor's table. I think back on

what Aba told me, about how he will rebuild the nobility of Uze, how he will restore us. I push away my worst conclusion. Aba can't be planning a rebellion. The satraps in the south paid for theirs with their lives. And yet, I know he has a plan, and it involves Lia.

I look up at the emperor's table on the dais. The emperor surveys us like we're his property. Vroni picks at her food while Mandla talks at her, not really paying attention to whether or not she's listening. My resolve steels. I will prove to Aba that I can be an asset. Whatever he's planning, I'll be a part of it.

CHAPTER 17

Lia

Gazidah's palace is a labyrinth. After wandering the halls, avoiding other people for about twenty minutes, I decide my safest course of action is to get outside and find my way to the smithy. So I get to the ground floor and take the first door that looks like an exit.

I take a while, and I end up having to ask the friendliest looking palace slave for directions, but eventually I find it. It's five times the size of the one at home, filled with men and boys I don't recognize. I catch sight of a boy from Satrap Paykhan's household, one whose family has joined my father's resistance. I call out to him.

He turns around, and his eyes widen. "How did you get here?"

Instead of answering, I ask him, "Where is my father?"

The boy guides me into the smoke, past blazing furnaces and dark pools of water until we stop at an anvil where a man hammers away at a red hot strip of metal. Aba. But he's engrossed in his work. If I distract him, he could hurt himself. I wait until he wipes his brow to alert him to my presence.

His recently mopped brow furrows as his eyes settle on me. "Lia? What are you doing here? How did you get here?"

"I asked for directions. I think I have to stay in the chamber they assigned me to, but—"

"Not here. Let's talk outside." Aba clasps my shoulders and leads me toward an exit, where a welcome burst of fresh night air brushes against my face. Outside the smithy, we stand against a wall without windows, looking over an empty stretch of land that ends at the palace wall.

"What do you need?" Aba asks. "Have they harmed you?"

I shake my head. "No. I'm fine."

"Are you a chambermaid for a man or a woman?"

"A couple. The delegate from Derian and her husband."

Aba's shoulders relax, and I try not to think about why he was anxious, but I can't help but worry about Jorra.

"They don't look kindly upon slavery in Derian," Aba says. "They should be decent to you."

I nod, but then I think of Obipae Kula. "Yes, but Aba, the delegate, she's… she's otherworldly."

Aba looks at me quizzically, and I explain. After a moment, he breaks into a smile. "I've heard of her, the princess touched by the Snake Mother. Your mother over-heard the satrap talking about her several years ago—you were too young to remember. She single-handedly stopped a rebellion in Derian. They said she has magic. Don't offend her."

My hands shake, and I tuck them under my arms. She's a princess? Why does she want to be called "obipae"? I've never met anyone with magic. What can she do? What would she do if I anger her? How did she stop a rebellion on her own? I think of the meeting in Menewos and the subsequent punish-ment. I haven't seen any of those men and women since we arrived.

Aba must read my thoughts. He shakes his head. "She's not

from here, but find out what she needs from the emperor. If we gain their sympathy, Derian can become an ally."

My heart pounds. "What will you—"

He puts a hand on my shoulder. "Soon. I will let you know when we are ready."

"Aba I—"

A vaguely familiar voice breaks into our conversation. "You, slave girl, what are you doing here?"

A man approaches us, wearing more finery than a slave but less than a noble. I take a moment to place his face. The palace's chief steward. He frowns at me. "I'm sure I assigned you to a chamber."

I'm amazed that he recognizes me. He barely glanced in my direction as he rattled assignments off to us.

"The delegate is attending the banquet. I thought—"

The steward's frown deepens. "No one gave you permission to think."

He turns to Aba. "This is your child?"

Aba bows again. "Please forgive her, sir. She has never worked anywhere as large as the palace."

The steward shakes his head. "Well, if you have enough time to tour the palace, the kitchens have work for you."

I nod, and he turns toward the smithy's entrance, but I have to call after him. "Where are the kitchens?"

The steward rolls his eyes, but he looks into the smithy and calls someone's name. A boy I don't recognize comes running. "Yes, sir?"

"Take this girl to the kitchens."

I glance at Aba before following the boy. Aba gives me a slight nod, then he follows the steward back into the smithy. My nervousness grows as the boy leads me back into the palace proper. There are several quick turns, but it seems the kitchens aren't far. The boy leaves me at the door without saying a word.

When I step inside, the room is bustling with activity. From the look of it, the banquet has ended, and most people are cleaning up. But one woman at a table next to the door is preparing a tray. She glances at me and says, "You there, help me."

I scramble over to her, and she hands me a handful of spices and nods toward a mortar and pestle, saying nothing more. I take the spices and watch her as I grind them finely, careful not to spill any. My caution means that I work slowly, but it's a small amount of spices, so I hope no one notices. What am I making? The aroma is sweet but not overbearing.

The woman arranges dried fruit and candied nuts on the tray, then she disappears and returns with a pot of hot water, two cups, and a dark blue blanket draped over her shoulder. I'm making tea, I realize. A search of the workstation reveals thin strips of gauzy fabric on a lower shelf. I grab two of them, fill them with the spice mixture, and tie them securely.

The woman nods toward the tray. "Follow me."

I drop the tea bags on the tray and pick it up, rushing to keep pace with her. She speeds through the halls and up several flights of stairs, and I'm glad I'm not the one carrying the hot water because I certainly would have spilled half of it by now. Both my legs ache—not just my weak one—by the time we settle on a floor.

We pause in front of a heavy wooden door, and the woman knocks. The door opens from the inside, and I follow her into the room. A guard holds the curtain back for us inside the room. There are two guards here—one by the tapestry and one by the main entrance. The room resembles Obipae Kula's antechamber, but the decor is even more lavish. The ceiling is decorated with carved wood depicting stories, though I don't stare long enough to determine which myths are there. Incense is burning somewhere. Though I can't locate it, a rich scent of smoke and spices hangs in the air.

The woman spreads the blanket out on the table in the center of the room and places the water and cups on it. I put the tray down beside them and rearrange the sweets that had fallen out of place on the walk here. I'm about to replace the last one when the woman grabs my elbow and pulls me away to stand back from the table. The room's main entrance door opens, and an older man and woman walk in, followed by two more guards. I recognize the man immediately and stifle a gasp. This is the emperor's chamber.

The emperor walks by and glances at us, and I struggle to breathe normally. The woman who'd brought me up here bows, and I do the same, praying he doesn't look at me. But when I straighten, my eyes meet Emperor Pakel's face, a frown cut across it.

"Who is this?" he asks. His voice seems more gravelly than it had in the throne room, less regal but fuller of disapproval. Though he's still in his finery, he stands shorter than he'd seemed in the throne room, his age leaving its mark on his posture. He looks back and forth between me and the slave woman, who studies me for the first time.

"Forgive me. She has slave's cuffs and was in the kitchens…"

"She can speak, can she not?"

The woman turns to me. I keep my eyes to the ground, and my voice is barely more than a whisper. "I am of Satrap Paykhan's household, your majesty."

Please don't let him ask which Satrap Paykhan, I pray. Please let him move on.

"Really? Look up," the emperor says.

I wince inwardly but try to keep myself from shaking as I look in his general direction without looking at him.

"Your face is familiar…"

"What is your interest in the slave?" the emperor's wife asks as she sits on the sofa and picks up a handful of candied nuts.

Her voice is demure, but there's a bite to it. "Certainly you'd want a more attractive new consort for your collection."

Emperor Pakel turns to his wife but says nothing in response. He glances at me again before he sits next to her.

"Today is a day of celebration, Shaha."

My ears perk up at the use of honorifics with his wife's name. The emperor defers to the empress in private? She must be older than him, I reason, though she doesn't look it.

Shaha Saretha nods slowly. "Are you pleased now that your bloodline is secure for another generation?"

Emperor Pakel scoffs. "It won't be secure until the girl gives birth to an heir."

Shaha Saretha doesn't respond. Instead, she rolls up her voluminous sleeves to pour water into the emperor's teacup, and I stifle another gasp. She has the same tattoos as I do.

I study her face more closely, looking for any sign of familiarity. I remember my birth mother's face, and the emperor's wife doesn't have it. My birth mother had a round, youthful, beautiful face, and while Shaha Saretha is elegant and regal, she doesn't have a face I'd call beautiful or youthful. Still, she looks too young to be my grandmother, but then, she could just be healthy. Did my grandfather have consorts, or did my father? I never learned of any, but I was too young. Would the emperor be so bold as to marry one of the Asil wives or consorts?

I glance at the emperor's own wrists, but they are without tattoos. Either he didn't keep up the practice, or the last artisan truly died in the war. I resist the urge to pull my arms in toward me. My tattoos are safely hidden beneath my cuffs.

I feel eyes on me and look up to find Shaha Saretha looking at me now. She frowns. "You are dismissed."

The woman with me and I bow and retreat through the tapestry. As we walk, the woman says. "Our work is finished. You may return to your post."

I ask her how to get to my post. She clicks her tongue but tells me. It's on the other side of the palace, but at least it's on the same floor.

"If there is anything else I can help you with—" she starts.

I know she's being sarcastic, but I ask my question anyway. "What did the emperor's wife mean by 'your bloodline'?"

The woman crosses her arms. "You don't know?"

I shake my head.

"Shaha Saretha is barren, as was the Emperor's first wife. Emperor Pakel's heir is his first consort's son."

Barren? Barrenness is a curse for royalty. It's a wonder that Emperor Pakel didn't replace her and make his first consort his wife. Unless there's a reason he couldn't. If his first wife was barren too, perhaps the curse is the emperor's. None who become his wife can have children. In that case, maybe his consorts didn't want to be promoted.

I ask my last question. "Is Shaha Saretha of the previous dynasty?"

"No." The servant woman looks at me quizzically. "Why do you ask?"

"Her wrists…" I let my voice trail off.

"You saw her tattoos?" The woman shakes her head. "I don't know how she got those, but I worked here before the… before. I never saw her."

The tattoos would remain a mystery, then. I return to the delegate's chamber, but when I push the tapestry aside and step into the room, Obipae Kula and Enipae Gowan are already there, reclining on a sofa, deep in conversation.

I rush forward. "Forgive me. I was trying to find my way around the palace."

Obipae Kula shakes her head. "There's no need for forgiveness. We had no need of you. But could you bring me that tray?"

I glance over to the table beneath the window and take a

step toward it before I realize that Obipae Kula's last sentence had been spoken in Derian, not Elisyan. I turn back to find both her and Enipae Gowan staring at me, their eyebrows raised.

Enipae Gowan nudges Obipae Kula. "I knew it."

"You speak Derian," Obipae Kula says. Her voice isn't accusatory, but it feels like an accusation.

"I didn't want to seem like I was eavesdropping."

"So you avoided it by eavesdropping?" Obipae Kula's eyes flash, and I wince. Is this where I get turned into a toad?

Enipae Gowan stands. "Why did the emperor assign a servant who speaks Derian to our suite?"

"It was a coincidence," I insist. "He doesn't know I speak Derian. He doesn't even know me."

Obipae Kula's brow furrows. "That's quite a coincidence."

I'm feeling desperate, and my words fall over themselves to leave my mouth. "I know it's hard to believe, but my father speaks Derian. He grew up near the border. All my siblings speak it. We—"

Obipae Kula waves my comments away. "We'll look into it. For now, though, you may retire."

My expression must be one of confusion because Obipae Kula laughs. "It's not a trick. Go to bed. We'll see you in the morning."

I'm still not sure I trust it, but I bow anyway. "Thank you. Goodnight then, Obipae Kula and Enipae Gowan."

I cross the space to the tiny room that belongs to the chambermaid. Before I close it completely, I hear Enipae Gowan say, "can't be older than thirteen. Just a tiny thing."

I glance down at my petite frame. I'm sixteen, but I've always been small, and I look young for my age. Being plain doesn't help me look older either. I appear like a common child.

Obipae Kula must agree. "I wonder what her usual work is."

My usual work is anything anyone tells me to do, I think bitterly as I shut the door. I obey the satrap, his family, my parents, Aba and his freedom fighters, and the emperor and his servants.

I sit on the bed, a small pallet on the floor and fold my legs underneath myself. I'm a toy whose arms and legs are moved by others. When I close my eyes, the emperor's face flashes before me. He said I looked familiar.

The memory makes my skin go cold. I rub my arms and try to convince myself it was nothing. Aba reassures me in my mind. The emperor will forget me. He sees many faces and has killed many people. He won't connect my face to a single man from years ago, no matter how important that man might have been.

But my breath goes shallow, and my arms won't warm up. Soon, the emperor will see me again, and nothing will keep him from recognizing me then.

CHAPTER 18

Enra

I turn over in bed and try to push my thoughts away, but I've been unable to sleep for several hours. Vroni is officially betrothed. She'll be married at the end of the festival. Aba and Uncle Comar expect it to be a boon for us, but it still feels underhanded.

Marriages are made for political convenience all the time. Even my own… But when we leave after the wedding, Vroni will be here alone. Aba has provided enough for her to take care of herself and then some, but will that be enough to protect her if Emperor Pakel decides she's no longer valuable?

There's so much happening right now. Aba plans to let Benar go through with letting Lia claim the end of slavery. We're prepared for it. Aba has supported Benar and hidden Lia, and he's built our household to weather any damage the changes would cause. He'll wait and see which side of history it falls on and leverage the result for our benefit. In case things don't go well, and even if they do, he has Vroni. He'll use Vroni as a vein through which to feed influence into the young prince who will be emperor. He'll use Lia and her family as tools to build the foundation on which we will stand.

I feel sick as I think about it. But to protect my family, I have to do what's necessary. They will hate Lia and blame her for ruining the lives of many. If things don't go well, she may start another war. But she's here, and that's knowledge Emperor Pakel doesn't have. And my family has each other. The satraps and the malik of Uze don't wield the power they used to, but there must be some strength in our positions. We sided with the emperor early enough that we convinced him none of us held Uncle Tusun's reservations in high regard.

It makes sense that Aba would help Benar. One way to ensure our own power is to diminish that of others. Taking a third of the economy out from under their feet will accomplish that faster than any political machinations between the palace's pillars ever could. It'll be devastating, but I know Elisya is resilient, and according to my studies, other nations have survived such shifts before. We can't remain passive, like we've been for the past twelve years. I know that. But it's hard to justify what we must do in my mind.

My chest hurts as the image of whips tearing slaves' backs open returns to my memory. Aba proposed such a brutal punishment to keep up appearances. So that no one would believe it if anyone were to claim we allowed our slaves to build a revolution under our noses. But it still seems like too harsh a punishment to me.

Will the same happen to Lia? No matter what she does, she'll face punishment for it, and there will certainly be investigations into everyone close to her. What will we have to do to prove we didn't know all along? How deeply will we cut the ties?

They go deeper than Lia knows. I still don't understand why Aba kept all the betrothal contracts in order, unless he intends to exploit them. Exploit. It's such an ugly word, and yet it's the most accurate. Even if it is an exploitation, how does it benefit us?

Unless, I realize, Aba thinks she'll succeed. And in that case, those contracts will leave her at least better off than she is now.

I rub a hand over my face. I'm trying to justify my desire to use her. How does that make me any different from Emperor Pakel? Certainly my motivations are better. I'm not just after power. I want to save my family, my people, my province. And Lia can enable me to do that.

If I reached out to her, it would take time, but she might accept me. And then… Then what?

Maybe instead of cutting ties, we could bind them closer. We can keep supporting Benar silently if we have to, but once he gains enough power, we can step into the sunlight and stand with him. We may even win over other maliks with Aba's support. But it would require Lia's trust. And if we're going to get to Lia, we have to go through me.

The light in my room grows brighter, and birds chirp outside. I sigh and swing my legs out of bed. Aba will be awake already. He always rises before the sun. I might as well speak to him now before I lose my nerve and before he gets caught up in any other serious business for the day. I throw on a tunic and a belt and pad out into the common room.

Aba is sitting on a sofa eating and nods in greeting. "I was wondering when you would come out."

"You knew I was awake?"

"I could hear you tossing around. What is it you want to say?"

He motions to the cushion across from him.

I take a deep breath and sit down. "It's about Lia."

Lia

I stare at the ceiling as light seeps into the room from the space between the floor and the door. I slept fitfully all night, plagued by dark dreams and jumping at every noise the palace made.

But I have to get up. The obipae and enipae will be awake soon, so I need to make sure the room is ready for them. There's chatter on the other side of my door, and I spring up. I'm already late. The women's voices mingle with the dull, irritating scraping of pottery. They're delivering the morning meal, and I should be out there setting it up.

I throw a dress on over my sleeping tunic and hurry out the door to the disapproving clicks of the servant women.

"Are you just now waking up?" one asks me. "What does Satrap Paykhan permit in his house?"

She doesn't require an answer, but I give one anyway. "I was awake. I just—"

Another hands me two bowls and points to a covered pot. "Dish out the food. We have other people to feed."

I nod and remove the pot's cover, releasing the thick, savory aroma of spiced grain and milk into the room. My stomach rumbles despite me, and the clicking of tongues resumes. "You should have eaten earlier," the first woman says. "Now you'll have to wait until midday."

I nod again, but even though my stomach is growling, I doubt I could eat anything. Not with my nerves the way they are now.

When the food is served and waiting on the table for Obipae Kula and Enipae Gowan, the women pack up to leave. I hold the door to the servants' hallway open for them. As they pass me, the second woman stops.

"Oh goodness, I almost forgot." She pulls a small scrap of wrapped parchment from her skirt and hands it to me. "You're to report to the smithy this morning."

"The smithy?" I take the note from her and open it.

The woman shrugs and walks off, and I turn my attention to the note. It's short, written quickly but signed with an official seal.

The bearer of this note shall have their cuffs refitted and replaced.

The floor tilts beneath me, and I have to use the door to steady myself. Why? Why would anyone order this now? And why me? Could the emperor be that suspicious? I close my eyes. Of course he could. He's a man willing to do whatever it takes to protect his own power. If even the spark of a thought of danger crosses his mind, of course he'll snuff it out. Another door opens and closes behind me. The obipae and enipae are awake.

"Good morning, Lia," they say to me in Derian. They must have dispensed with speaking Elisyan since they know I understand them. I think I respond, but I'm not sure. They settle into their seats to eat. I close the door to the servants' hallway and let the tapestry fall. I should straighten their room before I go to the smithy.

"Is something wrong?" Obipae Kula asks me as I pass them.

"N—No, Obipae," I stutter.

I must be unconvincing because the two of them share a glance before Obipae Kula speaks again.

"Are you sure?"

"Yes, Obipae."

I bow and retreat into their room. For a moment, I wonder if maybe they can help me. Can I claim asylum from Derian if I'm not in Derian?

I can hear them talking in hushed voices from the other side of the door, and I set about airing and resettling the sheets and blankets and mindlessly arranging anything that seems out of place. I'm doing my best to prolong the inevitable, but I know it's not going to work.

I go back into the common room and bow to the obipae and enipae. "May I be excused? I must report to the smithy, but I will…" I hesitate. "I'll return soon."

That may not be true, but maybe if I say it, Juae will hear me and have mercy.

The couple exchanges a look again, but then Obipae Kula says, "You may go. We have no need of you this morning."

I had almost hoped they would keep me, but perhaps it's better this way. Maybe I should get things over with quickly.

The walk to the smithy is even longer than it was yesterday. Every step feels like a hundred years. But Aba is there. The emperor didn't say who should replace my cuffs, just that they should be replaced. I can ask Aba to do it. Then maybe the truth will stay hidden. I can reveal myself in my own time. My spirits rise then sink again. Can anything stay hidden from Emperor Pakel in his own palace?

A different boy meets me at the entrance today. I ask him to direct me to my father, and he leads me to the same booth where he was before. Aba is already frowning over a sheet of metal when I arrive, his face drenched in sweat, but his frown deepens when he sees me.

"Lia? Again? I told you—"

"Here," I cut him off, handing him the note.

He opens it and reads it. As he does, his hands tremble a bit, but his expression remains the same. He crumples the parchment in his hand. "What happened?"

"I served the emperor tea yesterday—"

Aba's jaw drops open. "You did what?"

I start to answer, but Aba holds up a hand as he glances over at the servant boy. "Say no more."

There will be an opportunity for more explanations later.

I hold my wrists up to him. "Will you change them?"

As a response, Aba calls for the servant boy. When he comes closer, Aba tells him, "Go get me two new slave cuffs."

The boy nods and runs off, presumably to the treasury, where unused slave cuffs would be. After all, they are solid metal, and they still have value even when they aren't on the arms of a slave.

While we wait, Aba has me sit in the corner next to him while he works. We talk through the noise of the smithy. In his years of planning, Aba has become skilled at being heard only by those he wants to hear him. He talks beneath the din instead of above it.

"He saw you?"

"Yes."

"Did it seem like he knew who you were?"

"No, but…"

"But?"

I sigh. "He said I looked familiar."

Aba looks at me sharply. "He recognized you?"

I shake my head. "It didn't seem like it. But… But there's something else."

"What's that?"

"His wife, she has tattoos like mine."

At this, Aba drops his hammer. He stoops to pick it up. "That's impossible."

"I know."

My cuffs chafe my wrists as I think about Shaha Saretha's tattoos. I don't know what it means.

When the boy arrives with the new cuffs, Aba dismisses him before unlocking mine. My tattoos glisten beneath the surface of my death-colored skin. My wrists never see the light of day, so they're several shades lighter than the rest of my arms. I rub them both, willing color into them. But before any change happens, Aba claps the new cuffs onto them. I know it's better to be quick and safe, but I still miss the semblance of freedom as soon as it's gone.

Both of us glance around like guilty thieves, but no one is paying attention. Slaves' cuffs get replaced often. People get older, their bodies change, and a slave isn't as useful without hands. It's not an important occurrence. But I can't help but feel my life is at risk now. Somehow he knows.

But why? How?

"We're done," Aba says. "You should return to your assignment."

"But what did this—"

Aba shakes his head, and when he speaks, his voice is low. "Come to the slave quarters tonight. We'll discuss it then."

When I reach the Derian delegation's suite, Obipae Kula and Enipae Gowan are here, and they have others with them, several men and women in Derian clothing. They're discussing some kind of policy but fall quiet when I enter the room.

"She's the one who speaks Derian?" a man asks.

Obipae Kula nods and waves me over. "So, your father is a blacksmith?"

"Yes, Obipae." She did mention she would look into my background when they found out I spoke Derian, but I'd forgotten in the chaos surrounding the emperor.

"And he speaks Derian?"

"It's his first language. He grew up near the border, and soldiers captured him as a boy."

"And all your siblings speak Derian?"

I nod. "Aba spoke it to us growing up. We aren't as good as he is, but—"

Obipae Kula's brow furrows. "Why did he feel the need with you all living in the north? When would Derian be useful to you?"

The rest of the Derianite group stays quiet, watching this exchange, waiting for my response. Obipae Kula is in charge of this conversation, and a part of me envies her. What is it like to be the most influential, the most powerful person in the room?

I can't tell her that Aba wanted me to learn Derian to make me a better politician. I can't tell her he taught it to Atar and Jorra so they could flee to Derian and try to make a life there. Instead, I say, "I imagine he wanted to preserve his heritage. You'd have to ask him for his reasoning."

It isn't a total lie. I know Aba misses his life in the mountains and wonders what became of his family often.

Obipae Kula raises an eyebrow. "Perhaps I will."

She dismisses me to my work, and I go through my usual tasks for the day, but my mind isn't with me. It's traveled hours ahead to this evening, to tomorrow, to the future. Dark possibilities swim in my thoughts, but I try to anchor myself in some kind of hope, though it continually eludes me.

After the sun sets and everyone has gone to sleep, I slip from my room and into the servants' corridor. The hallway isn't empty—people still have work to do after dark—but no one questions my movements. There are hundreds of guests in the palace right now, and they have many requests. If anyone asks, I can tell them Obipae Kula sent me on an errand. No one will be rude enough to ask what the errand was.

The slave quarters are technically outside the palace, though they're still within its outer walls. They're on the far side of a pasture where some of the emperor's smaller herds graze. They are far, and they're under guard, but the guards are more concerned with people going out than people coming in. I join a group of women walking from the palace to the slave quarters. They barely even register my presence as we walk through the gates.

Inside the camp, the fragrance of spicy boiling vegetables chooses my direction for me. My family will be where the food is. Sure enough, I find Atar filling a bowl next to a blazing fire.

He looks surprised to see me. Maybe no one told him I was coming.

He waves to me. "Follow me."

We walk to the building where the rest of my family is living—a low slung, clay structure with a thatch roof and no windows. There is a heavy straw mat in place of a door, and Atar pushes it aside to let me in.

CHAPTER 19

Jorra is the only one inside when we arrive, crouching over a low flat table, kneading together what will be the rest of the evening meal. She too looks surprised to see me, stopping her work with her hand hovering over a mound of dough.

"Aba told me to come," I tell her.

She nods. "He asked me to as well."

Atar ducks into the room behind me after pinning the mat back to let the firelight from outside in. "Seems like something's wrong."

"Yes," I admit. I might as well tell them so they don't have to glean half-formed information from other conversations. "The emperor had my cuffs replaced."

Atar's eyes go wide, and Jorra gasps. "Does he know who you are?" Jorra asks.

I shake my head. "I don't know."

"What would he do it for then?" Atar wonders.

I have no answer for him. The dim room is so quiet that I can hear conversations outside, though I can't concentrate on what anyone is saying.

After a moment, Jorra says. "It must be a coincidence. How would he know you were alive?"

I sigh. "He saw my face, and there was no way he could have confirmed my death in the first place."

Jorra sits back on her knees. "What do you mean?"

I can't bring myself to face her as a horrible realization dawns on me. It's possible the emperor has known about me all along. "Not everyone was dead when I… when I fell."

Jorra and Atar have heard the story I tell at Aba's meetings, so they know how I was thrown from a window, how Ima found me, how she and Aba hid me and raised me. But I never tell the story of how I came to that window. People assume that the emperor's men threw me out in an unsuccessful attempt to kill me, but it was actually a successful attempt to save me.

Atar leans forward. "What happened?"

"The memory is still so clear," I admit, falling into the memory that always lurks in the back of my nightmares. "I wasn't an only child."

I don't look up, but I'm sure both of my siblings are surprised. My parents know about Duin, my infant brother, but I've never mentioned him to Jorra and Atar. "My baby brother was already asleep. Our nurse and I were in the antechamber. I was playing with a toy. There was a loud noise. My nurse went to the door, but before she could get to it, my mother came in. She was beautiful, glittering, wearing the finest clothes I'd ever seen."

I don't know why that image of her stands out so much in my mind. Maybe it was the contrast of her shimmering robe, headscarf, and jewels and the terror on her face. Maybe somehow I knew it was the last time I'd ever see her.

Jorra takes my hand, silently urging me to continue.

"She shouted something, and she and my nurse pushed furniture against the door. But they weren't fast enough. Soldiers got in. My mother…"

I don't have to close my eyes to remember. I can still see it, even with my eyes open. A man grabbing my mother's head, my mother pushing him away, the nurse struggling against the man's arm, trying to pull him away to no avail as his spear runs my mother through, my mother crumpling to the floor, my nurse being thrown beside her, men walking over their bodies, bypassing me, walking into the nursery where my brother cries. He heard the noise, our mother's cry, our nurse's scream. He wails, and then he's silent. My nurse stirs, tears staining her cheeks. Her eyes meet mine.

"My nurse picked me up and ran, but she couldn't get far. She threw me from the window before the soldiers reached her. But she was alive."

They probably got to her soon after I fell, and the first thing they would have done would be to look for me. Could they have killed her in the heat of the moment? If they hadn't, there was a chance—however small—that the emperor knew I had lived.

"She could—" I start, but movement at the entrance of the room stops me.

Aba comes in with Ima and a couple of familiar men. They're also from Satrap Paykhan's household and smile at me and my siblings, but I can't return the gesture. Their eyes belie their expressions—they're worried.

"They were already suspicious," one man says. It seems like he's continuing a point he'd made before they arrived. "Since what happened on the journey, they've been watching us."

"All the more reason it could be nothing. They don't trust any of us. No one is singling Lia out," the other insists.

Ima sits next to Jorra and I, and Atar sidles over to Aba as he replies, "Then why replace her cuffs? They already split us all up. Even this small group could be too much. But we need to be ready."

"Ready for what?" I ask, even though I'm not sure I want to know the answer.

Aba holds a dagger out to me, the second I've been offered in my life, and I stare at him. "What is this for?"

"You need to protect yourself, just in case."

My hands go numb. "Aba, you can't mean…"

My voice trails off as he hands a similar weapon to Jorra. A dagger would do little to protect us from the palace's guards, and if we're found with a weapon, who knows what would happen to us.

Aba presses the dagger into my hands and closes my palms around its hilt. "It's important for you to know so you can be prepared. I want you all to be prepared, no matter where you are."

I can barely hear him over my pulse pounding in my ears, but he continues. "The day may come when you see smoke rising from the slave quarters. When you do, I want you to run. Find each other in Menewos, and keep running. Don't look back until you reach Derian or the sea."

My hands shake, and I look to Ima for help, but she just nods. Jorra is dumbstruck, but Atar looks ready for battle. Has Aba given up on me? Maybe he's decided I wouldn't have enough power to make the change we need. A few months ago, that thought might have hurt, but now it fills me with terror. He and Ima are preparing to die. They're going into danger for me again.

They'll all be killed. A gruesome vision flashes through my mind—bodies broken, strewn around the palace's courtyards. Slaves murdered without mercy for attempting to stand up for their freedom. Aba executed as an insurgent.

"Aba, please," I plead, "You don't have to do this."

But instead of answering me, Aba lifts Atar, Jorra, and me to our feet. "Go. You can't afford to be caught here after curfew without permission. Eat in the palace."

My eyes dart between him and Ima. They both look resigned, like everything has already been decided. I have to stop them. The realization dawns on me even as my heart races. And there's only one way to do it.

If I can prove who I am before Aba's rebellion begins, there will be no need for it at all. I need to get to the judges, but first, I need to remove these cuffs.

MY HEART IS RACING SO FAST that I'm afraid it'll stop at any moment, but I need it to stay with me for a little while longer. It's late, and there are few people around since most are eating their evening meals, but there's still fire in the smithy. I stop at the entrance. Even if someone is inside, they'd be breaking the law by helping me take my cuffs off. No one would do that for me, a stranger and a slave. But I can't ask Aba to lend me the keys. He'd know what I was planning immediately and would do anything he could to stop me.

I pace in front of the doorway, pondering my options, the desire to give up growing stronger. But every time I resolve to walk away, the image of my family destroyed a second time by the emperor flashes through my mind. I can't let that happen. I have to at least try to stop it.

After too many moments of fear and doubt, I take a deep breath and step across the threshold, staying as close to the wall as I can. My eyes adjust quickly. While several contained fires are still burning, no one is inside. There could be blacksmiths close by, eating their meals away from the smoke while monitoring the building to make sure nothing goes wrong. But if I'm fast, maybe I can get out of here before they investigate the sounds I end up making.

I've watched Aba often enough to recognize several tools. He's only had to remove my cuffs with his key, but there are pliers, hammers, and tongs I've seen him use on stronger metals than gold. One of them should work on these.

A glance around assures me that no one is watching, so I approach the nearest work bench and grab the first tool that looks sharp. It's enough to bend the metal around my left wrist, but after a few moments, I realize it's not going to cut through, and I move to a different one.

After several trying minutes full of starts and stops as I pause with every noise, I find a small, sharp pair of shears that cuts through my cuff like it's cloth. I grit my teeth as I wedge it under the bands around my wrists. I'm not being as careful as I should, and sometimes I cut my skin along with the gold, but I don't have time to worry about that.

When my cuffs are off, I glance over my torn wrists. They look bad, but I don't have time to treat them. I've been here too long, so I need to go. Figuring out how to leave the palace undetected is still a mystery, but my current priority is evading capture in the smithy. I toss my mangled cuffs into the nearest fire and slink out the door.

CHAPTER 20

Outside, the night air blows warm across my skin, making my wrists sting. Without my cuffs, I'm not as easily identified as a slave. Unless someone has seen my face before, they're unlikely to know who I am. My plain dress and simple appearance make it obvious I'm no one of importance, but maybe I can slip into a group of Gazidah's lower class workers going home for the evening.

I hurry to the nearest gate, tucking my arms in close against me, and I send a prayer of thanks to Juae when a couple dozen men and women come into view in front of me. Hopefully, the guards won't notice the addition of one more, and none of the workers are vigilant enough to bring me to a guard's attention.

I slide into the rear of the group, nodding at those nearest me but keeping my eyes on the ground. As long as I remain unnoticed…

Someone touches my arm, and I startle, looking up to see an older woman with her hair covered and an expression of concern on her face. "Are you injured?"

She glances from my torso to my face. My dress is smeared

with a smattering of blood, darkening the fabric where I'd held my arms close to me.

"Oh, I…" I scramble to come up with an explanation. "I cut myself at work, but I'll take care of it when I get home."

The woman gives me a quizzical look but nods and turns away. It would be unusual for the palace to send a wounded servant home without treatment, but most people don't want to ask too many questions for fear of getting themselves too involved with a stranger.

The guards at the gate survey us as we leave, but they don't seem incredibly concerned with identifying everyone in the group. These guards prioritize tracking the people who enter the palace rather than those who leave, so as long as we don't possess any valuables, they leave us alone. Once we're out in the street, people say their goodbyes and go their separate ways. I follow a polite distance behind a few strangers and head toward a tall, rectangular building.

There are only three places in the wealthiest part of Gazidah that tower over the rest of the homes and businesses —the palace, the temple, and the Halls of Virtue, which house the judges. If I'm going to see them, that's where I need to be. The palace is behind me, and a quick glance into the sky assures me that the temple is the building with the three spires that threaten to pierce the stars, so the Halls of Virtue must be the only building left. That's the direction I take.

The roads wind and meander, and though the Halls of Virtue are obvious, it doesn't take me long to realize that they aren't close, and when the buildings of the city crowd into the street, I easily lose sight of it. I try to keep to the main roads, not taking myself down alleys or side paths unless absolutely necessary.

The walk to the Halls of Virtue is quiet enough on the main roads. Few people are out of their homes in the evening. Most are sharing their evening meals with their families and only a few workers, shopkeepers, and untrustworthy sorts meander around. I count my footsteps on the path, only stopping when I lose count well into the thousands. The numbers serve as a distraction from my racing heart, allowing me to focus on my purpose—the tower in front of me. I just need to get there.

When I start to think I've lost myself in a maze and will never find the exit, the doors to the Halls of Virtue loom above me. The building is dark and as quiet as a graveyard, but a lone guard stands outside, leaning against a tall ceremonial spear. He straightens as I approach, looking alert but not wary. The Halls of Virtue allow all Gazidans, regardless of their station, so even though I appear out of place, I have every right to be here.

Still, the guard calls to me, and I stiffen. "Halt. The judges are no longer…"

His voice trails off as his eyes trail over me, lingering on my blood-stained dress, and his expression turns into one of pity and caution. He's an older man, and his face seems kind as he shifts his stance. He shoots a glance over my shoulder. "I cannot leave my post, but if you need treatment, I know of a place where you'll be safe."

My heart is pounding, but the man's kindness strengthens my will enough for me to pry my arms from my sides. The guard's eyes go wide as my tattoos glint in the moonlight.

"I need to see the judges." My voice is barely louder than a whisper.

For all this guard knows, I could be a criminal with illegal tattoos, but even if that were the case, the judges would need to determine my guilt.

The guard pounds on the door, and when there's no answer, he repeats the action. My heart beats along in my ears. After a few moments, a servant appears from a side entrance, looking tired and annoyed.

"The judges are required," the guard says.

"It is late—" the servant starts, but the guard interrupts him.

"This is a matter of utmost importance."

The servant studies the guard, his expression quizzical, and then he glances over at me. Distaste flickers across his face, but he gapes as he takes in my arms. As quickly as he'd arrived, he disappears through the side door.

A few more moments later, an elderly man in a pale tunic exits the building to meet us, still tying a sash around his waist. The colorful sash with deep blue tassels denotes his station as a priest.

"What is this about?" His voice is still thick with sleep.

"Forgive me, your excellency," the guard says, "But you are about to have a dilemma on your hands."

The priest raises his eyebrows, and the guard gestures to me. "Your excellency, I believe this is Asil Liani, Hara Elisya."

The ground spins as the guard says my name, a name I hadn't expected him to know. Am I that recognizable? If so, it was certainly wise to keep my tattoos covered all these years.

The priest stares, speechless, then he laughs. "This slave girl is the dead hara?"

The guard nods to me, and I fight back nausea as I expose my bare wrists. As I do, and my golden tattoos' faint glow lights up like the flame of a weak candle, the priest's laugh dies down. He reaches for my hands but stops short of touching me. He covers his mouth. "Juae have mercy."

He waves toward the tower. "Inside, come inside, Hara."

I think I may vomit on the tower's ground, but I keep my empty stomach from heaving.

"Come with me," the priest says.

He takes me inside, through a maze of hallways, and upstairs, leaving me in a richly appointed room with a sofa but no bed. I imagine the Halls of Virtue don't have many overnight visitors.

"What's going to happen to me?" I ask the priest before he leaves.

He shakes his head. "Only Juae knows, my dear. But for now, you are safe."

As he closes the door, I look out the window in time to see a figure running from the Halls of Virtue toward the palace. The news will be there soon.

Safe for now, indeed.

Enra

The palace is abuzz with wild rumors this morning. Rumors that the old emperor Asil has returned from the dead. That his son was found alive. That a slave girl who's actually a princess was just discovered.

The last one sounds true.

I don't know exactly what happened last night, but apparently Benar made his move. From what I can glean out of half-truths and ignorance, Lia went to the Halls of Virtue in the night. But there hasn't been any action from the emperor.

That is surprising. I expected Emperor Pakel would put up more of a fight. He tried to kill an entire royal family and just found out he had failed. Certainly he wouldn't want that coming to light. And yet, he's done nothing about it. That's more unsettling than anything he could have actually done.

When I'm dressed, I make my way down into one of the palace courtyards where a morning meal is being served for several noblemen and their wives. Supposedly, the emperor will attend this banquet, so it's crowded when I arrive. People mingle and chat before the food is served. Aba and Ima are already here somewhere, and I'm sure Vroni is in attendance as well.

I bow politely in greeting to some familiar faces—local nobles I've encountered at the festival's earlier events—and see Vroni among them. She beckons me over with a ladylike wave. As I approach, I overhear their conversation. Like everyone else, they're discussing the resurrected heir.

"I heard she claims to be Emperor Asil's daughter," one woman says as she adjusts her shawl.

Another scoffs. "How many people have made those claims over the years?"

A nobleman about my age chimes in, crossing his arms confidently. "My servant told me it is not a woman but a man, possibly the child prince. He saw him leave the palace last night."

An older man in a billowing bright green tunic shakes his head. "The prince is dead. And even if he was…" he lowers his voice, "alive, he'd be no older than twelve. Certainly not a grown man."

"If it were a prince, the emperor wouldn't have let him live," an elderly woman admits.

"Good morning, Enra," Vroni says. "I assume you've heard the… news."

I nod. "Does anyone actually know for sure what happened?"

"My servant—" the young nobleman starts, but the green-robed man cuts him off.

"Anyone who knows is certainly not telling us. But that doesn't keep people from speculating."

The others murmur in agreement.

"What have you heard?" the woman in the shawl asks me.

I may be one of the few who falls into the category of "anyone who knows," I realize. I weigh my words, trying not to give anything away while also not seeming like I know more than they do and am hiding it. It's easy to lie to seasoned politicians, but it's difficult to avoid being caught doing it.

"I haven't heard much that would be new to you." It's true. I haven't "heard" much that would be a revelation at all. And I'm not going to tell them what I know. "Someone said the old emperor had been resurrected. But I heard it was a woman," I admit. "So unless the old emperor came back as a woman, they can't both be true."

This suggestion gets a laugh from the group.

"Surely you know something, Hara?" the elderly woman asks Vroni. Everyone turns to her expectantly. Vroni fidgets a bit, but her movements are so small I'm sure I'm the only one who notices.

"If any of it is true," Vroni says. "I'm sure the emperor will do what he thinks is best for Elisya."

It's the most diplomatic response—entirely appropriate for the emperor's future granddaughter-in-law. But it's not the response the group wanted. They all offer half-hearted agreement before dismissing themselves, leaving my sister and me standing awkwardly on the stone walkway.

Vroni watches them go. "I think I disappointed them."

I shrug. "Let them be disappointed. You said what was right."

Vroni's voice drops to a whisper. "I'm not sure it is right, though."

"What do you mean?"

Vroni twists her fingers together. "It's just… I sleep in the women's wing with the emperor's wife and consorts, and I overheard him talking to Shaha Saretha last night. I don't know what they were saying, but it sounded heated."

So he is worried. But then why hasn't he done anything? The question won't leave me alone. I start to respond to Vroni, but the morning meal's arrival overshadows my voice. Servants set out low tables and cover them with an array of dishes. The courtyard gets louder as people exclaim how beautiful and delicious it looks.

Then Emperor Pakel and Empress Saretha appear at the entrance of the courtyard. The people grow quiet and everyone bows. As we look up, the emperor and his wife step into the courtyard, greeting the courtiers nearest them. Emperor Pakel looks a bit tired, but Empress Saretha is unbothered. Whatever they discussed last night, it doesn't appear to have distressed her in the slightest. Perhaps Vroni heard something or someone else.

I glance at her, but she's watching her new in-laws.

All conversations about rumors have ceased. No one would dare talk about a challenge to the emperor's throne in his presence at his own banquet.

But while we're here eating and discussing everything except the topic everyone is thinking about, Lia is at the Halls of Virtue, probably safe, and certainly creating more news for us all to gossip about later.

CHAPTER 21

Lia

A knock on the door wakes me from a fitful sleep on the sofa. I take a moment to orient myself to where I am. A room in the Halls of Virtue, in the priests' wing, where those who are on duty live while they serve outside the temple. The knock sounds again.

I get up and open the door. A servant woman waits on the other side with a basin full of water, a cloth, and a dress tossed over her shoulder. I reach out to take them from her, but she moves her arms away from me.

"I can carry them, Hara," she says.

Hara?

That's me. She's talking to me. I step aside to let her into the room. She sets the basin and cloth on a table and lays the dress out on the sofa. It's a plain cream in a simple style, but the linen is finer than anything I've ever worn before. She pulls a strip of beaded fabric from where it hangs on her own wrap skirt and lays it on top of the dress. It's a belt, the fanciest belt I've ever been expected to wear.

"Please dress at your leisure, Hara. I will return with your meal."

She bows and disappears through the doorway.

I stare at the dress for a moment before using the basin to wash. Whatever they plan on doing with me, they want me to be clean and appropriately dressed for it. I wash the blood from my dress in the basin and lay it out to dry. Then I try on the new dress. It's slightly too big for me, but the beaded belt fits it to my waist. As I tie it, there is another knock on the door.

I cross the room to open it, and on the other side, the same servant woman, now holding a tray of food, gives me a baffled look. "Hara, you may simply tell me to enter, and I will open the door. You do not need to open it."

"Oh…" I say.

I can't think of anything else. Opening doors has been my job my entire life, just as it is this woman's. We could switch our places, and I would do everything she's doing now. I am as much a servant as she is.

"What is your name?" I ask her.

"Ndondo, Hara," she answers.

She puts the tray of food—a thick porridge with milk and spices—down on the table and picks up the water basin and towel. If she notices the blood in the water, she doesn't say anything. "You have visitors who would like to speak with you. Shall I send them away?"

My heartbeat picks up speed. The emperor is already here. I might as well not put it off. "No, thank you, Ndondo. I will see them."

At least he can't kill me on the Halls of Virtue's grounds.

Ndondo retreats through the door again, and after a few minutes, there's another knock. I stand to open it but then remember myself. I shouldn't frustrate Ndondo any more than I already have.

"Enter," I call, trying to imitate the nobles I serve, but my voice sounds thin.

Ndondo opens the door, but instead of the emperor, Obipae Kula sweeps in with Enipae Gowan close behind her.

"Well." Obipae Kula's eyes flash as she smirks. "My chambermaid is the long-thought-dead princess of the Asil dynasty."

I stand and bow. "Good morning, Obipae."

"Don't bow to me," Obipae Kula says. "We are equals."

"Of course not, Obipae!" I insist. She must be feeling so offended. I can't imagine her reaction at being told her rank was equal to mine. Even if that were true, her age alone would give her seniority. "I would never presume—"

"No presumption is necessary. You were born my equal, so that is what you are. Call me Kula."

"I—I couldn't possibly—"

Obipae Kula sits at the table and slides the tray of food over to me. "Yes, you can possibly. Eat. You'll need your strength."

She gestures to the chair opposite hers, and I sit. "Thank you, Obipae."

"Kula," she says.

She glances at her husband, who's standing next to the window with one hand resting on the hilt of a dagger at his belt. Obipae Kula cocks her head at him. "What are you doing?"

He takes a moment to realize the question is for him. He glances over at us and then back out the window. "Keeping watch."

"For what? There are guards already outside the doors."

"You can never be too careful."

"*You* can."

They exchange a look, then both of them laugh and turn away from each other—Enipae Gowan back to the window and Obipae Kula back to me.

"How long have you known?" she asks.

"My whole life," I admit. The secret is already out, so there's no use in trying to keep it.

"Then why now?"

"I—" I know Aba would want me to say, "I want my people to be free," and I do, but if I'm being completely honest, I'm just trying to make sure everyone stays alive. "I just want to save my family," I say.

"Your family?" Confusion flashes across Obipae Kula's face for a moment, but it is quickly replaced by a neutral smile. "It seems you'll get the opportunity for that soon enough."

It's my turn to be confused. "What do you mean?"

"The judges are preparing to present you to the court."

The floor tilts, and I have to grab the table to keep from fainting. "They what?"

"They've prepared a test—to see if you're truly Emperor Asil's living relative—but everyone seems certain you'll pass. Apparently, you look like him. Once that's done, they intend to take you to the emperor."

"How do you know all this?"

Obipae Kula shrugs. "Information has become easy for me to acquire over the years."

It's happening. Aba was right. They're going to give me the chance to make a blood claim of restitution. But Emperor Pakel will fight. He's burned the city to the ground once before to kill my family. There's nothing to stop him from doing it again. The judges didn't stop him the first time, and they won't be able to stop him now if he thinks I'm trying to stand between him and his power.

My hands shake, and my heartbeat pounds in my ears. If this will save my family from an unwinnable rebellion, I'll do my best.

"Is something wrong?" Obipae Kula asks me.

Everything is wrong, but I can't say that. There's another knock on the door, and Ndondo comes back in.

"The judges have requested your presence, your highness."

Obipae Kula also stands, but Ndondo tells her, "It will not be long if you'd like to wait and continue your conversation."

Obipae Kula nods and sits. "I'll do that."

I stand and walk to the door as if I'm in a dream. The floor beneath me seems to be gone. It's all happening so fast.

Ndondo leads me outside to a building constructed of thin wooden branches packed tightly together with a cone covered in clay as its roof. Several bright strips of fabric hang from the roof and dance in the wind like a rainbow. The building looks like a cough could blow it down, but I know it has stood longer than every other structure in the Halls of Virtue's compound. It's the first court, the structure in which citizens of Gazidah used to come to resolve their differences before they built the surrounding compound. The cone roof represents the building's purpose—taking our petitions before Juae—though it's no longer used for that. Instead, it's the place where I'll face my first test.

Ndondo gestures for me to go inside, so I walk past her and into the shadow of the small building. Inside, three judges wait for me in their official robes. bright cloth wrapped around their waists several times and slung over their bare shoulders, held in place by beaded collars. I can tell they're men by their dress, but a wooden mask of an animal obscures each of their faces —a bird, a camel, and a cat. A guarantee of impartiality. You can't influence the judges outside of court if you don't know who they are. And you can't read their faces if you can't see them. They sit on the ground and indicate I should do the same. Between us is a low table with only one item on it, a small clay vial.

I sit in front of them, and they stare at me for what feels like hours but is probably only a few seconds. Then the judge to my right—Camel-Mask—pulls a tablet from behind him and reads it.

"You are Asil Liani Hara Elisya daughter of Asil Nahan Datu Elisya?"

It must be my birth record from the palace archives.

"Yes, I am," I answer. My voice trembles, though I will it not to.

The judge nods and turns to the one beside him—Cat-Mask. "You may begin."

From the center, Cat-Mask leans forward and grasps the vial. "Please hold out your arms."

I put my arms on the table with my hands facing down, but the judge turns them so my wrists face upward. My tattoos glow in the dim room. He then opens the vial. "If you are false, confess now and be cleansed."

I stay silent. He nods and then pours the vial out onto my tattoos. The liquid feels like water, cool and clear. But when it hits my skin, my tattoos fade. Their glow dies, and then they disappear altogether. I gasp. Were they fake this whole time? They've never washed away before.

The judges' masked faces are unreadable, and my heart races. "I thought… I promise, I never…"

The judge to my left cuts me off. "This water negates all magic. When it dries, your marks will reappear. We have determined your claim to be true. In an hour, we will present you to the court."

I exit the building in a daze. When Ndondo appears to escort me back to my room, I tell her, "I passed."

She nods. "Yes, Hara."

Obipae Kula and Enipae Gowan are still waiting for me in the room. With no one else to talk to, I describe the test to them. "They're going to present me to the emperor."

"To make your claim?" Enipae Gowan asks. When Obipae Kula and I look at him in surprise, he shrugs. "I had the occasion to study Elisyan law several years ago. You may claim restitution for your family. But since your family was the former emperor, you can ask for basically anything."

"I know," I say.

"You don't sound pleased about that," Obipae Kula notes.

Aba wants me to ask for power, for a position in court, and for the abolition of slavery. Given the lives that were lost, none of that is unreasonable, but the emperor will fight. Asking for power would be equal to asking the emperor for his life, and I'm sure he's not going to give either up. It will be a battle—either literally or figuratively—but I'm not prepared to fight. That's what I'm trying to avoid.

Could I forego the position and power and just ask to abolish slavery? That way, the emperor wouldn't feel threatened, and perhaps he would set us free. But no. Aba's voice rings through my mind. You need power to change the law. Even a blood right cannot do that. If I wanted to use my blood right to empty Elisya's coffers, I couldn't do it. That would be against laws of thievery. To change a law, a noble must present the change to the court and get it accepted by the emperor. No common person can do that, and even though I was born noble, I'm a commoner now.

And even if that were possible, Elisya now stands on the backs of slaves. Emperor Pakel will not easily release his footstool, even if that was all I attempted to claim.

I let myself fall onto the sofa and put my face in my hands. What was I thinking? I need help and time, and I have neither. I'm not sure how long I've been silent, but Enipae Gowan and Obipae Kula are staring at me when I look up.

"Is there anything we can do to help?" Obipae Kula asks.

"I don't even know what I need to do." I sink deeper into the seat, dejected.

Enipae Gowan leans on the window frame. "You can ask

for anything you want. Did you come here without knowing what you desired?"

Yes, and no. I came here wanting to stop my father from losing his life in a violent uprising. I wanted to show him I could do what he wanted, but mostly, I wanted to save him, to save them all. But I may have rushed ahead too early. I need more time to figure all this out.

That could be the answer. Aba told me that the right to make a claim is mine for my entire life, unless I waive it. If I hold on to the right, the emperor has no reason to kill my family. He could kill me, but that would put him at odds with the judges and with Juae himself, since I'm under their protection until I make a claim. Even he can't afford to make an enemy of the Halls of Virtue.

I nod and stand. "Will you accompany me to court?"

Obipae Kula and Enipae Gowan quickly agree. It feels good to bring someone with me of my own accord, even if they aren't my family. And at least any assassins will have a more difficult time killing me if I'm accompanied by Derian nobles. An international war is the last thing Elisya needs.

Ndondo returns with two priests and a judge, Cat-Mask. "Are you ready, your highness?"

I'm not, but I say I am anyway.

The judge leads the way outside, and more join us as we walk. By the time we leave the tower's confines, I feel like I'm surrounded by a marriage procession, but this is not a joyful occasion. They are leading me to a decision I'm not prepared to make.

CHAPTER 22

The palace looms even higher than it did the first time we arrived, and my heart pounds as we walk through the gates. We are a column of people—me at the center, a wall of priests surrounding me, and the judges at the front. Obipae Kula and Enipae Gowan are directed away before we enter, probably to join the rest of the onlookers in court. I'll have to walk in alone.

The priests begin a chant at the doors. My stomach roils with the rumble of their voices.

I want to ask everyone to pause and let me figure out what to say. I just need to make my presence known. The judges can protect me, and Aba and the others will know we're moving ahead. They don't have to fight, and they don't have to rush. As long as I know we're all safe, I can figure out how to do what needs to be done. But I need to know how to do that, and the time for me to learn has run out.

I tap the priest closest to me on the arm, a younger one. He shrugs and tries to ignore me, continuing the current verse, but I try again.

Finally he turns to me, his voice a low hiss. "Yes, Hara?"

"What do I say?"

The young priest looks at me like I've lost my mind. "You announce your claim for restitution."

He faces forward again and resumes his chant. Is that all he thinks it takes? I tell the emperor what I want, and the world changes? That would be too simple. I glance toward the obipae and enipae as they go inside before us. Obipae Kula shoots her husband a meaningful glance, and he pats her arm as if to reassure her. Do they know something I don't? The thought makes me laugh darkly to myself. Everyone knows something I don't.

The courtroom is once again crowded with people, Elisyan nobles and dignitaries from other countries. I don't know how many of them know what's actually going on, but they all decided they had to be here to see it.

The emperor sits at the front of the room, Shaha Saretha beside him with no sign of her tattoos today. They're hidden beneath a wealth of beaded bangles adorning her wrists and forearms. Shaha Saretha looks bored, but the emperor glowers at me and then exchanges a glance with the judge at the head of our party. The judge nods.

The courtroom is silent as the emperor speaks. "Welcome, harbingers of justice. What have you brought to court on this day?"

"What" not "Who." The distinction doesn't escape me, but I don't have the energy to be offended. My heart is already racing too fast.

The judge—Bird-Mask—straightens himself and declares, "We have determined this to be Asil Liani, Hara Elisya, heir of Asil Nahan, Datu Elisya, and sole descendant of Asil Niotek, whose lives you took."

The noise in the room swells as waves of whispers pass over the gathered crowd. I wince. I hadn't expected the judges to be so blunt about the emperor's crimes. The emperor raises an eyebrow. Perhaps he hadn't expected it either.

"She appears before you," the judge continues, "To make a claim of her blood right of restitution for her family."

Emperor Pakel looks directly at me. "Is that so?"

I feel hands on my back as the priests push me forward until there's no one standing between me and the emperor. I'm exposed, and Emperor Pakel scowls at me.

"Go ahead, heir of Asil Nahan. Make your claim."

He's goading me, making me the subject of a joke I don't understand.

All eyes in the room are on me now, a few I know and most I don't. At the side of the dais where the servants are, I recognize a couple of my father's allies. Aba himself isn't here, but they watch me in his place, confused and, it seems, expectant. I can't disappoint them.

"I am—" My voice stalls in my throat, and I try again. "I am Asil Liani, Hara Elisya."

The emperor purses his lips and leans forward on his throne. Though the movement is slight, its pressure bears down on me like iron.

My hands shake, and I grip the sides of my dress to steady them.

"I have—" My voice shakes as violently as my hands. "I have a blood right to claim restitution."

"Is there proof of this claim?" the emperor asks.

At this, one priest behind me steps up and reaches toward me. I realize he's asking me to raise my wrists and expose my tattoos for all the court to see.

It's like he's asking me to expose my naked body in front of hundreds of people, but I do as he asks, raising my arms and flipping my hands toward the ceiling. My tattoos glint in the sunlight that fills the room.

"We have determined the royal tattoos to be authentic and given in accordance with the law," Bird-Mask asserts.

The emperor gives a solemn nod. "I see. I recognize you as the sole heir of Asil Nahan."

Bile threatens to rise up in my throat as the emperor stares at me, his expression as serious as the grave, but the slightest smile at the corner of his lips.

He's not worried. Of course he's not. This is his court, his empire, his world. He knows what to do here, and I don't. But I have to at least try.

Before anyone else can speak, I raise one sparkling wrist a little higher. My voice squeaks instead of ringing out. "In restitution, I ask for slavery to be abolished—"

The room erupts with voices, cutting me off. I pause, stunned, and then I try to continue, "—abolished in Elisya…"

No one hears me. The fervor of the court drowns my voice out. The two slaves in the front gape openly at me.

I know the request is unprecedented, but I had assumed they'd at least let me finish my demands.

The Bird-Mask judge returns to the front and stands beside me. As he does, the room quiets. Even amid courtly chaos, the judges inspire respect.

"You may request your recompense after your right has been established." Bird-Mask's voice is low.

"But…" I hesitate. I hate how unconfident I sound. This is the voice of a scared child, not a hero. "But he's already acknowledged me."

Bird-Mask nods. "There are other things that must be done." He turns back to the emperor. "As this has been established and acknowledged to be Asil Liani, we recognize her status as a citizen of Gazidah and renounce her designation as a slave."

I blink at him as the court chatter picks up again. I'd forgotten it, but Aba told me about this as much as he understood it. According to Elisyan law, no native Gazidan can be a slave. The lowest rank they can have is that of an indentured servant, and the time they may serve is strictly adhered to.

The first emperor created that law when he made his first campaigns of unification into the surrounding territories. He wanted those in Gazidah to be superior to those from the other kingdoms. That's why Gazidan records are so carefully kept. Proving that your lineage in Gazidah has been established since before the founding of the empire ensures the security of your rank.

"In addition," Bird-Mask continues, "We establish the right of Asil Liani to claim restitution and recompense for what was lost to her, life for life, honor for honor, breath for breath."

The emperor clutches his chest, remorse on his face, though it's as much a mask as the ones the judges wear. "I must acknowledge my guilt before Juae."

It sounds like he's reciting something, some kind of script or ritual I don't know about.

"We accept your acknowledgment of guilt," Bird-Mask says. Then he turns to me. "Do you require the life of Pakel Hechede in restitution for his crimes?" he asks.

"I.. His life? I..." I scramble for the right words. "I don't need his life, I just need—"

Emperor Pakel leans forward in a bow or a deep nod on his throne, his eyes fixed on me, and my words falter. What do they need me to say?

Bird-Mask tilts his head. "Do you release your claim on the life of Pakel Hechede?"

Releasing the claim is the last thing I want to do. The eyes of everyone in the court bore into me, but I have to press on. "No, I don't, I just... I don't want his life."

When will they ask me what I do want?

"If you do not require his life, you offer him forgiveness," Bird-Mask says slowly, as though he's afraid I won't understand.

And I don't understand. What is he asking me to do? Do I need to forgive the emperor to ask for the end of slavery?

"I—I do not require his life, so I suppose I do… forgive… him. But, I—"

"You extend him your forgiveness?" Bird-Mask asks.

"I—yes?"

My agreement is a question, but Bird-Mask treats it as an answer. He holds a hand out to me. "Let it be recorded that Asil Liani, daughter of Asil Nahan, has relinquished her claim—"

"What? I didn't—" I try to interject, but the judge continues, and the chattering court drowns my voice.

Apparently, I've done something so surprising that even the judge's voice can't deter the gossip. Bird-Mask has to shout the rest of his statement.

"And forgiven Pakel Hechede for his crimes against her family. We honor her in the tradition of Magebe under the blessing of Juae."

"You didn't let me—"

Emperor Pakel stands and bows to me, a deep, low bow reserved for those to whom you are indebted. "I accept your forgiveness with unworthy gratitude and extend peace with my right hand. You will celebrate with us as part of Elisya's noble history."

His family follows his example, those younger than me even kneeling. My own knees threaten to buckle.

"I—"

The courtiers break out in applause as if they've seen an amazing show, and just as quickly as I entered the courtroom, I am ushered out into a warm, dim side chamber. The racket of conversation dulls as the door shuts behind me.

My breath catches in my throat as I choke back a sob. What have I done?

CHAPTER 23

The door creaks as it opens again, letting in more noise and two figures. Obipae Kula charges in followed by her husband.

"Thank you," she says to the guard at the door, though by his expression, it doesn't seem that he wanted to let her in.

The tone of Obipae Kula's voice shows she didn't give him much of a choice, either. As the door closes, she turns to me.

"That was… a display."

I put my head in my hands.

"What did I do?" I ask through my fingers. Tears spring up at the corners of my eyes, and I don't see any reason not to let them fall. I may have guaranteed my father's rebellion. After my failure, he'll see no other way. How could I have caused the one thing I was trying to prevent?

Obipae Kula puts a hand on my shoulder. "You made life much easier for Emperor Pakel. He can hold you up as a symbol of peace. Your 'forgiveness' marks the true end of the last dynasty and the civil war. You've made him legitimate."

I wince. I didn't really expect her to say something encouraging, but that stings more than false platitudes would right now. "Was this what he wanted the whole time?"

"Perhaps," she admits.

"And the judges were on his side?"

Enipae Gowan sighs. "Maybe. Peace serves them too right now."

"But how could they know I wouldn't know what to say?"

"It's a safe guess, since you're a child alone," Obipae Kula says. "A child who's been living as a slave with no political education to speak of. It's hard to imagine the emperor dreaming up someone easier to manipulate."

Shame washes over me, followed by a wave of anger. I want to curl up into a knot, and I want to run back into the court and scream until someone listens to me. The two emotions pull at each other. This is my fault, I know. I was unprepared, but I went ahead anyway. I thought I could change things. Aba told me I could. But he was wrong. He never should have built me up like this, not without knowing how far I could fall.

But it's not just my fault. It's the emperor's fault too. He's the one who talked his way out of his guilt. He's the one who'll never pay for my birth family's murder now. He's the one who'll keep my family and hundreds of thousands of others enslaved for their entire lives.

I have to find my family. I need to explain, so they know I tried, even if it provides no comfort. Maybe, since the judges acknowledged my position in front of everyone, I can free them at the very least. I'll figure out what else to do from there.

I stand and cross the room to the door. Outside, the guard stands facing the hallway—to keep people out or to keep us in, I'm not sure. His weapons and simpler clothing identify him as a justice guard, not a palace guard. He bows to me.

"May I help you, Sali?"

He uses the term for "noblewoman". I may not be royalty, but I suppose being a descendant of the former emperor still garners some respect, even when you've made a fool of yourself before the entire empire and several of its allies.

"I need to—" I stop. Do I need to tell him where I'm going? I'm no longer counted as a slave. "I will return," I say.

Instead of questioning me, he nods, but when I walk away, he falls into step behind me. I glance over my shoulder a few times, but he's still there. Should I tell him to stay behind? Having him overhear talk of Aba's plans will do no good for anyone. After a few turns with him still behind me, I give up. Perhaps I can get him to wait outside the smithy for me.

Thoughts of how to get rid of my guard distract me from my surroundings. I turn a corner and run directly into Prince Enra.

Enra

I always forget how small Lia is. As she plows into me, she knocks me aside, but she herself crumples to the ground. A guard behind her and I both go to help her up, but I get there faster than he does.

Lia winces. "Forgive me, Suan."

I chuckle. "Lia, you don't have to call me 'Suan'. You're a princess. I should call you 'Hara'."

She straightens her belt and rearranges her dress, and I avert my eyes politely.

"I'd rather you didn't," she says. "I'm used to you calling me Lia."

With a smile, I quickly check if it's appropriate to look at her. "Well, you can call me Enra, and we can consider ourselves even."

She winces. "That will also take some getting used to, but

alright Suan… Enra. You don't seem as surprised as I expected to discover my identity, if you'll forgive me for saying so."

"Oh, well," I shrug, trying to think of a good explanation. "It's nice to see something throw the court out of its formality every once in a while. But it is strange, a princess living within our walls…" I think of Vroni. "Another one, at least."

I decide to change the subject, trying to figure out what happened in the courtroom. "I was surprised that you forgave the emperor. But then, I know you're kindhearted."

Lia cringes. "I…" She sighs. "It wasn't my intention. It was all very sudden."

"That is true." I got the feeling that things didn't go the way she wanted them to, though they might have gone the way Aba expected. How could he have predicted something like this? I'll have to ask him later.

Lia looks like she may cry or scream, and part of me wants to reassure her. They really took advantage of her in there. However she was taught, whatever she was told to say, she was woefully unprepared to face Emperor Pakel and his court. They're nearly all his pawns. But Lia isn't yet. So I need to get on her good side. I'd like to gauge where her thoughts are, how willing she might be to accept our family's hand.

"What will you do now that the truth is out?" I ask.

Her expression deflates, and she lets out a long sigh. "I… I should…"

She doesn't finish the statement. Instead, she gives me a weak attempt at a smile, though her eyes glisten.

"I don't know," she says.

I stop short of grimacing. How does Aba do this so easily? Getting people to tell you what you need to know is even harder than it looks, and it looks hard.

I change the subject. "Where are you going?"

Her smile falls away. "I need to see my father and explain…"

"I'll escort you."

"Oh, no—" she starts to protest but then pauses. Her shoulders deflate, and she nods. "Thank you, Enra."

The way she says my name catches me off guard, and I push away the twisting in my heart. That's not a response worth examining right now.

We chat as we walk. I try to keep the conversation as light as possible, discussing how large the palace is, how easy it is to get lost, how there are so many faces that you could never meet everyone. And I avoid any further conversation about Lia's newly revealed identity. But every time we pass a slave, Lia winces like she's been struck.

There aren't very many people inside the smithy when we arrive. Lia asks after Benar, and the page boy directs us to an older building in the palace that is being updated. The roof needed patching, and Lia's father and some others were directed to repair it. Benar is standing on top of the roof when we reach the building, but he climbs down when he sees us. He bows to me. They probably want to be alone.

"I'll wait over there." I nod politely and point to a nearby tree that's out of hearing distance.

Lia looks grateful, but Benar's frown doesn't move. He says, "Thank you, Suan," though.

If Lia's nobility now, shouldn't her family be as well? It doesn't make sense for those who raised her to be so far beneath her, to be held in slavery. I should talk to Aba about freeing them. That's the least we can do.

I sit in the dust and grass beneath the tree and fold my legs, picking at grass and waiting for Lia to finish talking to her father. I know what kind of conversation that can be, and I feel even worse for her. I hope it goes well—as well as it can. They stand close together and speak in hushed tones. I can tell even though I'm far away.

But I don't intend to eavesdrop. I don't need to know what Benar is planning. As long as Lia knows I'm waiting for her, that's all that matters.

CHAPTER 24

Lia

Aba's movements are stilted, but I can't read any emotion on his face. My best course of action is to apologize. "Aba I—"

He shakes his head. "Are you well?"

My voice stops in my throat, and when I don't respond, he continues. "When you disappeared, your mother and I panicked. We searched the palace for you, and then rumors started up…"

His voice trails off. What must they have thought, hearing that a descendant of the old emperor had appeared? They would have known it was me.

"I'm sorry Lia."

Aba is apologizing to me?

"I pushed you too hard."

My heart falls into my stomach. I wish he would just get angry. Then I could be angry. His disappointment is so much worse. I've failed him.

"No Aba, I wanted to—"

"I know you were only doing what you thought was right. It's not your fault."

But it is my fault. I panicked and rushed ahead. I left him and the rest of my family behind to save them myself. I was supposed to save them myself. I haven't just failed Aba, I've failed everyone who was relying on me.

Aba puts his hands on my shoulders.

"Don't worry," he says. "This won't stop us. We've been ready for every contingency."

"You have?" I didn't think I could feel any worse, but I do. I know what he's going to say, but I have to ask. "What will you do?"

He shakes his head. "It's better if you don't know. You're in a different place now."

"But maybe I can still help," I offer.

Aba is unrelenting. "You'll be safer where you are. You can do no more now."

That feels like a rebuke, and my face warms. I can't help but blurt out, "Why didn't you tell me what the judges would ask?"

I prepare for an argument, but instead of getting angry, Aba touches my face. "That's how I failed you. I didn't know."

He looks away. "I wanted to ask others, those who know the ways of Gazidah now better than I do. It's been years…"

He doesn't have to finish his explanation. He didn't have time to find out and teach me because I rushed ahead without him.

Aba pats my shoulders. "You should go. Things will change for you now."

"But maybe I can—"

He shakes his head as he turns me around, back to where Enra is waiting. The thud of hammers against wood rings in my ears. "Go."

I want to stay, to convince him I can fix this, but if I'm being honest, I don't know how. So I leave, looking over my shoulder several times as I walk, but Aba has already turned back to his work. My pulse pounds in my ears. All I've done is make things worse. I've pushed them into the rebellion I was trying to avoid.

Enra stands as I approach, and I step back. I wish he would act normally. This new behavior is burdensome. But then, Aba is right. Things will change for me now.

My new guard has been watching at a respectful distance, and he keeps it as we move. Enra walks quickly, and I try to keep up with him, but I'm lost in my own thoughts. There has to be something I can still do. I try to tell myself that I should give up and let Aba handle things his own way. But for a long time, I was his way. I have to believe I still can be.

We walk back to the palace in silence. Enra is the first to break it. "What did he… Was everything alright?"

I nod. "Yes."

I don't feel like saying any more, and he doesn't ask.

When we get back inside, I'm accosted by a collection of women. Enra disappears as hands grab my arms and a half dozen voices speak at one time.

"—Not ready at all—"

"—Almost hopeless cause—"

"—About her hair—"

"—Taken to the empress."

The last speaker is the most final one, and the others defer to her. I search frantically for my guard, but when I lay eyes on him, he doesn't seem concerned.

"Who are you?" I ask. "What's happening?"

The authoritative woman blinks at me like I'm a simpleton. "Shaha Saretha has called for you. You are not presentable, but nothing can be done. Come."

I don't have time to reply before I'm swept through a hallway, across a courtyard, and onto a ground floor pavilion where the empress reclines alone with her meal. She's dressed differently than she was earlier today, in a brightly patterned wrap dress belted around her waist with bejeweled cords and a blue scarf covering her hair.

The women bow to her, and she nods. "This is her?"

"Yes, your majesty."

Shaha Saretha squints and studies me intently. I feel her eyes on me, but I glance at her arms. The beaded bangles that adorn her arms conceal her tattoos completely. I can't help but be curious. Is she related to me, or did she get the tattoos illegally, at the risk of her life? How many people in the palace know she has them?

Without warning, Shaha Saretha's laughter breaks through the silence. She laughs as if someone has poisoned her with mirth, her head thrown back and a terrifying grin on her face. After a few minutes, she wipes tears from her eyes as she asks, "Are you afraid?"

That's directed at me. "Yes," I admit, though I don't know why. The truth comes out unbidden.

Shaha Saretha nods. "As you should be. I imagine I too would be afraid if I were you."

She picks up a nut from a platter of food before her and pops it into her mouth cheerfully. "But you don't need to fear, at least not now. I have no reason to hurt you. You've brought quite a fervor into the palace."

A fervor seems like something I should apologize for, but the way Shaha Saretha says it, it sounds like a good thing. She beckons me forward.

"Sit. Let us talk comfortably. I have questions to ask you."

What could the empress possibly have to ask me? I sit warily across from her, and she pushes a tray of fruit toward me. When I don't take anything, she shrugs as if it doesn't matter to her whether I eat. I'm sure it doesn't.

"So," she says, "Why now? What do you want?"

She's blunt, but then I suppose empresses can say whatever they want however they want. But I don't know how to answer her questions. Why now? Because I'm a fool? Because I'm a failure? Because I was trying to keep my family safe, and instead I pushed them into the arms of death? Because I had no other choice? And what do I want? Does that even matter? It's not like I can receive it by telling her. But I have to tell her something. I scramble for a respectful response so she doesn't have me flogged.

"As I stated before the emperor…"

Shaha Saretha waves her hand. "Yes, yes. The end of slavery. Of course, you'd ask for that after being a slave most of your life. But why now?" She stresses the last word. "What is it you truly seek?"

I think for a moment. "The circumstances of my… revelation were not entirely in my control."

That's honest enough. I made the choice to go, but the only reason I did it was because my father was going to start a rebellion otherwise. I sigh. He's certainly going to do that now.

Shaha Saretha nods. "I suppose they weren't. What circumstances could be in your control?"

She laughs as if she's told a joke, but I don't find it funny. I suppose I wasn't meant to because her attendants remain silent. They probably know when it's appropriate for anyone other than the empress to laugh.

"How did you live?"

I've never told this story to anyone who wasn't a slave. It feels like a betrayal to explain how my parents are my saviors to the empress. She's certainly powerful enough to do them harm and wouldn't hesitate to do so if it served her.

I answer as carefully as I can. "I was saved by slaves."

"Thus the quest for their freedom."

Shaha Saretha purses her lips. Then, faster than I can react, she reaches out for my right arm. Her grip is firm as she turns my wrist over and studies the tattoo. I hold myself still, stunned, as Shaha Saretha taps the golden design with a sharp fingernail. I wince. That hurts more than it should. But the tattoo sparkles, a bit of magic running through it as if it wants to prove itself to her. I've never seen it do that before.

Shaha Saretha smiles wistfully and nods. "He was skilled. I'm sorry he's dead. The art is lost forever now."

Before I have a chance to wonder what that means, she releases my arm and gets her attendants' attention. "Prepare her. She'll attend tonight's banquet as my esteemed guest."

"Yes, Shaha," the women behind me respond in unison.

Two women help me to my feet as though I'm a fragile bird, ready to break at any moment. They surround me as they shuffle me away, but over my shoulder, I glimpse Shaha Saretha chuckling to herself.

CHAPTER 25

The women whisk me away, back into the palace. As soon as we're out of the empress' sight, their conversation picks up. They discuss what to do with me to make me presentable enough for the empress' standards for the banquet this evening, talking around me and picking at my hair, dress, and skin like I'm a doll.

The dress I'm wearing is the finest dress I've ever worn, to my memory. The judges gave it to me this morning before they tested me. But according to Shaha Saretha's attendants, it's too old-fashioned and plain, not nearly grand enough for any palace occasion.

A part of me wants to interject, if only to ensure they won't throw it away, but every time I speak, it seems like the women don't even hear me. They respond, though, when a stooped, elderly man blocks us in the middle of a hallway.

The same authoritative woman from before steps forward, exasperated. She nearly shouts at the man. "Gelen, is there something I can help you with?"

The man turns toward her voice, but his eyes don't meet hers. It seems he may have lost his vision at some point, and perhaps his hearing has suffered as well. But he answers. "Yes. The emperor has summoned the sali."

The woman takes a step back as I stifle a gasp. The emperor wants to see me? Now? Why? My mind and heart race. I did throw his court into turmoil. It would make sense he'd want to see me. Will he finish the job he started and kill me now?

"The empress has tasked us with preparing her for the banquet," the woman says, though she shows the older man more deference than she had before.

The man shakes his head. "I will return her to you."

For a moment, relief washes over me. If I'm coming back to these women, that means I won't die. But then, this man could be lying.

There's a moment of tense quiet, and then the women shuffle me forward from amongst their ranks, leaving me facing the old man.

He turns without glancing in my direction. "Follow me."

I want to refuse. The empress seems safer than the emperor, though not by much. But I don't imagine I have much choice. At least he sent an elderly man and not ten guards.

The man, Gelen, walks with speed and precision through the palace hallways, so quickly that I wonder if I was wrong about his eyesight. But people give him a wide berth and pull whatever they're carrying out of the way.

Gradually, the walls and ceiling around us get lower and tighter. We're in an older part of the palace, a part that was certainly here long before my family was killed. When we reach the end of a hall, Gelen opens a small wooden door. "Please enter."

I hesitate. We're on a lower floor, possibly partially under-ground, judging by the cool air, and there are no nobles or guards anywhere in sight. Why would the emperor want to meet me here? My heart races, but I go inside the room.

Emperor Pakel reclines at a low table and looks me up and down. I avoid his eyes, but I can feel him studying me.

There's a small open window above his head, but the room is stuffy, and the air is stale. My eyes lose focus, and for a moment, I think I might faint, but I don't. Instead, I just stand there, and the emperor stares at me.

I take a deep breath and raise my eyes from the floor. Up close, it's easier to see the emperor's age, and he seems shorter here than on his throne, though he's no less menacing.

After an eternity of scrutiny, he speaks. "Sit."

I try to sit gracefully, but my knees betray me, and I half-sit, half fall to the floor next to the cushion.

I think he laughs at me, but it might have been a cough. "You're a slave of Paykhan's. Or at least, you were."

I don't answer, but he doesn't seem to mind since it wasn't a question. It is strange to hear Satrap Paykhan referred to so casually, but if anyone can do that, Emperor Pakel can.

"When was the last time you were here?"

I shake my head, answering truthfully. "I don't know."

I don't add any honorable titles. Even if he kills me, I can't bring myself to do that.

He shakes his head. "No, you wouldn't. But I do."

My hands shake, and I tighten my fists around the fabric of my skirt. I can't let him see that I'm afraid.

"I'm sure I know more about you than you know about yourself. You were born here, in this very room, to be exact. I was with your father when it was announced."

My attention is focused on the floor. I know I'm shaking, and I press my lips together to stop, but it doesn't help.

Emperor Pakel truly laughs then. "You have nothing to fear from me now, girl. Though I am curious by what miracle you survived."

Nothing to fear from the man who tried to kill me and failed? I would echo his laugh if I could.

"I knew your face was familiar. Your father and I were close once. His blood is apparent in you."

It almost sounds like the truth, but it can't be. Certainly, he knew my birth father, but no one can be so heartless as to murder their friends.

"He would have been shocked at your appearance today," Emperor Pakel continues. "And doubly shocked at your lack of decorum."

He would probably have been most shocked to learn that you killed him, I think, but I say nothing.

The emperor pulls a piece of parchment from beneath the table and slides it across so it's within my field of vision. "I am a man of my word—what was your name—ah yes, Lia. You go by Lia. I tell you nothing but the truth."

I should at least face my family's murderer. He's the guilty one here—though I've accidentally pardoned him. I struggle and wrap my arms around my waist, but I lift my eyes to Emperor Pakel's face. But instead of anger, his expression is one of interest, almost amusement.

"I told your grandfather I would replace him, and I did. Now I tell you I will not kill you, and I won't."

"Why?" I ask, my voice a whisper despite my best efforts. "Why wouldn't you kill me?" The word "now" sticks in my mind.

Emperor Pakel smiles. "Your life means nothing to me. What threat do you pose? Any power in your name died with your father. You are a relic of a bygone era."

I clench my fists against my sides despite myself. He's not wrong. I'm as good as powerless without the blood right, and my only allies are slaves or dead.

"Besides, you have forgiven me," the emperor continues, "That's suits me better now than killing you would."

He taps the paper between us, and I look at it for the first time. It's a statement saying that Asil Liani Hara Elisya will live out the rest of her days in exile from Elisya as a political refugee. He left the country I'm being exiled to blank.

"You will stay here for the duration of the festival as a testament to Elisya's peace. After that, you can go wherever you like," Emperor Pakel says. "Derian, Susheph, even across the sea, if you fancy that. Take your family too, whoever they are."

He sounds so casual, like he couldn't possibly care less about what I do with my life or who my family is. But this must be important to him, and he must want to keep it a secret. That's why the only person outside the door is an elder who may be both blind and deaf.

"You may want to go north," the emperor continues, tapping the parchment. "Since that's the direction your brother went."

I take a moment to understand. My mind whirs. My brother? Then I realize. Duin. My infant brother. The emperor is a cruel liar as well as a murderer.

"My brother is dead," I say with more force than I realize I had left in my body.

"Is he?" Emperor Pakel asks, his voice tinged with humor. "The last I heard, he was alive and well. A healthy boy capable of any work. Sold north to a band of mercenaries."

I study the emperor's face despite myself. It can't be true. It can't possibly be true. I was there when he died.

But I didn't see it.

All I heard were the cries and then the silence.

It could be possible. A hope grows in my chest, though I try to tamp it down.

I reach out for the paper instinctively, but the emperor snatches it back. "That was several years ago. He may be dead by now. It doesn't matter to me. But I am curious. Why are you really here?"

Empress Saretha asked the same question. For a moment, my panic returns, and I feel like I did just before walking into court. But I've already faced him there. Why are they both so curious? What is it they're afraid of?

Before I can think of a more appropriate response, I bite out. "You instructed the satrap to bring his entire household."

For the first time, I sound angry, like I blame the emperor for all this. And I suppose I do. If he hadn't made that demand, we'd all still be in Ragien. I wouldn't have ruined Aba's plans, and he wouldn't be starting a rebellion now.

The emperor nods as if he'd forgotten. "Yes… Paykhan is an obedient dog."

The insult of the satrap feels foreign. Even at the most heated meetings, Aba and his supporters never spoke about the satrap that way. But the emperor can say what he wants about his nobility, I suppose.

"This is my offer for you," Emperor Pakel says. "Be a good, presentable noble. Then leave. Never return. And all will be well."

I stare at the agreement. Aba wouldn't want me to sign it. He wouldn't want me to do anything the emperor wanted. But for the first time, I see an opportunity. If the emperor doesn't see me as a threat, maybe I can find a way—any way—to end slavery where I am. Then no one will have to fight, and no one will have to die. And if, by some miracle, the emperor isn't lying, and Duin is still alive, maybe I can find him too.

So I take the paper and sign my name at the bottom. For a second, the emperor seems surprised I can write, but I don't feel the need to explain my education to him. When I'm done, Emperor Pakel takes the paper and rolls it up, a satisfied expression on his face.

He calls for Gelen. "Take her away."

Gelen reaches a hand out to me to help me stand, and though my legs are still shaking, I don't need his help. I adjust my skirt, avoiding the emperor's eyes. Perhaps it's good if he thinks I'm scared. The more assured the emperor is of my fear, the less he'll need to watch me.

Gelen bows to the emperor—I don't—and then he leads me through the halls, back to the waiting arms of Shaha Saretha's attendants.

CHAPTER 26

The servant waiting at the door to the palace courtyard keeps glancing at me. I'm sure I'm making him uncomfortable, standing here trying to work up the courage to enter the banquet, but I'm uncomfortable too.

Shaha Saretha's attendants have scrubbed my skin off, treated the raw flesh beneath it with oils, braided my hair into a fan that perches precariously on top of my head, swaddled me in soft blue fabric that turns out to be a dress in the latest style inspired by fashions in Susheph, and laden me with more jewels than I've ever seen in my life. The women fussed over what to do with my hair. There was a discussion of whether they should style it to hide the scars on my face or to accentuate them, and the group in favor of accentuating them won the argument. So they beaded and pulled my hair away from my face, pierced my ears with golden cuffs—which still sting—encircled my neck with delicate wood and gold necklaces, and adorned my feet with glittering slippers. But they've left my wrists bare. When I asked why, one woman told me, "The shaha says guests will want to see them."

They'll want to see my tattoos. The proof I had hoped to

use to save everyone I love has become nothing more than a curiosity.

So even though I'm standing in a corridor wearing more finery than I've ever dreamed of touching, I feel exposed. I pull my arms to my torso and shiver. I'm a spectacle, and I'm expected to go out into the palace courtyard and perform.

This has been one of the worst days of my life, and as I stand here, the arguments for it being the absolute worst continue to grow. Before now, I would have considered the worst to be that day twelve years ago when Aba and Ima rescued me. But today I've failed to rescue them. Worry over my family fills my mind, and thoughts of Duin echo among them.

If the emperor is telling the truth, he's alive, and he's been living without the protection of a family like mine. He's been all alone for twelve years, and no one knew.

A part of me realizes the emperor could be lying. It would make sense for him to lie. Why would he leave another heir—one who could actually inherit the throne—alive, and why would he tell me about it?

It can't be true, I tell myself, but I can't seem to crush the hope that it is. If it is, maybe I can rescue him. Maybe I can still rescue all of them.

A familiar voice calls out behind me. "I hardly recognize you, Lia."

Obipae Kula and Enipae Gowan approach. I start to bow but stop myself. How am I supposed to greet people now?

Obipae Kula smiles, amused. "We tried to find you after you left, but your guard told us you were with the empress."

"Yes, Obipae." I can't bring myself to call her by her given name.

She frowns, but Enipae Gowan puts a hand on her arm.

"Are you alright?" he asks.

I hesitate and then nod, opening my arms to gesture to my outfit. "She gave me this."

Obipae Kula gives me a quizzical look. "She's picking her battles, then."

I don't know what to make of that statement, but Enipae Gowan must. It's his turn to frown. "Why?"

Obipae Kula shrugs.

I'm still being used, but I don't even know what part I'm supposed to play. I'm so tired of being a tool for people. The emperor used me in court earlier to free himself of his guilt, and Shaha Saretha is using me now. I sigh. Even Aba had been using me as an instrument of freedom until I ruined things. When do I get to choose what I am?

Obipae Kula walks over, lifts my chin, and straightens my shoulders.

When I'm standing straight, she nods. "That's better."

She points to the doors ahead of us. "Nobles eat fear. If they sense it, they'll devour you to get at it. Don't let them."

She gestures ahead like this was encouraging and I'm equipped to go conquer them all now, but my stomach turns. I don't think I can do this.

Enipae Gowan smiles pityingly at me as if he's heard my thoughts. "We'll watch out for you."

I take a deep breath and walk forward, nodding to the servant to show he can open the door for me, and his shoulders relax. I wonder if he's a slave, if there's somewhere else he'd prefer to be, if there's something else he'd like to be doing. He's wearing long sleeves, so I don't see cuffs, but they could be hidden. As horrible as I feel, I know I'm not the one suffering the most in this palace. A wave of guilt washes over me. If I had been stronger, braver... I shake my head. Maybe I still have a chance to be stronger and braver now.

The door opens, and the weight of hundreds of eyes falls on me from around the courtyard. They've been waiting. The conversation doesn't slow, but as I walk past, people lower their voices. What are they saying? Do I even want to know?

Someone gasps to my right. A man is staring, terrified, but not at me. He looks past me, and I turn. Obipae Kula and Enipae Gowan enter the courtyard. I hadn't noticed in the dim hallway, but Obipae Kula is wearing green, which makes her eyes flash in the outdoor firelight. Her wrap skirt and shawl, traditional in Derian, glitter like there's gold woven into the fabric. Next to her, Enipae Gowan is imposing in a dark tunic embroidered around its collar and sleeves, his handsome face impassive. It seems like Obipae Kula expected a reaction—like she orchestrated it—because she smirks at the party-goers who stare at her. Enipae Gowan only nods politely. He alone is impervious to the effect Obipae Kula has on the crowd, which somehow makes him seem even taller than he is. They're taking the attention away from me, if only a bit, and even if it wasn't intentional, I bless them for it.

The Nehim family sits near me, and Enra waves in greeting. I return the gesture in a daze.

Someone touches my shoulder, and I whirl around, surprised. An older woman in a cream and yellow dress smiles at me disarmingly. "Hara, you have brought great joy to my heart."

"I have?"

She takes my hand. "I was a member of your grandfather's court. It is a blessing to know that his legacy has not been destroyed."

"You knew my grandfather?"

I study the woman more closely. She's old enough to have been a courtier during the former regime. How did she survive the coup?

"Please come to me if you need anything," she says. "I'm more than willing to help."

I try to smile. "Thank you…"

"Lady Eme," the woman says.

Someone else reaches out to me. A man this time. He doesn't touch me but captures my attention. He too is older. "It's a miracle you're alive, Hara. Truly a miracle. Juae must have smiled upon your father's life."

A third person approaches with similar sentiments, and then a fourth and a fifth. The fifth woman adds, "You are truly gracious to extend forgiveness to the emperor. I will teach my children to follow your example."

I wince. My failure shouldn't be an example to any children. But how are these people so confident in praising me for being alive? It seems like saying such things would be an insult to the man who tried to ensure that I would never hear these blessings. I glance around and find Emperor Pakel seated with his immense household on a dais at the far end of the courtyard. I suppose he's well out of hearing distance, but he must have allies everywhere. These people being here means they're his allies. Whatever they once meant to my grandfather, they were quick to replace their allegiances when the person in power changed. Why go out of their way to express their gratitude to me?

I notice that in all their praise, no one mentions my demand that slavery end. They all dance around the topic, as if breathing a word of it would bring curses down on them. So even in embracing me, there are still things they can't—or won't—do.

Obipae Kula and Enipae Gowan approach, and the small crowd that's formed around me disperses.

"I hope you're prepared to be popular," Obipae Kula says.

"I'm not," I admit.

The banquet overwhelms me. All the people, the food, the noise. I close my eyes and imagine myself back in Paidashar Fadir, but instead of being in the satrap's house, I'm outside a home of my own near the water. We're free, my family and I, and I'm drinking in the sun and the sea air.

My own shame and frustration breaks into my fantasy. That isn't my reality, and right now, it may never be. I ruined it. I open my eyes and take a breath. Since I ruined it, I have to fix it, even if no one thinks I can.

CHAPTER 27

Enra

Lia is being mobbed, or at least that's how it looks from here. I had just caught her attention when she was surrounded by courtiers eager to be the first to lay claim to the latest fascination in the imperial court, though it's doubtful any of them will be successful.

She's not prepared for this, and she has no one to protect her. A wave of guilt washes over me. I'm also trying to use her, but at least I have a good reason. I'm protecting Vroni, protecting my family, making sure we have a foot in every avenue of influence in Elisya, so we'll be safe. Still, I have to admit they probably have their reasons too. Many of them had the same choices my father had, and while some of them were willing participants in Emperor Asilo's takeover, most were forced to do what they needed to do to survive.

Aba clears his throat, drawing my attention to him. He nods toward Lia. I should go. I can ask her to sit and eat with us. That way, she would be associated with my family still. But would that be strange for her, eating with the family that used to own her life—and still owns her family's?

Aba raises an eyebrow at me. I can almost hear his thoughts. What are you waiting for? I stand and adjust my tunic, trying to appear nonchalant, but my heart pounds as I walk over. As I approach, the delegates from Derian speak to Lia, and the surrounding people disperse like they've all forgotten an important appointment. Obipae Kulebra Uhero is an intimidating figure. Few in the palace are brave enough to even cross paths with her, let alone cross her, and her husband used to be a guard, if I understand correctly. He still has the physique for it. They're an imposing pair, and I consider giving up and sitting back down, but the crowd around Lia is gone, and she can see me. She and the Derian delegates are staring right at me.

I rush to give them a polite bow. "Sali. Obipae. Enipae."

Enipae Gowan returns my greeting. "Prince Enra. It is an honor to meet you."

Obipae Kula—as she insists everyone calls her—smiles at me. Her unusual eyes flash as though highlighted by her grin, and my stomach sinks despite myself. I resist the urge to flee. "Suan. Are you here to meet Sali Liani?" she asks.

I shift on my feet. "Ah, no. We—we already know each other…"

Obipae Kula laughs. "I know, Suan. But you seem very uncomfortable, so I guessed you were here to greet her as an equal."

"Oh…" My voice trails off. Should I invite them all to eat with us?

"Hello again, Suan," Lia says.

If I could shrug at myself, I would. It's worth trying. "May I invite you all to join us for the banquet? There is plenty of room."

Enipae Gowan and Obipae Kula exchange a glance, then Enipae Gowan bows. "We would be honored, your highness."

I give them my most welcoming smile. "And Lia, please call me Enra."

She tries to smile back, but it's more of a wince. "Thank you… Enra."

Aba's expression is inscrutable when we approach the table, and he greets Obipae Kula and Enipae Gowan politely. When he meets Lia's eyes, she shuffles and lowers her gaze like she doesn't know what to do. She doesn't know that he's known who she was this entire time. A wave of guilt washes over me. She doesn't know that I've known either.

"Welcome, Sali," Aba says.

Lia bows. "Thank you."

Her voice trails off. Aba gestures to the table. "Please join us."

Obipae Kula and Enipae Gowan sit opposite Aba, but Lia takes a seat next to Nalkendi. She hunches her shoulders like she's trying to shrink out of view, but she's failing miserably in her new dress. The blue gown captures the light and shimmers with her movement. The beads in her hair and the jewels around her neck glitter in the firelight. People at other tables turn around to see her, and I don't blame them. Lia has always been pretty, but whoever helped her dress today must have wanted her to stand out. She's a sky full of stars.

Nalkendi stares at Lia, and Lia gives her a rare genuine smile, the first I've seen from her today. Nalkendi touches the sleeve of Lia's dress in awe. "I didn't know you were beautiful, Lia."

Lia chuckles. "I'm not. You're confusing me with the clothes."

I shake my head. "No, she's not."

Lia glances at me and then quickly averts her eyes to the table. My skin flushes. I'm glad the light is dim. Why would I say something like that?

Nalkendi nods. "See. Even Enra said so. I want a dress like this."

Lia pats her hand as a cloud comes over her expression. "I'm sure you may have one. I'll ask the empress' servants for you."

"The empress?" I ask.

Lia nods. "She's taken me under her wing, I think."

She doesn't sound pleased with the prospect, and I can't blame her. Shaha Saretha is an intimidating woman, much like Obipae Kula, given a few more years. Some say she carries herself like she even outranks the emperor, and from what I've seen of her, I wouldn't dispute that. She's confident in the power she exerts over the court. I exchange a glance with Aba, but he doesn't seem worried. I doubt he'd show it even if he were, though.

Obipae Kula chuckles, the first sound we've heard from her since she sat. "It is interesting."

Aba lifts an eyebrow. "How so?"

Obipae Kula leans forward. "Is your empress prone to taking on proteges?"

Aba shakes his head, and Obipae Kula nods.

"In all the time I've known her, Shaha Saretha has stayed at arm's length from others." She turns to Lia. "So what is it she needs from you?"

Panic crosses Lia's expression, though she catches it quickly. "She needs something from me?"

Obipae Kula nods, then she meets my eyes. "Don't you agree, Suan?"

"Ah, yes," I say, trying to sound knowledgeable. "That is, I wouldn't be surprised. Even though she and the emperor are family, she may find it useful to ally with you."

Lia snorts. "Ally with me? For what? I'm no one."

"You may have been no one before," Enipae Gowan says,

"But now you're the person who pardoned the emperor for his crimes. He is indebted to you, and that's valuable."

"Besides," Obipae Kula adds, "No one has forgotten your declaration about ending slavery, though they may pretend they have." She gives a pointed glance around the room. "They need to know what you have the power to do and whether you know you can do it. You are unprecedented."

Lia stares at the table, and a servant comes by to refill our glasses and set a tray of food in front of us. The conversation continues at tables around us, but for a moment no one at our table says anything.

But then Aba raises his glass. "You have suffered greatly, Sali, but may you prosper from now on."

The rest of us toast to Lia's prosperity, and she gives us all a half-hearted smile. I wonder if she's thinking of her family. If I were her, I would be. I cut a generous portion of meat and place it in front of Lia. When she meets my eyes, I smile.

"It'll be alright," I say.

Her face says she doesn't believe me. If I were her, I wouldn't believe me either.

CHAPTER 28

Lia

The banquet lasts well into the night, as banquets tend to, and by the end of it, I'm willing to sink into the dirt if it means I don't have to meet and pretend to remember the name of another Elisyan courtier or foreign dignitary.

But thankfully, a couple of hours past midnight, the emperor and his family retire to their rooms, signaling that the rest of us can leave whenever we want. Although Shaha Saretha had me adorned to attend this banquet, she and the emperor seemed content to ignore me for the entire night. It was just as well. I'd prefer to avoid them as much as possible. I wait a polite half an hour before I get ready to leave, as I'd seen guests at the satrap's home do.

Enra stands as I do. "Are you leaving?"

I nod. "I just… need to rest."

It's been a long and disastrous day. Nothing has gone the way I'd hoped or even the way I'd feared. I didn't free my family, and I also didn't get executed as an enemy of the crown. So I've failed in every way possible. I need to think of a way to turn things around and to find out if what the emperor said about Duin is true.

I take the servants' hallway back to the Derian delegates' suite as a force of habit, and it isn't until I'm in the antechamber that I realize I don't know where I should sleep.

Obipae Kula and Enipae Gowan come in through the main door just as that fact dawns on me.

Obipae Kula cocks her head at me. "Have they not given you your own room?"

I shake my head.

Obipae Kula frowns. "The empress probably has a room for you. If you want to—"

"Could I stay here?" I ask, interrupting her for probably the first time.

After a moment, Obipae Kula nods. "I suppose so. You can use the extra room until you find out where you should go."

"Thank you."

I move my meager belongings from the servant's room to the spare guest room by myself, and then I shut the door behind me. As I remove the jewels and the dress that adorn me, I replay the day in my head, trying to think of any way I could have made things turn out differently.

I started out this morning in the Halls of Virtue, sure that I was going to free my family or die trying. Instead, I've been treated like a child, or worse, a child's toy, all day—something to be tossed around, played with, used. Still, there must be something I can do.

I may have lost the option of using my blood right to abolish slavery, but there must be other ways of changing the law in Elisya. I can't imagine that all laws have been the same since the founding of the empire. If they are, what is it that the courtiers and politicians do all day?

But if there is a way, I don't know what it is. I need an ally, someone who'd know the politics of the empire. I remember

Enra walking me to see my father. He'd know the law. His upbringing focused on preparing him to become the malik of Uze, and a malik has to know all kinds of things. I don't know if he'd help me, but I can at least ask.

And Duin… He'd be twelve now, on the brink of becoming a man, if he's alive. My heart and my mind contend with each other, one unable to believe the emperor could leave him alive and the other grasping for reasons he would. How do I find out? It's unlikely that there would be any records of him. The chaos after the coup alone would have meant it would be easy to steal away with an infant.

The memory of Duin's cries being silenced repeats itself over and over in my head. But if it's true that he lives, if it's even remotely possible, I have a duty to find out.

I take a while to fall asleep, and once I do, I sleep fitfully. My dreams are nightmares, and in one, Jorra calls out to me.

"Lia… Lia!"

I stir. Jorra's actually here, at the edge of my bed. I sit up and try to rub the confusion from my eyes.

"Jorra?"

She wrings her hands, on the verge of being frantic. "I've been trying to find you for an hour!"

Her distress dispels the last of my sleepiness.

"What's wrong?"

"It's Aba—"

My heart drops into my stomach.

Jorra grabs my hand, but it seems more like an effort to steady her own than to steady mine. "They got caught."

I force myself to breathe. It can't be. They've been so careful. But then, by exposing myself, I may have exposed them, and we were already under suspicion since the meeting in the mountains. Of course, people would be watching now. What was he thinking, meeting on the night of my failure? What was I thinking, not warning him?

"What punishment will they give him? Is the satrap going to sell? I can talk to him… He ate with me tonight—"

Jorra interrupts me. "No, Lia, it's worse than that. They fought back. The guards came in with force… some were killed."

I shake with panic. Aba can't be…

"They've been charged with treason."

"Treason! Isn't being murdered by the emperor's guards enough? They were trying to gain their freedom. There are enough punishments for that."

Jorra shakes her head, falling more than sitting on my bed. "The guards were the ones who died. They say… they say Aba struck the first blow."

The room spins around me. Aba, a murderer of an imperial guard? That can't be true. It's impossible.

I try to find words. "How… Where did they take him?"

Jorra shivers. "They're all in the palace prison."

I stand and take Jorra's hand. "We need to go."

"Where?"

"I need to know what will happen to him. They'll tell me now." I motion to the fancy room around me. "They have to."

I drag Jorra from the room. "Where's Ima?"

"She went to the prison. All the wives are outside of it, mourning. The guards are sure to stop them soon."

I nod. We'll go to the prison first then. "And Atar?"

Jorra shakes her head. "I don't know. Aba forbade him from going with the men, but he's so stubborn. I didn't see him when they put Aba in prison, though…"

She trails off, and I pray Atar had a moment of sense and didn't follow Aba without his permission. Even as I pray, I know Atar would have been there, like he was last time. But if he's not in prison, where is he?

There's a lot more activity in the palace than usual for this hour of night, but that's not surprising since several slaves have just been arrested. My heart pounds, and I grip Jorra's hand as we dodge past servants and courtiers and try to get to the prison.

I hear it before I see it. The prison isn't far from the smithy, and there's a crowd outside of it. Onlookers surround a group of women on their knees, wailing at the prison windows. They scoop dust from the ground and smear it onto their arms and faces. Even in the torchlight, I can tell that most of them have muddied their faces with a mixture of tears and dirt. My heart breaks as they cry out, begging for mercy even as they sing funeral songs and weep openly. They know their husbands might as well be dead, even though they plead for their lives. Their families will be torn apart because of this, because they dared to try to free themselves from the foot of slavery pressing down on their heads. My family will be torn apart by it too.

I shake my head. No. It won't be. No one's family will be torn apart. There must be something I can do. Ima is not among the wailing women, but then she wouldn't be. She's much too proud to beg for Aba's life, and even if she weren't, he wouldn't want her to. But she will still be here.

We find her on the other side of the mourners, but she, several other women, and a few men and boys—probably those who hadn't run—stand between a row of guards and the mourning women. They face the guards, arm to arm, forming a wall of protection for the women. The guards can go around, but they don't. They're impassive, waiting. If they'd received orders to put an end to this, they would have done it by now, so I suppose they haven't yet. For now, Emperor Pakel has let this display be. Who knows why?

Ima notices us, and her firm expression breaks for a moment. We run toward her in front of the guards. She opens her arms to us. "Jorra. Lia."

Jorra bursts into tears. "What's going to happen to us?"

Ima wipes Jorra's eyes. "Don't weep. Not here. We will be fine."

"What can I do, Ima?" I ask.

A frown cuts across her face. "Lia, you shouldn't have come."

My face stings as though she'd slapped me. "What—"

Ima glances around, and I follow her gaze. While the mourning continues behind us, a lot of attention has shifted to us. To me. Onlookers whisper, and even the slaves with Ima glance at me with distrust. My heart falls. I'm no longer one of them.

There's no place I belong anymore. I'm neither nobility nor slave. Wherever I am, I'm a misfit. Still, there must be something I can do. I have to fix this. If I had just demanded freedom this morning, we wouldn't be here right now.

"What should I do?" I ask again.

Ima shakes her head. "Go back inside. There's nothing to be done now. We must wait and see if Juae delivers us."

I take a couple of steps back. The surrounding scene is one of catastrophe, but it's not like the one I feared would occur yesterday. Aba is still alive, and as long as there's life, there's hope. There must be something I can do.

CHAPTER 29

Enra

Noise startles me awake. I blink as my eyes adjust to the darkness. There isn't even a hint of sunrise on the horizon yet, but there's shouting outside. I throw on a tunic before I leave my room to figure out what the commotion that woke me up is about. Khanda and Nalkendi lean out by the far window, Khanda on the tips of his toes.

"What's going on?" I ask.

Nalkendi glances over her shoulder at me. "They brought prisoners in. There are women mourning. You can hear them."

She puts a hand to her lips to show I should be quiet, but there's no way I could miss them. There's lots of talk down in the courtyard, but wails and cries overpower all the other noise. They're cries of mourning. Someone has died.

My pulse jumps, and my thoughts turn to Lia. But Emperor Pakel wouldn't kill her the day she pardoned him. He's too cunning for that.

Ima steps out of her room, her braided hair covered with a scarf. "Your father has gone down already."

I raise my eyebrows. It must have been an important death. "Who died?"

"Three guards."

"Guards?"

All this for guards? After that thought, I feel guilty. They have families, loved ones, those who will miss them, mourn them. They must have taken the murderer to the prison. But why was Aba called away?

Ima must expect my question because she answers before I can ask. "Our slaves were involved."

Her expression is grim, and I take a moment to grasp her meaning. When I do, my heart sinks. "There was an attack?"

"An attempted escape."

"Attempted?"

The unrest must be serious. This is the second time slaves have caused trouble this month. The crack of a whip breaks into my memory, and I wince. "They were caught?"

Ima nods. "No one actually got away. But it's a serious offense, anyway."

They must have heard about Lia's declaration in the throne room. Although the nobles are avoiding the subject as the emperor did, the slaves and servants must have discussed it. Would Benar have tried to use the surprise of Lia's appearance as an opportunity to start a rebellion?

I shake my head. No. He's smarter than that, or else Aba wouldn't trust him. But then what really happened?

I need to get down there. I throw on a belt and rush from the room barefoot. The stone floor inside is cold, but outside, the ground is still warm, echoing the summer heat of the day. People race around me, their voices hushed even as they try to be heard over the mourners. But one person catches my attention. I recognize her tiny frame as she wanders from group to group, speaking but getting no response. She seems frantic.

"Lia?" I call out.

She meets my eyes, and her expression goes from panic to recognition. "Suan… Enra. Please help me."

"What do you need?"

"My brother—"

"Atar?" I ask.

She nods. "I need to find him. Our father…"

Her voice trails off, and realization dawns on me. Benar truly was involved. Guards must have detained him.

"Did Benar try to start…" I trail off, trying to think of the right words to ask what I want to ask without drawing attention to us.

Lia looks at me sharply. "Aba didn't start anything. They were…" She lowers her head. "They were caught. It's my fault. I need to find Atar."

Well, at least, according to Lia, it wasn't a full on rebellion. Her father was caught, but her brother wasn't. Where could he be? Where would I go if my father was arrested as a traitor? The idea hits too close to home, and I refocus on Lia. Hesitation has replaced her desperation.

"I'll help you," I say, but her caution doesn't dissipate. I don't blame her. This is a catastrophic situation, and she can't possibly know who to trust.

Even so, I need her to trust me. "It will be…" I stop short of saying "alright."

It may not be. Honestly, it probably isn't. Her father tried to escape without her. How desperate must he have been? If people died, it will cost them their lives.

I need to stick with promises I can keep. "Perhaps he escaped. Maybe there were some that got away…"

Lia gives me a confused glance. "Got away?"

"In the escape," I clarify.

Her brow furrows. "There was no escape. It was—no one was trying to escape."

That's news to me. Apparently, what Ima heard was inaccurate. Lia would probably know better than we would.

"Then he must be here somewhere. We'll find him," I assure her.

I follow Lia's lead, and while she wanders a bit at first, she soon starts to follow some kind of path. It takes me a moment before I realize we're on our way to the slave quarters. I've never been there before, and it's a bit out of the way of the main castle buildings. There's a wooden fence that surrounds it, and a single gate watched by several guards. Someone probably sent them to keep the peace.

They examine us, and one man near the front intercepts us at the gate.

"What is your business?"

Lia shrinks back and averts her eyes. I'm not sure if it's out of habit or from the stress of the day. But either way, she's not going to command this situation well enough to get us inside, so I step forward.

"I'm here for one of my slaves."

I can't help but glance at Lia as the words come out of my mouth, and shame creeps up the back of my neck. It's a new sensation, but I hold my head high. I'm recognizable enough among most in the palace. Guards would have been instructed to memorize noble faces.

Sure enough, the guard squints at me, and recognition crosses his face, though he doesn't seem to remember my name.

"Of course, Suan."

He steps aside to let me through, and I stride forward with all the authority I can command. Maybe if I'm important enough, the guard won't look twice at Lia, who shuffles through the gate behind me, even though she's probably more recognizable than I am right now.

When we're a long enough distance away, I whisper to her, "Where are we going?"

She gives me a quizzical glance like she's just realized I've never been here. "This way."

The buildings here are squat and bare, with simple clay walls and thatch roofs. Faces peek out at us as we pass, but no one is moving around. It's as quiet and still as the palace is busy. Lia winds through tight corridors and stops at a small building in front of a long dead fire. I don't ask where we are. This is probably her family's house.

Lia takes a deep breath, closes her eyes for a moment, and then pushes the woven mat that covers the doorway aside.

I reach out to hold it for her as she steps inside the room.

Her voice is little more than a whisper, but she calls out, "Atar?"

It's deafeningly quiet for a second, and then there is shuffling.

Lia scrambles into the room and drops to her knees in front of a figure that is no doubt Atar.

I turn away to give them privacy.

"I failed him…" Atar says. "It was so fast. I couldn't do anything."

Lia sighs. "No. It's alright. He's alive. That's what matters. We'll… we'll figure this out."

"We were supposed to be free right now."

Atar's voice is accusatory, and I wince on Lia's behalf.

But she just sighs. "I know."

She passes by me and says over her shoulder. "I'll tell Ima and Jorra you're here."

We walk quietly back through the slave quarters. I glance at Lia a few times, but she keeps her eyes on the ground.

"Was he hurt?" is all I can bring myself to ask.

Lia pauses a moment before answering. "No."

As we leave the slave quarters, a servant approaches us and bows. Someone must have seen us leaving the main palace.

He addresses Lia. "Empress Saretha requires your presence, Sali."

Lia's eyes go wide. "My presence? Again?"

The servant doesn't respond.

Lia glances at me, and I'm at a loss. If the empress has called for her, she has to go—that's not the issue. I'm trying to figure out how I can go with her. But Empress Saretha didn't summon me.

"I'll escort you," I say to Lia, hoping that ignoring the servant will allow me to come along. He may rather do that instead of contradicting a noble.

He doesn't seem put out by the idea of me coming along. He nods and says, "Follow me."

I gesture for Lia to walk ahead, but I pick up the pace to walk beside her.

It must be even later, or earlier rather, than I thought because the sun is sending signals it will rise soon. The sky turns a dark gray, lightening toward the horizon, but it's still dark inside the palace. We walk for a while. Wherever Empress Saretha is, it isn't nearby. Lia and I walk in silence behind the servant. I hazard a few glances at her, but she keeps her eyes on the floor, watching each of her footsteps.

When we reach one of the interior palace gates, the servant turns to me. "Please wait here, Suan."

I sigh. So much for getting in to see the empress.

The servant opens the gate, and I nudge Lia. She startles.

I give her a small smile. "Don't worry," I whisper.

Lia grimaces. I know she doesn't believe me, but one way or another, things have to work out.

She follows the servant through the gates, leaving me behind. I'll have to see her later to find out what they discussed.

CHAPTER 30

Lia

The empress taps a finger on her cheek, reclining beneath a garden pavilion where she'll take her morning meal. Although the sun is still low, I expect everyone will be awake early to join in the gossip. The thought makes my skin crawl.

"I hear your father has been detained," Empress Saretha says.

Though I'm sure she doesn't need me to confirm it, I nod. Why would she call me here to tell her something she already knows?

"And I'm safe to assume," she continues, "that you would prefer him to avoid the judgement of death."

She doesn't say it like it's a question, so I don't answer it. Of course, I would want my father to avoid death. What child wouldn't want to save their parent if they could, especially a child in my position? I should be trying to do that instead of standing here silently confirming the empress' assumptions. But I'm certain I can't just leave.

Empress Saretha nods. "I have a proposition for you. I can

ensure your father's pardon and release. He will be absolved of any guilt. All I need to do so is for you to become my ward."

My heart pounds as my thoughts catch up with her words. To save my father, she wants me to let her adopt me?

"Why me, Shaha?" I ask.

Shaha Saretha studies the garden that surrounds us. "I have no children. You won't inherit the throne as a ward of mine, but your presence will serve my purpose."

"What is your purpose?"

Shaha Saretha glances at me and smiles. "That is none of your concern. You will merely live as a princess and an ornament of the palace, and your father will be returned to his place."

That's all it would take? Me becoming a figurehead? Giving up whatever future I might have to be an ornament from a bygone era? Is it worth it? My thoughts churn. The empress is the most powerful woman in the empire. Even as her tool, I'd be in a more secure place than I am now. Being her ward would make me legitimate in the present order of the palace, not just the old regime. I don't know exactly what it would give me the ability to do, but it has to be more than what I can do now.

"Forgive me, my lady," I say as carefully as I can, "but that seems too good to be true."

She nods. "I suppose it would. The choice is yours."

I stifle a bitter laugh. Is the choice mine? To save my father or not—it's not really a tough decision to make. I don't know how she'll do it, but if anyone has the power to see he's absolved, Shaha Saretha does. But it seems like it will cost me more than it does on the surface. Still, I'd be getting something in return.

I turn the decision over in my mind for a moment, but I already know what my answer will be. "Very well, your highness. Let it be as you require."

Shaha Saretha's pleased smile is unnerving, and I regret my decision instantly. But Aba will be safe. That's all that matters. And even though I don't inherit the throne, it may give me more leverage for effecting change in the empire.

"Wonderful," the empress says. She motions for one of her servants to approach. "Get me an audience with my husband this morning."

"Yes, your majesty," the woman answers. She slips from the pavilion and into the palace.

Another servant slides a contract onto Shaha Saretha's table and places a quill and inkwell beside it.

Shaha Saretha gestures to me. "Sit and sign this."

This is the second agreement I've gotten from the imperial couple in less than a day. I wonder if they know about each other's contracts. The terms seem clear enough. Shaha Saretha claims me as her ward, placing me under her protection and guidance. She'll be like a third parent to me. I get a title and allowance, and she gets my loyalty.

Once again, I sign my name. When I'm done, I hand the contract back. "What do you need from me?"

"Nothing yet," Shaha Saretha says, "You may spend your time at your leisure. I will summon you when I have use for you."

Use for me. That seems to be everyone's goal. No one around me sees me as anything but useful. The realization chafes at me, but I get ready to leave. If they must use me, fine. I'll use them too.

I'm not sure what my strategy will be yet, but I'm sure I can find some way to take this new position and do what I couldn't do before.

My first instinct is to find my mother. She'd want to be the first to know that Aba will be released.

She's been sent back to work. In the time I've been gone, the palace guards have broken up the demonstration and sent the slaves back to their duties, though they keep watch. Three guards keep watch at the edge of the garden where Ima works, picking the season's vegetables and filling a basket that rests on her hip. She straightens to wipe sweat from her brow and notices me. I close the distance between us and take the basket from her to relieve her of the weight of it and also to spare her the hazard of dropping it and spilling its contents when I share my news.

Her face scrunches into a frown, and I can't help but notice the dark circles under her eyes. She must be exhausted.

"Lia? What are you doing here?"

I give her what I hope is a reassuring smile. It feels like my first smile in days, and the sensation is strange but welcome. "I have good news."

Ima's frown deepens. "What good news could there be in times like this?"

She bends to pluck the leaves from the nearest plant.

I bring the basket close so it's easier for her to fill it.

"The empress gave me an offer."

Ima's expression is one I can't read.

I continue. "She wants me to be her ward in exchange for Aba's release."

Ima tilts her head at me. "She wants what?"

"She's made me a ward of the throne. Her ward. So Aba will be absolved."

Ima's face turns pale. "You agreed to this? Lia, what have you done?"

I blink in confusion. Why doesn't she understand? "What do you mean? Aba will be free, and I can—"

Ima shakes her head. She lowers the leaves she's holding to the ground and takes my arm. "What were you thinking? What of your father's honor? Do you think he would leave the others in prison to save himself?"

"I just..." My voice trails off. I kept him from being

executed for treason, and I secured myself a better position, one where I may actually be able to do something.

Ima continues, her voice low. "He would rather die than take the emperor's mercy, especially mercy granted because his eldest daughter begged for it."

I hang my head. She's right that Aba would chafe at being pardoned for this. But Ima is wrong about one thing. "I didn't beg. She called for me. She said she'd do this for me. I didn't ask her to. And I can—"

Ima grabs me by the shoulders. "We will fix this. I don't know how…"

I imitate her gesture, placing my free hand on her shoulder. "Ima listen. I think I can use this." I hope my voice sounds more convincing to her than to me, though I keep it low like she did so guards don't overhear. "While I may not belong to the imperial family, I have more influence than ever. I can do something with this."

Ima holds my gaze. Then she nods. "Very well. When are they releasing him?"

I'm actually not sure, I realize. I didn't think to ask Shaha Saretha when he'd be released.

"It will be soon," I say, though I know I don't sound certain.

But Ima doesn't seem to notice or care. "We need to find your siblings."

"Oh," I say, just realizing I never had time to tell her. "Atar was at home. He was…"

My voice trails off as Ima nods. She gets my meaning without me having to say anything, and the relief on her face is palpable.

She bends to the ground again. "I'll have time to rest in an hour."

I could go find my siblings myself, but I don't want to leave Ima behind. I follow her with the basket and help her fill it, the new ward of the empress trailing behind a slave woman, making a strange sight. Guards' and nobles' eyes follow me as they pass. But I don't want to leave. They all already know where my loyalties lie. I said as much yesterday.

The hour passes slowly in the morning heat, but it gives me time to think. The emperor wants me to put on a show, and the empress wants me to… well, I'm not sure what she wants me to do, but her goals seem to differ from the emperor's. They've made me an ornament of the throne, but that should give me access to people and places I wouldn't have had access to before. I just don't know how to use that access.

That's where Enra comes in. My stomach does a small flip at the idea of asking him for help, but he's the closest person to me who may know what I need to learn. Will he be willing to help me? I don't know, but I won't ever know until I ask.

Asking Enra for help isn't something I ever thought I'd do, and yet here I am. I went through proper channels, sending a steward to request a moment of the suan's time, so no one can accuse us of being improper or plotting in secret. That's not my intention. I want to be obvious, as obvious as I was before the emperor. That way, if he tries to kill me and succeeds this time, everyone will know why. Maybe this time, someone will do something about it.

I count the lines in my upturned hands as I sit on a lush sofa in Obipae Kula and Enipae Gowan's receiving room and wait for Enra to arrive. The noble couple is out doing whatever diplomatic business they came here to do—I've heard that the obipae is quite the negotiator—so I have the suite to myself for the time being. The minutes pass slowly and painfully, but then there's a rapt knock at the door.

I stand to get it but then sit back down and call, "Enter."

The steward I'd sent steps inside and holds the door open. "Suan Enra, Sali."

Enra enters, looking about as awkward as I feel. "Sali Lia... You wanted to see me?"

I nod and gesture for him to sit on the sofa across from me. "Yes, there's something I'd like to discuss with you."

I figure I should get straight to the point. When he sits, I say. "I need your help, actually."

Enra raises his eyebrows. "My help?"

"Yes. I'm trying... I need to know how to change the law, but I don't know where to look, and I think you do."

He starts to answer me, but I interrupt him, my words spilling out of my mouth. "I know you don't have any reason to help me—you'd be losing your slaves too—and I'd understand if you refuse. People would hate you as much as me if they found out you were helping me. But you're the closest Elisyan noble to me, and I..." My voice gets quieter. "I don't have anyone else to ask."

Enra purses his lips, his face scrunched into a frown. This was foolish, I tell myself. What made me think he'd be willing to give me his support? But I really don't have another option. I wish I had a way to be more convincing, or some kind of leverage I could use. An idea occurs to me, and I blurt it out before I lose my nerve.

"If you need something in return, something my position can afford, ask me, and I'll get it for you."

I seem to be a popular commodity around here, at least to the emperor and empress. That may offer something of value to Enra. It may not be enough for him to trade his family's status, but who knows? I can only try.

With my request and offer out in the open, all I can do is wait for Enra's response. After a few painful moments, he asks, "What do you need from me?"

"I need..." My voice trails off as I search for the right

words. "An ally. I can only think of one way to stop my father, and I need help to do it."

I pray Enra doesn't ask what I'm trying to stop my father from doing, and he doesn't. "What's the way?" he asks instead.

I take a deep breath. "I need to abolish slavery."

Enra gapes at me. I know he was there when I made my request in court, but perhaps everyone assumed I'd give up after that spectacular failure. But I won't give up. I can't.

After a moment, Enra asks, "How will you do that?"

"That's where I need your help," I explain. "Obipae Kula can teach me how to navigate the court, but she doesn't know all the laws here, not like you would. If there's anything I can use, any path I can take, I need… would you help me find it? If there's no actual way to do it, then there's no point, and I'll just have to abandon it. But I can't do that until I've at least tried. What do you think?"

The silence between us is painful, and I want to fill it, but I'm scrambling to think of something to say.

"I think…" he pauses.

I'm afraid to hope, but I can't help it. Even if Enra says no, I'll have to find another way. I need to do anything I can.

Finally, Enra nods. "Very well, Lia. I'll help however I can."

"Really?" I blurt out before I can stop myself. "Why?"

Enra is focused on something else, though I can't tell what. "I don't know how else to say it, but I agree with you. Something needs to change, and you're the only one brave enough to do it."

I don't know if I'd categorize myself as brave, but I don't admit that out loud.

"Anyway," Enra continues, "I—and my family—aren't opposed to your desires. And I think you'll find others who aren't either."

"Thank you." I don't know what else to say. I had expected

to do more convincing than this. If everyone else is won over this easily, I won't have as much of a battle ahead of me as I feared. "Where do we start?"

Enra tilts his head. "Let me think about it. I'll arrange a meeting with you when I have some ideas."

I thank him again as the steward ushers him from the room. The steward will probably spread the contents of the conversation through the rest of the palace, and word will certainly reach the emperor, but I don't care. At least I've made progress. It doesn't occur to me until later that I should have asked Enra what he'd want in return.

CHAPTER 31

I hold Ima's and Jorra's hands as we wait outside the prison for Aba. Atar is a few feet ahead of us, like he's trying to apologize to Aba by being brave now. Occasionally, though, he glances back at us, as if to make sure we're still there.

The gate of the prison creaks as it swings open, and I hold my breath. First a haggard man exits and is greeted by a small child I hadn't even noticed until now. The man's shoulders sag, and his tunic hangs off his bony shoulders. His skin is ashen, and his face is sallow. He's not one of the men taken yesterday —he's probably been in the prison for a while. The man's face brightens as the boy calls to him. The boy wraps his arms around the man's waist, and the man holds him close for a while before they walk off. Father and son, most likely. How long had they been separated?

A cry from Jorra pulls my attention back to the gate. Aba steps through it without so much as a glance at the guards on either side, his head held high and his hands balled into fists at his sides. He strides forward, first to Atar. Atar bows, not too low, but enough to show his respect. Aba holds a hand out to him, and they grasp each other's forearms. It's the first time

Aba has greeted Atar like a man instead of a boy, at least to my knowledge. They turn to meet the rest of us together.

"My husband, you have returned," Ima says. Her voice is steady, but when I glance at her, I can tell she's holding back rare tears.

Aba touches her cheek. "It's a joy to see your face."

Ima nods.

Jorra sniffles, and Aba turns to her. She turns away to hide her tears, but Aba lifts her chin. "Head held high, young one."

Aba turns to me for the first time, and my face and arms warm in shame.

He puts a hand on my shoulder. "Lia."

I train my eyes on the ground. Aba doesn't lift my head like he did with Jorra. Instead, he squeezes my shoulder.

"This isn't over," he says. "We will continue. We must. But you need to leave."

My ears ring as if he'd slapped me.

"Return to your guardians in the palace. You can't be associated with us."

"But Aba…"

My voice trails away, and Aba grabs me by both my shoulders. "It's better for us all this way. Your presence here isn't safe."

Not safe for me or not safe for you, I want to ask, but I hold my tongue. I don't want to know the answer, and Aba would tell me the truth.

Jorra looks at me with pity and Ima with resignation. Atar refuses to look at me at all. I take a step back, and Aba nods approvingly. I blink back tears as I turn my back on my family and walk away.

None of them call after me. I knew they wouldn't, but my heart still breaks. They have abandoned me. I've been banished to the pit of vipers that control the empire. They've left me to fend for myself. But I won't let them fend for themselves.

Aba may cast me away from my family, but he can't keep me from helping him or at least stopping him from doing anything that could lead to him being thrown back in prison or worse.

I'll need help. But I may have help. Enra said he'd try. I don't know what he wants for his help, but he can be useful, and so could Obipae Kula and her entourage. If foreign influences are protecting me, and Emperor Pakel wants to stay on decent terms with them, he'll give me a wider berth than I would have under only the Empress' watch.

I lift my head and square my shoulders. Aba won't see me cower as I walk away. I'm determined, and I'll make sure they all know it.

As I approach the palace, the guards give me a quizzical glance, but they step back when they recognize me. I suppose everyone has heard about me by now. Although they give me space, they aren't shy about staring at me. My face warms, and I lower my head as I duck inside.

It's darker and cooler in the hall, but it bustles with people. Although this gathering is supposed to be a celebration, people are still working, trying to advance their own agendas while enjoying the luxury of the palace.

I find the obipae and enipae enjoying a meal alone, and I sigh in relief that they aren't in a meeting. Dishes clank, and they murmur, the noise obscuring their conversation, though I'm sure it's in Derian, anyway. I wait for their servants to notice me so I can get their attention. But before they see me, Obipae Kula speaks up in Elisyan. "Come in, Sali. You are an equal here. You must act like it."

Enipae Gowan gives her a knowing glance and then gestures to me. "Please join us. Are you hungry?"

My stomach growls in response. I don't think I've eaten a

full meal in a day, despite all the lavish food I've seen. When I sit, Enipae Gowan places a piece of bread in front of me and pushes a dish of stewed vegetables toward me. When I smile at him in thanks, he returns the gesture, and while he faces me, I notice the simple dagger at his side. It's less ornate than I'd expect a nobleman to carry, and its sheath is well worn.

Enipae Gowan glances at his hip. "I've had it since I was young, since my days as a trainee."

"Gowan is unchangeable," Obipae Kula adds, her voice tinged with humor. "He values reliability."

He squints at her, and she laughs, but then she turns to me. "What can we do for you, Sali? How are you adjusting?"

"I…" I fight the urge to avert my eyes. I must meet them as equals if I'm going to ask for their help. "Can I trust you?"

Obipae Kula and Enipae Gowan exchange another glance, eyebrows raised. Obipae Kula answers. "That depends on what you need to trust us for."

At least she's honest, but then, if the rumors about the obipae are true, she's always been honest to a fault.

"Well, this is about my father."

She raises her eyebrows. "Your father?"

"Not the prince," I explain. "My real father. I know what he wants, and I want him to have it, but I don't think he'll be successful if he continues the way he's going."

Obipae Kula leans in, an interested expression crossing her face. "We're listening. Please explain."

CHAPTER 32

I sit on a thick, fluffy pillow in a lavishly appointed pavilion and struggle to get comfortable. I know it's not polite to fidget, but I can't seem to help it. Life has become so strange. My heartbeat won't slow down, and I spend every waking moment worried for my family, but Shaha Saretha expects me to attend her routine midday feasts with the women here to celebrate the empire and the impending wedding. I still can't figure out why she wants me here. All I am is a source of gossip for the other women, and the only person who shows any genuine interest in me is Obipae Kula. I'm a curiosity.

Empress Saretha's guests divide their attention between her, Vroni, and me. I tear a piece of flatbread from a carved wooden tray and fiddle with it. Food isn't appealing when everyone is watching you as if you're a performance. A musician plucks a tune in the corner, but I don't recognize it.

A woman across from me whispers to the women next to her, and they snicker together. A second woman says a bit too loudly, "I always thought princesses were supposed to be beautiful."

"Naturally. But slaves aren't," another replies, and there's more laughter.

My cheeks warm, and I focus on my knees. This is unique torture. But for my family, I can endure it. I have to endure it to give them the freedom to leave. With Enra's help, they'll have what I can't soon. It's the least I can do.

The thought that none of these women have any idea what I'm planning bolsters me a bit. A part of me relishes the idea of them all being stripped of the slaves they rely on so much, as they mock them through me.

I think of Aba, Ima, and my siblings. I think of Enra and the earnestness in his eyes when he promised to help me. When he told me he'd do what he could, he meant it. I know him well enough to believe that.

It's surprising how easily he and his family have accepted me. I went from working for them to being considered their equal in a matter of a day. But Enra and his household have taken it in stride. If anything, it seems like they're trying to claim me as much as Empress Saretha is.

They must have ulterior motives as well, I think, but I push the thought aside. I have to trust someone. Enra has been nothing but kind to me, escorting me places, going out of his way to talk to me at functions like this—at least, at the ones where men take part—and even agreeing to help me change, or, if we can, abolish, an unjust law.

I bring myself back to the event at hand. We're all here to celebrate, but as beautiful as the day, pavilion, and array of food before us are, the atmosphere isn't very festive. It may be because the bride we're here to celebrate also doesn't seem very festive.

Vroni sits with her new family, flanked on either side by Empress Saretha and her future mother-in-law. Her own mother, Satrapha Edab, sits nearby with Nalkendi, who catches my eye and smiles. But while they're all chatting politely, no one seems genuinely happy to be here. A few of the more oblivious guests seem like they're enjoying themselves, but most keep glancing at the empress to gauge her attitude and how they should respond to it.

From the outside, everything nobles did seemed pretentious and fake. I saw the machinations that went on behind the scenes, the ways people tried to impress, win over, or insult one another at these kinds of functions, using everything from the colors of their clothing to the foods chosen to make a particular statement. But I always assumed that on the other side of it, this side, no one actually knew what was going on. That we servants were the shadow puppets, and no one knew the shape of the hands controlling us. They only saw the figure created with shadow.

But sitting here, I can tell that isn't the case. It is just as obvious from this perspective, but everyone pretends not to know.

I catch Obipae Kula's eye, and she gives me a knowing smirk, as though she can read my mind. I wouldn't be surprised if she could. She gives me a slight nod as if to say, "Watch this." Then she reaches forward and tears off a piece of flatbread from the center of the table, a subtle movement that still grasps most people's attention. She must be aware of this response because she uses the new attention to ask a question to no one in particular.

"Is it true the former emperor was on the way to abolishing slavery before he was murdered—oh, I'm sorry—before he died?"

The pavilion falls silent. Even the musician stops playing. I stare at Obipae Kula wide-eyed. A few women openly gape at her. Empress Saretha, who hadn't been paying attention, turns a withering glare to her, but Obipae Kula is nonplussed. Instead, she returns the Empress' stare, waiting patiently for an answer.

I can't bring myself to breathe. If looks could set fires, the palace would be burning right now. But after a moment, Empress Saretha raises an eyebrow and answers, "Yes."

"What happened?" Obipae Kula asks.

The empress dips her own flatbread into salt and spices and takes a bite. This functions as a signal for the rest of the women. The atmosphere under the pavilion cools several degrees, and people go back to chatting, satisfied that the contention is over and the empress and obipae won't end up starting a war between Elisya and Derian. The quiet strumming in the corner resumes.

I listen intently to Shaha Saretha's answer, though. I hadn't known my grandfather had been planning such a thing. Chances are Aba doesn't know either. If he had, he certainly would have mentioned it.

"It was imprudent," Shaha Saretha says, "to make such a change during a transition of power. Surely you can understand that."

Obipae Kula nods. "Of course. I'm quite familiar with the liberties some see fit to take when the leadership of the government moves from one set of hands to another. But why does the emperor not see fit to continue now?"

"The economy of Elisya is still fragile," the empress says.

"What better time to make changes?" Obipae Kula responds.

"There are plenty of better opportunities. For example, later."

"So he would consider it?"

Empress Saretha gives Obipae Kula a withering glance. "I couldn't presume to know what my husband would or wouldn't consider."

Obipae Kula nods. "Of course, of course. But it would cast his leadership in an even more positive light with Queen Niksele."

Empress Saretha smiles. "I will make sure he's aware of that fact."

That marks the end of the conversation, and I realize I haven't been breathing. Is there a chance that Emperor Pakel will actually make a move like that? Could he really be considering it? I shake my head. No. There's no way he would. Even if it were something he wanted to do—and he doesn't seem like the type of man who would want to set thousands of people free—he wouldn't have any desire to remind people of the previous emperor by fulfilling a policy he was considering. That much is obvious.

No, my best chance is still to take matters into my own hands, to at least try to find an avenue that doesn't require the emperor's input.

The rest of the party continues with little excitement. Obipae Kula must have gotten what she wanted out of her exchange with the empress because she's content to observe the rest of the pleasantries and superficial competition without contributing.

I don't take part either, but that's mostly because few of the women are eager to interact with me. I keep my head down and answer questions, counting down the moments until the party is over.

CHAPTER 33

I stand with my arms outstretched as three servant women fit a new dress to my body. The cream-soft fabric shifts as they pull and stretch it in various ways to make it suit me. I'm in Shaha Saretha's suite, but she's nowhere to be seen. Instead, her attendants have been coming in and out, getting me ready for a festival event. I haven't been able to determine what kind of event it is yet, and the servant women haven't told me.

Instead, they talk around me, discussing me as if I'm decoration or a piece of furniture. They fuss, preen, and argue, the tension weighing on them palpable. Whenever I try to ask a question, I'm shushed as they place a new item on me. It's important to them to get this right, but I'm not sure what "right" is.

When I'm laden with enough beads, gold, and fabric to fill a merchant's coffers twice over, the women deem me acceptable to be presented to society. They've left my wrists bare again, so onlookers can gawk at the relics of a departed era, and this time, they've styled my hair into braids that are loose at the bottom, leaving me with a cloud of hair around my neck. The braids at the top of my head are tight, giving me a headache that makes my eyes water.

Empress Saretha passes through once, scrutinizes me wordlessly, and nods her approval before leaving for whatever more important things she has to do. Once she's approved of my appearance, there is a collective sigh around the room.

Their work here is done. Now my job is to sit quietly and not destroy their masterpiece.

No one talks to me much, so I'm left alone with my thoughts, which race in several directions at once. Will I succeed? What will it cost me? Will I be able to pay the price? My hands tremble, and I press them into the cushion I'm sitting on. I don't want to muss the dress.

A part of me wants to laugh, but I'm afraid that if I open my mouth, a scream will come out instead. I force myself to take one deep breath and then another. I can't give in yet. Not until I've tried every option. Not until there's literally nothing left I can do but sit and be an ornament for the rest of my life.

There has to be something, and I've already decided I'm going to find it. I can't give up on it now. I have Obipae Kula's help and Lord Enra's. If I fail even with their support, then I can truly abandon all my hope. But until then, I have to at least pretend to be strong.

I sit on a cushion in Empress Saretha's suite for nearly an hour. The sun finishes its journey through the sky and is settling in for the evening by the time a page approaches me.

"Hara, allow me to escort you."

I want to ask, "Escort me where?" but I figure the question will yield no answers. So I just nod.

The page takes me downstairs and outside to a yard where several hundred people mill around aimlessly. There are blankets and cushions scattered around on the grass and dirt, and some people are already sitting. They all face the same direction—toward a large, empty patch of grass that all attendees are giving a wide berth. It's a performance, then. There's music wafting in from a corner, filling in the spaces left empty by voices. There aren't many of those, though. If there's anything nobles and dignitaries know how to do, it's talk.

People glance at me and some—those who've decided they're lower in rank than I am—bow. But they all whisper as they pass. Some whisper too loudly, letting me hear what they're saying.

"—as a slave," a man says.

The woman next to him clucks in understanding. "With a slave's manner, no doubt."

I sit on a blanket and try to convince myself I can't hear them. They're not talking about me. They're discussing someone else with "a slave's manner." But my mind is unconvinced.

"—heard her father is a stable hand," the man continues.

"Did she spend her days mucking after horses then?" someone new jokes, a younger female voice, getting a few polite laughs.

My fingers dig into my legs, gathering the beaded fabric into knots. The beads cut into my hands, and I'm sure they'll leave angry marks. Something in my mind tells me I should let the dress go, but I can't do it. Why do they insist on having this discussion so close to me?

"How did she end up there?" the young woman asks.

"Kidnapped, no doubt. I'm sure they thought they could get quite the ransom for her. But no one wanted a broken princess." The man sounds like an authority on my life, at least the one he thinks I've led. Is that what people here think happened to me? Someone kidnapped me, but no one was willing to pay the ransom?

"She must be delighted to have raised her station so much," the first woman says.

The man chuckles. "A worm in a bird's nest."

"My father is a blacksmith, actually."

I hear my voice before my mind realizes it's me speaking.

My voice shakes, but I turn over my shoulder. Not enough to see the gossipers but enough that they can tell I'm talking to them.

"He's the best blacksmith in Ragien, actually. Even free craftsmen come to learn from him."

Their eyes bore into me, and my face warms, but I continue.

"And I was rescued, not kidnapped. Who would kidnap someone who's supposed to be dead?"

The group behind me is silent. I keep my eyes trained on the blanket beneath me, but I laugh as if the concept is ridiculous, and they were fools to consider it.

"I thought maybe you'd want to know the truth, so you can spread that instead of lies."

A rolling drum beat indicates the show is about to start, and I shift to face the makeshift stage again. Voices pick up behind me, but at least they have the decency to whisper this time. I wipe my shaking hands on my dress before clasping them on my lap. Then I tune out the voices around me and focus on the show.

CHAPTER 34

Enra

I steal Lia away when the empress gives her a break from attending functions. She's been at more events than I have, but that's not surprising given who she is. Everyone wants to see—and talk about—her.

But I made her a promise, and I intend to do my best to keep it. The only thing I can think of to do right now is search the palace's library for any sign of a loophole we could use. It's not a great start, but it's better than nothing.

Lia trails behind me as we walk through the palace halls, and I slow my pace a few times so we end up walking side by side. People watch us as we pass, and some I recognize whisper. I don't mind the gossip—even though Aba would probably be furious with me—but it's got to be hard on Lia. She winces every time she notices someone talking.

She slows again, and I wave her forward.

"Yes, Su—Enra?" She asks.

"Stay next to me."

She cringes. "People will talk."

I shrug. "They'll talk worse if they see you walking behind me like a…"

My voice trails off before I put my foot in my mouth. Yes, Lia was living as a servant—a slave—until a few days ago. But I don't need to make a point of that. Especially since it was me she was serving.

But Lia catches my meaning even without my mis-chosen word. She frowns, but she picks up her pace and keeps step with me. Mostly, she keeps her head lowered, but now and then, it jerks up as if she hears a loud yell. She stays alert for a few moments before her eyes train back on the floor.

This must be so bizarre for her.

The library is a small, windowless room in an older corner of the palace. That is to say, it's small compared to the other rooms in the palace. There's still enough space here to harbor a couple hundred years of decrees and records. Rows of shelves piled high with scrolls disappear into darkness interrupted by an odd lantern here and there, and although no breeze may travel through, the air is chilly.

There must be a librarian here—I think there's one at all hours—but the library is so quiet I can hear the lanterns flickering in their cages.

"He—hello?" I call out, barely expecting a response.

"Yes?"

The voice comes from far too close beside me. Lia squeaks, and I gasp, leaning away from the voice as I search for its source.

The librarian is an older man, his curly black hair tinged with gray. He's almost a full span shorter than me, and his personal lantern makes the shadows on his face more prominent. His eyes narrow as he studies us, and I fight the urge to apologize, deciding to introduce myself instead.

"I'm Enra Nehim of Ragien, and this is—"

"Hara Liani," the librarian says. "I know who you are. I

know who everyone in the palace is. What are you doing here?"

I note the man's use of the title "hara" for Lia. He sees her as a royal—not just a noble. That's probably dangerous. It's a good thing we're the only ones here. "This is the library, isn't it?"

The librarian frowns in response. "You should be celebrating with the rest of the revelers."

I nod. "We will be, but we have some… things to read about."

The librarian squints at us, his eyes becoming black beads in the dark. Then he shrugs. "Very well. Nothing may leave the library. If you have questions, call for me."

He turns on his heels and walks away, traveling farther in a few steps than I would have thought possible.

"My name is Lia Benarvela," Lia says, her voice barely a whisper.

But it was enough for the librarian to hear. He turns around and gives her a pity-filled glance, the first emotion other than mild annoyance he's shown, before dipping into a graceful bow.

"My apologies, Benar's daughter."

Then he continues on his way, and we're alone once again. I don't even know where to look, or what to look for. But I can't very well ask our disapproving librarian if he knows where we should search to find a way to abolish slavery. He may be sympathetic to Lia, but that's no guarantee he wouldn't report us.

Each shelf is identical. There isn't much to distinguish the contents of one from another. Lia watches me expectantly, and I resist the sheepish desire to grimace. She thinks I know what I'm doing.

Well, the oldest documents will probably be in the back.

Maybe. I wave toward what I hope is the back wall. "Let's go this way."

We walk until we run into a dead end, a row of shelves against a wall. "Let's see…"

I pull a scroll from a random shelf that seems somewhat full and whisper a quick prayer that it's a copy of the Ajudakai Akori. I open it and squint at the ink on the page, unable to read it in the dim light. A lantern hangs on the wall nearby, so I angle the scroll into the light.

It only takes a moment for me to realize that this is not the Ajudakai Akori. It's not even that old. I sigh, and Lia asks, "What's wrong?"

I shrug. "Oh, nothing. I don't think this will help us."

I scan a couple of paragraphs. Perhaps I was wrong. While this isn't an old document, it discusses history—one of the earliest Gazidan wars against the provinces, before they were united. It reads like a modern scholar wrote it, and it discusses the origins of the practice of slavery. I whisper a thank you to Juae and close the scroll before handing it to Lia.

"Actually, hold on to this. It may be useful."

Lia nods and takes the scroll carefully, as if she's afraid her touch will destroy it. I chuckle. "You don't have to be that careful. This one is fairly new."

"Still," she says, "I don't want to harm it."

She gives me a cautious smile. As careful as it is, it brightens her face, and I can't help but return it. "Fair enough."

I return to the shelf that gave me that scroll and pull another from its ranks. Lia and I go through them two at a time, each of us holding them open in the dim lantern light, struggling to read what they say.

They're mostly historical commentaries, discussions of Elisya's founding and historical figures. The authors theorize about our founding king and his advisors' motives, desires, and intentions. We read for a few hours, trading our scrolls in for new ones as necessary. Every once in a while, we run across a discussion of the laws that endorse enslavement. So far, it seems like an unbreakable foundation of our nation, but foundations can crack. That thought gives me a bit of hope that maybe Lia's dreams can come true, and perhaps Aba's with hers.

When we're about to leave, the librarian reappears, presumably to ensure we won't be leaving the library with anything that doesn't belong to us.

"Did you find what you needed?" he asks.

"Not yet," I admit. But soon we just might.

CHAPTER 35

Lia

The morning after our visit to the library, my leg aches. I'm not sure if it's because bad weather is coming or because Enra and I spent so much time standing yesterday. Either way, it's a pain I'm used to, and I pull myself out of bed anyway to prepare for Empress Saretha's orders.

The obipae and enipae wake soon after I do and eat the breakfast left for them in the common room. I still find it strange to eat a meal brought by servants, but I'm so hungry that I can't help but join them.

"How are you adjusting?" Enipae Gowan asks.

"I can't say I am," I admit. "All this feels… wrong."

Obipae Kula's emerald eyes bore into me. "Why is that?"

I hold back a shudder and fight to meet her eyes. "This isn't where I should be. I should be dead, or serving this—" I lift a piece of flatbread, "—with my family."

Obipae Kula shakes her head. "Perhaps, but whether that's true or not, you're here now, and you have things to do."

I shrug. "Enra and I didn't find much yesterday, at least,

nothing that helps me. I'm afraid I missed my chance. Bargaining with the emperor was the only way."

Obipae Kula gives me a smile. It's not as unsettling as it was the first time I met her. "There's always another way. You just have to find it."

After our meal is over, the obipae and enipae leave for their day's appointments. Empress Saretha still hasn't called for me, so I wander around the palace, avoiding everyone until I stumble across a small, relatively empty courtyard.

I find an unoccupied corner of the courtyard and sit on a sun-warmed stone. I take a deep breath and let my eyes adjust to the sun, when I see Enra approaching with a bit of a trot.

"Come with me!" Enra says. He's bouncing on the balls of his feet like a little boy, and I can't help but chuckle.

"What is it?"

"Just come! I have an idea."

My heart leaps. "Really?"

He takes my hand and pulls me up so I'm standing right next to him. My heart flutters, but I push the sensation away. Enra is not someone I can consider. I can't consider anyone. I'm a bird in a cage. And besides, romance isn't something I can focus on right now. Not with the weight of thousands of lives on my shoulders. I have to keep my promise to Aba, to everyone.

Enra pulls me along through the palace and out to the front courtyard, where an open carriage pulled by two oxen waits for us. Enra apologizes. "It was the first method of transportation I could find."

"Oh, it's perfect," I reply. "But where are we going?"

Enra grins. "You'll see."

We ride through the city and off to a portion of the noble quarter that's older than the rest. It's likely a part of the old city, from before it was burned—before Emperor Pakel took over. A tall rectangular building looms over the road ahead of us.

"Is that where we're going?"

Enra just smiles, but the carriage pulls up in front of the building.

Enra helps me step out of the carriage, which is a change. I'm used to helping others, not being helped. But it isn't unpleasant. His hand under my elbow is firm and reassuring. I won't fall flat on my face the first time I get out of a carriage.

A solitary guard sits on a low part of the wall beside the door, but he stands as we approach. "Welcome back, Suan," he says to Enra.

Enra nods in response.

When we step inside the door, we're surrounded by hundreds of shelves filling the room. They are each stacked high with rolled up parchments. The scent of paper and ink fills the air, along with the rhythmic scratching of several people writing.

"Is this an archive?" I ask.

"It's *the* archive," Enra answers. "The one with all the nation's oldest historical documents and many from the palace that survived the fires."

"So then they would have—"

Enra nods. "Anything left from your grandfather's era would be here."

I take in the space. It's filled to the brim with records. Where do we even start?

As if he's read my mind, Enra takes my hand and pulls me forward. "I've already asked the archivists to gather a few records on slave rights. There's got to be something there."

A table with benches attached to it has several dozen rolls and stacks of parchment spread out across it. It's far more than any person could go through in a day. An archivist waits nearby, trying his best to watch us without seeming like he's watching us. Enra and I approach it, and we each reach for a parchment.

I open mine, but before I read it, I catch Enra's eye.

"Thank you for doing all this." I try to ignore the warmth in my cheeks.

Enra grins. "I'm happy to. Now, let's see what we can find."

Most of what's here appears to be dull day-to-day pronouncements of the emperor that someone saw fit to record. There are records of laws, statements on gifts of loyalty, ratifications of treaties with other nations, declarations of important events, and an exorbitant amount of money and property being moved around.

"Is there something in particular we're searching for?" I ask.

Enra shrugs. "A guarantee that the laws for slavery are just like all the others."

"Why does that matter?"

Enra smiles. "If it's a standard law, we might be able to change it."

The archivist, who has been listening and failing to hide it, nods. "You intend to use the Ajudakai Akori."

Enra raises his eyebrows. "Yes."

"What is that?" I ask.

They both turn to me, the archivist with surprise, Enra less so. "It's the founding document of the empire. It outlines the law as set down by the first emperor, your ancestor."

"And there's a way to use it for this?"

Enra nods. "If we can convince enough nobles to side with you, we can present a change to the emperor, and with enough pressure, it will be in his best interest to propose the change."

The archivist blinks at us. "Any noble can do that."

This time, both Enra and I gape at him.

"What do you mean?" Enra asks.

The archivist shrugs as he picks up a few tablets and scrolls and hands them to us. "This is why people should visit more often. They don't even know what their own rights are," he says under his breath.

Then he says to us, "Though the emperor would like his subjects to believe otherwise, any noble can propose a change to the law, and with enough support from noble houses, it will change. The Ajudakai Akori exists for the empire, not the emperor."

Enra and I still gape.

"You mean…" I start, but I can't bring myself to finish the statement.

Enra's expression changes from one of surprise to one of excitement. "I can convince my father, and with him in agreement, the rest of my family will follow. And if we convince a few more families who are still our allies, that should be enough. How many people do you need?"

The archivist pauses in his work, his arms full of parchment and stone. "According to the Ajudakai Akori, a simple majority. Any number over half the registered nobles will do."

"And I count as a noble too…"

It's more of a statement than a question, but the archivist answers me, anyway. "Of course, Sali."

The hope I've been afraid to feel solidifies a bit more in my heart. Getting half the nobles of Elisya to agree seems like a daunting task, but it's more possible than trying to pressure the emperor. We may do this yet.

CHAPTER 36

Enra

Aba and Uncle Tusun are taking their evening meal together when I find them. The remnants of garlic and onion are still fading from the air. I'm not sure what they were discussing, but they don't seem surprised to see me when I get to our suite. We exchange a bit of small talk before I launch into the speech I'd been rehearsing the entire walk here, asking my father to support Lia in abolishing slavery.

"I know you've been prepared for any eventuality since... for the past decade, and I know you've prepared for this change. And I know you prefer to work behind the scenes, but I believe this opportunity requires us to step forward."

When I'm finished, I study Aba, trying to gauge his thoughts, hoping he'll choose to believe in me, knowing he may not. He listened in silence, his expression giving away nothing, but I can almost hear him saying, "I knew I shouldn't have trusted you" already.

Uncle Tusun, on the other hand, smiles at me and gives me a reassuring nod. At the very least, I've convinced him. But I'm not sure I can say the same about my father.

Aba shakes his head, and my heart falls. "So instead of letting the girl be a distraction, you distracted yourself."

"I'm not..." My voice trails off. Maybe I am distracted. Instead of helping restore my family's influence, I've been trying to help Lia provide her family with freedom. But that doesn't seem like a poor trade to me.

"Well, perhaps I did," I admit, "But at least I haven't been getting in your way."

My attempt at humor falls flat with Aba. He just stares at me in silence with an eyebrow raised, but Uncle Tusun gives me a polite chuckle.

I cringe but continue. "Besides, imagine the influence we'd have as the family who ended slavery."

Uncle Tusun nods. "Enra has a point. He is attempting something new in this empire. It will certainly have an impact."

Aba's silence is deafening. I clasp my hands in front of me and wait for his judgment.

"I'm surprised," he says finally. "You never cease to amaze me."

"Is that..." I pause, afraid to ask. "Is that a good thing?"

Instead of answering, Aba just smiles. "And you know this will work?"

"We've had the documents set aside by the archivists, and I read it all twice myself. I'm sure it will work." I sound more certain than I feel, but we made every precaution. "If you'll side with her..."

Aba glances at Uncle Tusun, who gives him a nod. "The rest of the family will follow. But that won't be enough."

"I know," I concede, "but it'll be a start."

"Emperor Pakel will fight it," Aba says.

"But the law is clear, and the judges owe him nothing."

Aba's expression becomes serious. "If you fail, you are on your own. You acted alone."

I gulp, but I nod. "I know."

Aba meets my eyes and holds my gaze for a moment as if gauging how serious I am. Then he holds a hand out in solidarity.

"Very well, my son. You have my word. We will do as you ask, and I will speak to your uncles. But you must plead your own case with them."

Uncle Tusun grins and clasps his hands together. "I am proud of you, my boy."

Aba's smile returns. "As am I."

We grip each other's arms at the elbow as a sign of agreement, each of them taking one of mine. The sight of our clasped arms makes me choke back a tear. Aba is trusting me with this. Uncle Tusun is trusting me. Lia is trusting me. I won't let them down.

Lia

I mill around the throne room surrounded by nobles and Elisya's wealthiest subjects arrayed in finery. It's the prince and Vroni's wedding day—the culmination of the festival—and everyone strives to take full advantage of the situation.

The throne room is transformed with tapestries, lanterns, and gold, everything and everyone glittering in the early evening light. The emperor is missing from his dais in the front. This is the one event at the festival where he must take part as a family elder instead of presiding over the rest of us.

This is not where I thought I'd be when this journey started. I thought I'd be fighting, either for freedom or a in civil war, or I'd be dead by now, murdered by the emperor along with the rest of my family. Instead, I'm struggling to work up enough bravery to walk up to an Elisyan noble Obipae Kula introduced to me and speak to her.

Enra told me a bit about Lady Zemuri. She's an older woman titled in her own right—not through marriage—and she's known to be a gentle soul, at least as far as nobility is gentle. She was a member of my grandfather's court but transitioned her allegiance to the emperor during the coup, as most did. It was the only way to stay alive. But the most important thing Enra told me about her is that she has no slaves. Paid servants care for her household. So there's a chance, a slight chance, she might be sympathetic to me and my family.

I take a deep breath and force my feet to move forward. Lady Zemuri notices me and bows. "Good evening, Sali."

"Good evening, Lady Zemuri."

"It's a beautiful occasion. I pray blessings upon the families."

I nod. "May their union be…" I search for the right word. "…prosperous."

Lady Zemuri smiles. "Indeed, but it would seem you didn't approach me to discuss the wedding."

"Ah, yes." My face and arms warm, and I fight the urge to shrink back.

I hear Obipae Kula's voice in my head. "Be honest. You'd be surprised how many people can be convinced by honesty."

I'm not sure my honesty will be as convincing as hers, but I'm willing to try it. Lady Zemuri watches me expectantly.

"I'm sure you know of my upbringing," I start.

Lady Zemuri nods. "It is well-discussed."

Of course it is.

"I admire your filial loyalty," Lady Zemuri continues. "To maintain your ties with your family though they are low-born. Many would not have your honor."

I parse her words, trying to determine if they're an insult, but she appears genuine.

"My family's birth circumstances weren't their choice, but I would like to give them the opportunity to change their lives."

"You intend to purchase their freedom?" Lady Zemuri asks, but her expression belies a deeper meaning.

I decide to take a plunge. "I intend to do more than that. If I can, I intend to purchase everyone's freedom."

Lady Zemuri raises her eyebrows but says nothing.

"And I would ask you for your support in such an attempt."

Lady Zemuri nods, her expression unreadable. But before she can answer, a low horn sounds in the room, bouncing from the walls and alerting all party-goers that the wedding is about to begin.

The music is the first to enter the room, before any of the wedding party is even visible. The groom's song reverberates through the palace halls and into the courtroom. Then a priest appears, carrying a torch before him. Close behind him are the groom's family members, first the men, starting with the youngest behind the priest to the oldest men who walk in front of the women. The emperor and Empress Saretha form the junction between the two groups. Empress Saretha walks just behind the emperor, with the oldest women in the family surrounding her. They all sing the same song, one of love and devotion, extolling the bride's beauty and virtue while boasting of the groom's ability to provide for her.

Behind the women, the proud groom sings and dances as he leads a beautiful black horse that carries Vroni, who is fully shrouded by an opaque blue veil. Only her henna-covered hands can be seen as she holds onto the horse's bridle. Her own family follows her, reversing the pattern of the groom's family—the youngest women in the family follow behind the horse, then the oldest women, then the men. They sing a different song, of family, prosperity, and hope for the future. Together, the songs are dissonant, but it's rare for couples to coordinate family songs, at least at the weddings I've seen.

When the procession reaches the front of the courtyard, the two families split, the groom's family going to the left and the bride's to the right. The prince helps Vroni down from her horse, which is then taken by one of the prince's relatives, and the couple stands before the priest.

I don't pay much attention to the words the priest speaks. The language at weddings is much the same—passages of scripture about the duties of a wife to a husband and vice versa, expositions of historical love stories, admonitions on how to have a good marriage. I'm too distracted by my own thoughts to worry about any of that.

The bride and groom exchange gifts with one another and take turns honoring their elders, first the groom's and then the bride's. After the priest gives each of them a ceremonial drink of wine and declares that they are united before Juae from now until the end of eternity, the official part of the wedding is over, and the long celebration begins.

The prince grabs Vroni's hand and raises it high above their heads to the cheers of onlookers. I applaud politely to avoid seeming too out of place. Then the two sit down at a table brought out by four slaves. It's arrayed with an obscene amount of food, and we all have to watch the couple taste each dish before any of us can eat.

It's a long process, with each of them feeding each other—Vroni's veil has been put back for this portion—and conversations pick back up among the guests.

My heartbeat picks up speed as Lady Zemuri turns to me.

"Thank you for your honesty, Sali," she says.

I nod but can't bring myself to speak. Instead, I prepare for… rejection, denial, I'm not sure what.

"I will support you as you ask."

My jaw drops, and I snap it shut. Someone who isn't Enra or Obipae Kula has agreed to help me. Someone who's a veteran in the court and probably knows more people than all of us combined.

I scramble for words. "I—thank you—I'm eternally… You can't imagine my gratitude."

Lady Zemuri smiles and stops me. "You've only asked me to do what is right. It's the least I can do."

My heart pounds, and the world spins around me, but I have to ask. "Do you know of anyone else who may be sympathetic?"

Lady Zemuri nods. "I just might."

CHAPTER 37

I don't know what to do with myself after fumbling with my gratitude to Lady Zemuri. I try to find Enra to tell him the good news, but he's probably busy with the wedding festivities, since I can't locate him in the crowd. It is his sister who's gotten married, after all. I'm sure he has duties to attend to.

I keep to the outskirts of the celebration, picking up the odd taste of food here and there. It's hard to imagine eating a meal when my stomach seems to have feral cats running around inside it, but it's rude to refuse food at a wedding.

Even though I'm trying not to be noticed, I'm not doing a good job. People keep glancing at me, but few talk to me, and that's just as well. I know I have more convincing to do. Lady Zemuri discreetly identified a few people she thinks would be open to my cause, and for a while, I consider approaching them. But I don't want to ruin my chances by rushing. I'd like to take my time, to not become too obvious to the emperor too soon.

As if he heard my thoughts, the emperor appears in my line of sight, and I wince. He and Shaha Saretha are making a tour around the party, along with the rest of their family, receiving congratulations from all their guests. Even though

Empress Saretha isn't the prince's grandmother by blood, her status as the emperor's wife makes her the family matriarch, so well-wishes go to her whether or not she wants them to. And while she seems perfectly pleased when dignitaries are paying attention to her, her expression when they turn away says she'd rather not receive wishes of any kind.

The emperor, however, basks in the celebration's glow. He accepts guests' praise, blessings, and goblets of wine—though the empress drinks from them first. That is puzzling. The job of testing for poison goes to servants or slaves, but it seems the emperor has given Shaha Saretha that task. No wonder she seems to resent him. Their relationship must be quite strange.

They wind their way through the crowd, and I shrink back toward the wall, intent on avoiding their notice. But I fail. Shaha Saretha sees me, and she draws the emperor's attention. He makes a direct path to me.

I beg my feet to move, but they're frozen in place.

"Good evening, Sali."

My heart pounds, but I answer. "Heartfelt congratulations and blessings for your family."

My words sound stiff, and though I try to infuse them with genuineness, they get quieter as I continue to talk.

The emperor smiles and extends a hand to me.

"Walk with me, Sali Liani. The people need to see us interacting. It will reassure them. Saretha, my dear, continue to greet the guests. I will return."

Shaha Saretha glowers at him, and for a moment, all the torches in the room get brighter, flaring all at once. It happens so quickly that I'm not entirely sure I haven't imagined it. Emperor Pakel avoids the empress' gaze. The tension between them is so volatile that I'm surprised all the guests don't turn their attention to the three of us. But then Shaha Saretha gives the emperor a slight bow.

"As you wish."

Her expression turns into a serene smile, and she returns to the crowd.

The emperor leads me forward without touching me. He nods and laughs as revelers greet him with shouts of congratulations. But an aura of ice emanates from him, though only I seem to feel it.

He leans in to speak to me. "You have been busy, Sali."

My throat goes dry, but I squeak out, "I'm sure I don't know what you're referring to, your excellency."

The emperor chuckles. "You've done a good job of convincing the Nehims and Lady Zemuri to support you, but how quickly do you think their support will disappear when they discover you're a fraud?"

"Everyone already knows I was raised a slave." I sound confident, though a cloud of foreboding settles over me. He wouldn't call me a fraud for being a slave. The emperor knows better than that. He's threatening me with something. I just don't know what.

"Yes, a slave who's risen to the ranks of a princess by way of her birth." His voice becomes wistful. "I, of all people, know what it means to change your station in life."

He turns to me as we reach the front of the courtroom, where the ceremony took place. The partygoers are arrayed before us—Elisya in all its splendor. The suffering my family endures is so far from this.

I feel the need to defend myself. "I'm not pretending to be anyone I'm not."

"Oh, I know you're not. At least, not intentionally. But do you know what it takes to be a noble in this empire?"

I stay silent, the cloud of foreboding growing heavier.

The emperor smiles. "Land. Land and a record of your family name. But if anyone checks the records of your family, they will find the Asils dead and their land gone, sold to those loyal to the emperor years ago. You may have been born a royal, but you have no true power. You are nothing more than a slave and a pretender, Sali Liani."

He spits out my name like it's a curse, and I wince, each syllable piercing my heart.

"What change can you make as a fraud?"

My hands shake, and my knees threaten to buckle beneath me, but I scramble for the hope I'd had earlier.

"Someone else will do it then…"

"Who?" the emperor asks. "Enra, that traitor's heir who follows you like a calf? He and his family are powerless, and they will remain so until they die off in their hovel of a kingdom. And as for anyone else… Who do you think will take up your cause when you've died in shame and disgrace?"

Fear spikes in my mind, leaving me dizzy. I whisper the words, confirming what I've feared. "You intend to kill me?"

"Of course. Smile, dear. The people are watching."

The emperor gives a gracious nod to some passing nobles who toast to him. "Not now, as I've told you, or even soon. Saretha seems to have taken a liking to you." He shakes his head like I'm a strange pet she's dragged home. "But when you've been trotted around long enough and lost your usefulness, I will let you rest with your ancestors."

My usefulness. Even now, trying to fight for my family, I've been "useful" to the emperor. I swallow the bile that threatens to escape my throat.

"You won't—" My voice fails me, and I try again. "I'll—"

"Tell someone?" The emperor laughs and leans in conspiratorially. "Who will stand up for you? None of these people could challenge me for your grandfather. What makes you think they'd do it for you?"

I reach weakly into the air, hoping for something to grab to hold myself steady. But nothing is there. The emperor bows politely, as one should to someone who has spared their life, and walks away, leaving me limp at the front of the party like a puppet without a master.

Enra

The wedding was a blur. I remember singing through Vroni's entrance, standing for the ceremony, and then shaking far too many hands and hugging an uncomfortable number of people. Some people even asked me when I would celebrate my marriage. I don't know how I answered, but I'm sure I didn't tell the truth, whatever the truth may be. I don't even know at this point.

I tried to find Lia, but by the time I located her, Emperor Pakel had his claws in her. He dragged her around for a few minutes—for appearances, no doubt—and they talked for a minute at the front of the party. I think most people were too busy celebrating to notice, but the color drained from Lia's face with every word Pakel spoke. I wanted to rescue her from him, but Uncle Tusun had me surrounded by my peers, other princes who would rule provinces, and they were distracted by the eligible noblewomen whose parents brought them by our table to "introduce" them. It didn't matter that most of the men have been betrothed since childhood. A surprising number of parents are comfortable with their daughters becoming consorts, as long as the one they're with is powerful. And all my companions were interested in entertaining a potential consort or two—whether or not their families would approve.

If I had left that parade of women to extricate Lia from Emperor Pakel's clutches, the princes would have had questions. I didn't want to make things worse for Lia by drawing their attention to her, and to be perfectly honest, I suppose I didn't want to make things worse for myself, either. After the princes left, I intended to find her, but she disappeared for the rest of the night after finishing her conversation with Emperor Pakel.

It's late morning now, and people are taking their time starting the day. There will be another party this evening and a third tomorrow, so guests will use the daytime to rest. Lia's got to be around here somewhere, unless Empress Saretha has her doing something. What she could be doing is beyond me— there's nothing going on this morning.

After a moment, I decide to go to the courtyard where I found Lia a few days ago. She seemed relaxed there, so it may be where she'd go to recover from the wedding and whatever it was the emperor said to her.

The courtyard isn't as empty as it was the other day. More people have time to relax, and they're taking advantage of it. But Lia is nowhere to be seen. Obipae Kula and her husband cross the garden, and I catch their attention.

"Do you know where Lia went this morning?"

"I believe she's still in her room," Enipae Gowan answers.

"Is she all right?" I ask.

Obipae Kula furrows her brow. "She was in bed by the time we left the wedding last night. Did something go wrong?"

"I don't know," I admit, but something doesn't feel right. "Would you permit me to visit her?"

Obipae Kula shrugs. "We can't stop you."

"Perhaps invite her outside, for propriety's sake," Enipae Gowan adds.

Obipae Kula laughs at him, but I nod my agreement and head off toward their suite. Behind me, the obipae teases her husband about propriety.

When I reach the door, I raise my hand to knock, but it opens in front of me, and Lia almost runs into my hand.

She jumps, and I jerk my hand back. "Oh, I'm sorry. I thought you were—"

"I was just coming to—"

We each stop and gesture for the other to speak. Lia's eyes are puffy and rimmed in shadow, and her shoulders sag more than usual.

"What happened last night?" I ask. "I saw you with Emperor Pakel."

"He wanted to talk to me," she says, even though that much is obvious.

I lead her away from the suite door and through the hallway. It would be better to talk outside, where people are less likely to eavesdrop in secret.

In the morning sunshine, we find a quiet corner where it's easy to see if someone is approaching.

"What did he talk to you about?"

Lia sighs, her breath a bit ragged. "He said I'm an imposter. He had my family's nobility abolished by selling our land, so I have no right to change anything. We've been wasting our time."

I'm sure Lia believes the emperor, but my mind won't accept it. "That can't be right. You can't just remove a noble family."

Can you? I search my memory for anything I've heard or learned to refute that.

Lia shrugs. "He says he did."

Since Emperor Pakel replaced the previous emperor, would that give him the power to treat the Asils as though they never existed?

If anyone can deny—or confirm, I admit reluctantly—that it's possible, they'd be at the old archive. I grab Lia's hand without thinking, and she stiffens. I drop her hand.

"Sorry…but let's go. The archivists will know for sure."

After a moment, Lia nods, but her expression remains

hopeless. The emperor said something else, but whatever it was, she's not ready to tell me.

It doesn't take long to find transportation. No one is in a hurry to go anywhere this morning. In fact, when Lia and I board our cart, no one else is in the courtyard. Even the driver's eyes are dark. The servants who had free time probably also spent some time celebrating last night.

But the cart driver dutifully helps us into the cart and sits at the front with a noticeable sigh, and after a few seconds of adjustment, we're off.

I give Lia what I hope is a reassuring smile, but she barely registers it. That's alright, though. I hope she'll be able to actually smile after this trip is over.

CHAPTER 38

Lia

I don't know how to tell Enra all this is pointless. The emperor is going to kill me. He certainly won't let me live long enough to change the law, even if it turns out to be possible. But Enra seems so determined to help me. He's been by my side, keeping his word through this entire process, getting nothing out of it, as far as I can tell. But if he keeps going down this path with me, will he end up stirring the emperor's ire as well?

He chats with me as we ride, talking about the city, the weather, the transportation—only meaningless things, and nothing about the wedding last night or the future. When we arrive at the archive once again, Enra requests the palace's records regarding me and my immediate family.

The archivist, the same one we'd met before, nods and collects the required documents, setting them on a table for us to peruse and waiting nearby to observe us.

"If he abolished your family's name," Enra says, "There would be a record. It would be in here…"

He examines the stacks of parchment and sighs.

"Somewhere."

I try to smile, to be reassuring, but my smile must be unconvincing, because Enra frowns like he pities me. He picks up a dossier and hands it to me before grabbing one for himself.

"It would be a newer decree, something from only a few years ago, probably."

I nod, flipping the wooden cover of the dossier open carefully to avoid spilling its contents. The first page is a decree from my birth father, as the crown prince of Elisya. I skim it. Something about a land purchase. I flip through some others. More transactions and documented alliances, scattered among records of the crown prince's daily activities, his schedules, who he met with, what he said, and even what he ate.

None of it is interesting, and none of it says anything about the current emperor. If he made a decree about my family, it isn't in this dossier.

As I close the dossier, a filigreed edge of parchment catches my eye. I gently tug it free, curious what it's doing in a collection of such dry documents. I skim over its contents—it too seems dull, belying its ornate borders. But then my name catches my eye, and then Enra's. I stop skimming and go back to the beginning.

In the presence of holy witnesses and under the eyes of Juae, let this pronouncement be made from the lips of Asil Nahan Datu Elisya with the blessing of his Imperial Majesty:

To honor his loyalty and service to the crown, Paykhan Nehim Satrap Ragien will receive the following promise with the consent of Tusun Nehim Malik Uze for the benefit of his heritage.

An alliance for all perpetuity through his son, Enra Nehim, Noble Prince, as malik of Uze, as signified by the betrothal of Asil Liani Hara Elisya, firstborn daughter of her house, to be the helpmate at his side through the rulership of Uze for the glory of their families...

There were other things listed—money, spices, textiles,

other resources—but I couldn't focus on any of them. Betrothal. It says I was betrothed. Was I… am I promised? To Enra?

My hands shake as I clutch the parchment. I'm afraid to ask, afraid that my understanding is accurate, but the words still slip from my mouth. "What does this mean?"

Enra glances over my shoulder. "What does what—"

He stops mid-sentence and fixes his eyes on the paper in front of him.

"Tell me," I insist.

After a long pause, he sighs. "It means that when we were of age, you were to become my wife."

"I was. Was this annulled as well?"

Enra pauses, and then, like it hurts him to do so, he shakes his head. He isn't surprised but… Ashamed. My heart pounds in my veins, and the trembling extends to the rest of my body as realization dawns on me. "You knew this."

It isn't a question. I know what his answer will be.

"Yes."

"You've known this."

"Yes."

"You've known who I am."

"…Yes."

"Your whole family knows this."

"Well—"

"And yet… and yet, you all let me work for you. You kept me as a slave in your house. You told me nothing. Even when I joined the court, you told me nothing."

Enra winces. "It was better—"

"Better for who? For you? For your father? Certainly not for me and my family. With this knowledge, you could have freed us immediately. None of this would have been necessary. We could have—I could have…"

My voice fades as I choke back tears. My entire life, I

thought no one knew my secret but my family, but Enra, the satrap, they all knew. Not only that, they knew I was betrothed to marry him, and yet, they left me in the dark.

I can't tear my eyes away from him, and yet Enra can't meet mine. All this time, he's claimed to be on my side, to want to help me secure freedom for my family. But they could have given that to us years ago. My stomach roils. "I thought I could trust you. I thought… But you're just using me, too."

Enra winces. "Lia—"

"What is it you get out of this? How do I serve your purposes? I think I deserve to know that."

I'm shouting at him, drawing all the attention in the archive. An archivist makes his way over to us, and I take a deep breath and lower my voice. "How could you?"

"It's more complicated than that."

"How?" I ask. "How could it be more complicated than that? What was so complicated?"

"You wouldn't…" Enra starts but then stops himself.

I fume. "I wouldn't understand? Of course I wouldn't. I don't understand any of this. But whose fault is that?"

I'm trembling with fury, but I can't think of anything else to say, so I slam the parchment back on the table, turn on my heels, and stalk toward the exit.

The day outside has turned cloudy, and I pass by the carriage that brought us here as I walk out into the street with no destination in mind. I just know I need to get away.

Enra

I chase after Lia, beating myself up. How could I have not caught that declaration first? How did I think I could get away with not telling her? How can she walk so fast? She's already out of sight by the time I get to the courtyard.

I should have told her the truth, I admit. Her response probably wouldn't have been any better earlier than it is now, but maybe it would have made a difference. At least then she would hear it from me.

"She wouldn't have understood then either," I hear Aba's voice saying in my head, but I shake it away. Lia's no fool. She would understand we were trying to keep her safe—to keep everyone safe. She would understand that now, if I could explain it… If I can find her.

But she's gone. I run out to the street, trying to find a slight girl in a simple dress and quickly realizing my search is hopeless.

"Lia!" I call out in case she's nearby. "Lia! Please wait."

There's no answer, but I didn't really expect one. I move to the side of the road to avoid being run down by carts and foot travelers. Lia doesn't know the city. Where would she go?

Forward leads back to the palace—chances are she wouldn't go that direction. Right leads deeper into the noble district, where the wealthy live, so she'd be unlikely to want to go that way either. That leaves left. I turn that way and start running, dodging the carriages and people in the road while scrutinizing every small woman in a cream dress I come across.

Some people do double-takes at a wealthy young man running through the streets of the noble district. But most don't seem to care who I am or what I'm doing. As long as I don't run into anyone or knock anything over, they're content to let me pass.

There are several women along the road who could be Lia but aren't. It takes me about 10 minutes of running to realize I don't need to go too far from the archive. I should go back and get the carriage. That's the best way for me to catch up with her. I do one last circle around the area before turning back, but as I go, movement between two buildings catches my eye. Something beckons me forward, and I don't know why I follow it, but I do.

The narrow passage forming an alley between two structures isn't long, and it lets out into a small public courtyard where the locals have taken the time to cultivate a shared garden with vegetables and trees. A few people sit out beneath the trees, enjoying some rest or a meal before returning to their day's activities. A winding path curves its way through the garden, and a familiar form brushes her hand across the leaves.

"Lia!" I call out, hoping she'll freeze instead of run.

She stops cold, and I feel a pang of regret at using her apprehensive nature against her, but I still jog forward to catch up to her. She turns away from me.

"Please listen to me."

She's silent.

"I'm sorry," I begin, not knowing how else to start.

"I'm sorry we—I didn't tell you, and I'm sorry we kept you in captivity. We thought it was for the best, but we—I didn't consider your feelings or wellbeing. You may never forgive me, and you don't have to, but I meant what I said when I told you I wanted to help you. I meant it when I told you I want your family to be free. You don't have to believe me. You can hit me, or yell, or curse me to the ends of the world. But please come back to the archive. I know we can do this. And when we've succeeded, you can cut all ties with me. I'll burn that betrothal covenant myself if you want me to."

Lia rubs a leaf between her fingers as she thinks. I hold my breath, my heart pounding.

"I'm not going to hit you," she says, finally.

I let out a surprised laugh. "It's fine, if you want to."

"I don't want to."

"You can break off the betrothal, too. You have the power to do that."

She doesn't respond. Instead, she asks. "How far are we from the archive?"

"Not far." I point in the direction I came from. "We can get back that way."

We walk in almost complete silence back to the archive, but Lia breaks the silence once.

"What do you really want, Enra?"

I pause before answering. "You know how my family survived the coup?"

Lia nods.

"We don't have… we aren't what we once were, and we'd like to be what we were again."

"And helping me gives you that?"

I answer honestly. "I believe it will."

Lia glances at me. "What if it doesn't?"

A part of me doesn't want to tell her the truth, but the better part of me does. "Aba's prepared for that—"

Lia nods again, but I'm not finished. "But even then, I… I want to help you."

Lia's quiet for a moment, and I figure we're done talking, but then she asks, "Why did you never end the betrothal yourself?"

The question catches me off guard. "What?"

"Why didn't you end the betrothal? You knew about it, and as long as it was on record, you'd never be able to have a wife, only consorts. What would you have done?"

Why is she worried about my marriage prospects? And why didn't I ever end the engagement?

"I never wanted to…" I let my voice trail off. Why didn't I? Is it because I knew she'd be restored? Because I valued the advancement an alliance with a deposed princess would give us? Because I… I wanted to marry Lia? I glance at her, her eyes focusing ahead instead of at the ground, set firm on her destination. My heart flips, but I brush the feeling away.

"I… don't know," I settle on.

Lia nods as though she expected that answer, which hurts me for some reason. Why wouldn't she think I wanted to marry her? I know the answer to that, and I don't like it. I push that feeling away as well. That's something to deal with later.

This system must go. The thought hits me with more force than it ever has. If I was determined before, I'm adamant now. I'll examine the reasons when I have time. For now, I allow the resolve to solidify in my heart. I'll do whatever I must for my family, for Aba, for Vroni. But I won't rest until Lia and her loved ones are free.

CHAPTER 39

Lia

My thoughts are racing the entire walk back to the archive, so I'm glad that Enra says nothing other than to answer my questions. The question of why he didn't end the betrothal lingers, but I try not to focus on it. Thinking about the fact that I'm promised to him and have been for my entire life makes me furious and anxious—and something I can't quite place—and none of those feelings are useful right now.

We reach the archive and pass the confused carriage driver as we reenter the building. I give him an apologetic nod.

When we get back inside, the archivist watches us emotionlessly, although I know he overheard everything. He has the decency to not address it, at least not to our faces, though the gossip among the archivists may heat up once we're gone.

"There's got to be something here we can use," Enra says, but it doesn't seem like he's talking to anyone in particular.

We flip through a few more dossiers and loose documents, and there are only a few that even mention the current emperor, mostly those daring to list him as contributing to my grandfather's and father's deaths. He isn't even named as their killer.

I come across a document in a language I don't understand. It's not written in Elisyan or Derian, but the writing is Elisyan.

I hand the document to Enra. "Can you read this?"

Enra reads it over, sounding the words out before shaking his head. "It sounds eastern, but I can only make out a few words of this dialect." He turns to the archivist. "Could you?"

The archivist peruses the parchment over Enra's shoulder. "It's in Eutu, a dialect of Min. It reads 'Asil Meti Diyan Elisya…'"

My heartbeat speeds up. My birth mother? Her face once again wafts through my memory, from the earliest smile she gave me to her final expression of terror.

"'Left to her firstborn… daughter?' I see…" The archivist squints, reading the parchment more carefully as my attention returns to him. What did he say?

"She left something to me?"

His eyes turn to me sharply. "Ah… yes. It would appear that when you were born, the diyan bequeathed her land and title as 'Sali of Eutu in the Min Kingdom and the rightful owner of the land of Onide to her firstborn daughter, she being the sole heir of the land with no male relatives…' It would seem to be a condition of her betrothal, to leave her title to her firstborn daughter."

My head spins. My birth mother left me land. And a title. Even without my father's land or Shaha Saretha's blessing, I'm still a noble, though not one of the imperial family. Still, that's more than the puppet I've been for the past several weeks.

I glance at Enra, afraid to be hopeful. "Does this mean…"

He gives me a wide grin. "The emperor didn't take away your rights after all. You can still use the Ajudakai Akori."

The archivist shrugs. He seems to have put together what

we're trying to do, though by his attitude, it doesn't seem to affect him much. "Well, technically, that is correct. But technically, Sali, you are also considered dead, and you have lived as a…" he pauses, trying to find a more decorous word and failing, "slave, for most of your life. So your ability to guide Eutu as a noble could be contested. You lack experience."

My heart falls, and the hope that had budded withers. The emperor still has a hold over my life and my future. But something solidifies inside me. This is the first and last gift my birth mother ever gave me. I can't let the emperor take something like that away from me again, especially not with the power it gives me—the power to finally change something.

"Is there no way for me to keep my place?" I ask.

"You can take the case to the judges," the archivist says. "They would determine your worthiness and ability and decide if you deserve the title the diyan left to you."

The judges. I'd have to confront them again. But at least this time, I wouldn't have to prove who I am. They already determined that for themselves, before they let the emperor use me as a plaything.

No. That was my fault for being unprepared. I won't make that mistake a second time. "What will I need to do?"

The archivist glances over the papers. "This kind of claim will require a formal audience. You'll have to request to see them. Given the nature of your claim, I'm sure they'll make arrangements quickly."

I nod. "Can I send a request from here?"

The archivist blinks. "Naturally."

He and Enra help me craft a request for a formal audience with the judges on the archives' official parchment. By the time the two of them have finished with it, it barely resembles the simple question I need answered, but I'm sure it's as official as the judges require. An archive courier takes it out to the court as soon as we're done.

"When will we hear back?" I ask.

"Soon, I'm sure," the archivist answers. "I wouldn't be surprised if they send a reply before the day is over."

I breathe a sigh of relief. "Good. That means the emperor won't have time to…"

I let my voice trail off. I almost said it out loud. Maybe Enra didn't notice. But he glances over at me.

"Won't have time to what?"

I wince and purse my lips, praying he'll drop the subject.

Enra turns to me more fully. "The emperor won't have time to what, Lia?"

"Kill me." I whisper the words, hoping it'll be too quiet for him to hear them, but the archive chooses that moment to become still as a tomb.

Enra stares at me, his expression unreadable. "Is that what he told you?"

His voice is low, almost the whisper mine was.

I nod. "But I expected he'd kill me. I'm surprised he didn't do it immediately. When he didn't, I got too comfortable, but I knew…"

I don't know why I'm trying to assure Enra that my murder at the hands of the emperor isn't a surprise to me. Maybe I'm trying to make him feel better about it. But it doesn't seem to work. Enra's expression grows darker by the second.

"It's alright," I say. "As long as I can free my family first, I'm… I'm fine with dying."

It's not entirely true. I'd rather live. I'd like to see Aba and Ima resting in a house of their own, to attend Jorra and Atar's weddings and see their children grow up. And that nebulous dream I'm afraid to hope for. I'd like to prove Duin is alive. I'd love to see his face again.

But if I have to die to give my family their freedom, I'm willing to do it, I realize. Just not until they're free.

"You're not going to die," Enra says sharply. "Emperor Pakel will not kill you."

"I have no way to stop him."

It isn't a question, but Enra still answers it like it is.

"You will once we confirm you with the judges."

Enra

He told her he'd kill her. Of course he did, and he would if given the chance. Lia said she was surprised he hasn't done it already. I'm not surprised, but my blood races.

I leave Lia at the archive, afraid to take her out into the street for fear Emperor Pakel will take the opportunity to rid himself of her while we're in public, especially if he's found out what we're planning. Our archivist is probably trustworthy, but Pakel has spies everywhere. I wouldn't be surprised if he learned about Diyan Meti's will for Lia soon after we did.

He wouldn't have had to worry about Lia while she was under Empress Saretha's thumb. He knew she had no true influence, so anything she did would amount to nothing. But with an actual title and land, Lia immediately becomes more of a threat. He'd want to get rid of her before that becomes the case.

When I get back to the palace, I make a beeline for my family suite. Most of my family, except for Vroni, is here in the common room, eating a leisurely meal.

"Where have you been all day?" Ima asks me when I come inside.

I give her a quick bow. "I'm sorry, Ima. There's been... It's been..."

I can't think of a good way to summarize what's happened, so I launch into the story, telling them how I found Lia this morning, what she told me, what we found at the archive, and how the emperor plans to kill her. As they listen, my family stops eating one by one, and by the time I'm done, they're all staring at me.

Aba raises his eyebrows. "You've certainly been busy."

"I know you don't want to get involved, but I need to make sure Lia makes it to the Halls of Virtue, and I can't do it alone."

Uncle Tusun lays his flatbread back on the table. "What do you need, my son?"

Lia

I feel just as anxious as I did when I started this journey of nobility. When I wasn't sure if I would live or die. Now I'm fairly certain I'll die, but I hope I can change the law first. With all the records here, according to Enra, they have no reason to deny me. But even then, it's still not a sure thing. By now, someone from the archive will have told the emperor what we're planning.

My archivist and a priest sit nearby and watch me fidget. I grow to like this archivist—Osman—more and more with each interaction. As soon as Enra left, Osman sent for a priest, ensuring that no violence can take place in the archive.

While the priest is here, the emperor can't hurt me, not without blaspheming Juae, desecrating the grounds, and losing the right to rule. But that doesn't mean he won't try something later.

There's a commotion as the archive doors open and footsteps hurry in my direction. I freeze, my heart pounding, but Enra comes around the corner with a courier in tow.

The courier hands me a roll of parchment, warm from his

touch. My hands shake as I open it. I read through it, having to read some lines twice because my eyes won't focus. When I'm done, I hand it to Osman to guarantee I've read it correctly.

Enra raises his eyebrows expectantly.

"They've granted my request. I think… I think they'll see me right now."

We both glance at Osman, who confirms my interpretation. "You'll have to see them alone."

My heart drops, but I nod.

"I suppose we need to leave."

The emperor may have assassins along the road. The dark thought occurs to me, and I don't even try to push it away. Even if that's the case, I still have to try.

As if he's reading my thoughts, Enra's expression is grim. "He may try to…"

His voice trails off, and I let out a bitter chuckle, more hysterical than humorous. "It's not like he hasn't tried before."

It's Enra's turn to nod. His face is so contorted with concern that even in my fear, I want to comfort him. I muster my bravery and reach out to touch his arm. "You don't have to come with me. You've already done enough. If you return now—"

"Stop it." He cuts me off, putting his hand over mine. "I'm going to see you, and this, through to the end."

Tears spring to my eyes. A spark passes between us, and my heartbeat jumps and picks up speed. Enra seems to lean toward me.

"Your highnesses, forgive me…" Osman's voice breaks into the moment. I feel Enra jerk away. "There are people in the courtyard to see you."

I FEND off dizziness as Enra and I walk to the courtyard. When Osman opens the door, a group of armed men wait outside, and I steel myself. This is it. They will either try to arrest me or kill me here. I tell myself I'm prepared for either, but I can't stop shaking.

Enra moves to place himself between me and them, but I stop him. "It's all right."

I have to do this. I move around him and walk down the short steps to the small militia.

The men form a crescent before me. I wait, watching for the leader to step forward and tell me of my fate. But after a few tense moments, no one approaches.

I hold my head up in an attempt to come across as dignified. "Who speaks for you?"

The men exchange glances before one says, "You do, Sali."

That was unexpected. I focus on the man who spoke. "What do you mean?"

He tilts his head in confusion. "We… we have come to escort you to the hearing. The houses of Uze sent us…"

The man's voice trails off as he registers my own confusion, but a wide grin spreads across Enra's face.

"You know something about this?" I ask.

He nods. "I didn't know if they'd be able to do it, but they found you protection."

"Is that why you left?" When he told me to stay at the archive, I didn't know where he was going, but he must have gone to his family.

"Yes," Enra admits. "I wouldn't be able to face your father if I didn't at least try to protect you."

My heart aches at the mention of Aba. My family's faces waft through my thoughts. All this is for them. Either they'll get what they need, or I'll die trying to give it to them. I give the group my best attempt at a smile. "Thank you. I'm ready."

I step into the group of men, and they part for me. As they

encircle me, I glance over my shoulder and relax as I see Enra. He gives me a reassuring smile, and I nod. It's time.

The men surround me and walk with me as I make my way to the Halls of Virtue, where the judges hold court. It functions like a temple—no violence is allowed on its grounds, so as long as I can get inside, I have a chance.

My breath is shallow, and my heart pounds, but the streets are eerily silent. It's late, but there should still be people busy at work, bartering at the market, preparing evening meals. However, we walk alone—a small crowd exposed to the elements.

A prickle goes up my neck as a voice calls out, "Halt, in the name of the emperor!"

The men in front of me come to a stop, and gradually, the rest of us do too. I crane my neck to see who's stopped us.

A tall man in military regalia holds a spear out toward us, and a blockade of two dozen soldiers is arrayed behind him.

He frowns. "Go no further. Disperse now, and no harm will come to you."

My hands tremble, and Enra puts a hand on my shoulder. "Don't worry," he whispers, but his own voice is shaky.

One man in front of me holds his ground. "We escort Hara Liani to the Halls of Virtue. Let us pass."

"There is no Hara Liani," the military captain scoffs, "And no one is permitted to reach the Halls of Virtue today. You remain here at the risk of your lives."

He waves his spear above his head, and there's a commotion in the surrounding buildings. I look up and my stomach drops. We're surrounded by archers on the rooftops. So much for "not now." The emperor must have been forced to move up his plans. He truly intends to kill us all.

CHAPTER 40

Enra

Archers surround us. The men with us huddle into a protective formation, but I know it won't be enough. Pakel's soldiers don't even wait for us to respond or give us a chance to surrender, but honestly, I wouldn't have expected them to. The warning was just a formality. They're here to stop Lia by any means necessary.

Just as I finish that thought, a volley of arrows arches through the air. I grab Lia's arm and pull her to the ground as the men around us raise their shields. There are shouts and cries and the grinding bite of metal clashing against metal. They have soldiers on the ground, too. How many people did Emperor Pakel send to kill one girl?

Lia's eyes are wide. The bottom of her dress is stained by the ground, wet with mud and worse. A scream forms on her lips, but her voice is silent. Or maybe I can't hear her over the fighting.

I grip her arm more tightly. "Come on!"

We crouch and crawl through the fighting, with me trying to shield Lia with my body as best I can. I wish I had a shield, a spear, a sword, anything. Instead, we have to dodge past the blows of our allies and enemies, trying not to get hit.

We just need to get to the Halls of Virtue. Once Lia's inside, she'll be safe. But she's the sole woman on a battlefield of men, and she's the one with the target on her head. I pull her behind me and pick up a sword as a man falls. I'm not sure who he is, but the sword is already stained with blood.

We duck into an alley, and I push Lia ahead of me. I need to see her to protect her. "Run!" I shout at her.

She glances past me to where the fighting is still going on. Her eyes are full of horror, and I can see her freezing. But we don't have time. Soon someone will follow us, so I push her forward. She stumbles a bit but starts running.

I call out directions to her as we run. We break through crowds of people as we dash through the streets, people who have no idea what's going on. The soldiers must have cleared our route as soon as they knew where we were going. At least Emperor Pakel isn't eager to kill civilians this time. But screams echo behind us as the fighting follows us.

The pace is punishing, but we have to keep moving. Any slowing will allow Pakel's men to catch up with us. And I can hear them getting closer with each step we take.

Lia gasps for air, and my own lungs burn, but I spur her on. "Keep going!"

The Halls of Virtue are finally in sight.

By now, the news of fighting has traveled through the streets, and everyone is running, whether or not they know why. Even though it's been years, the fear of the coup is still in the city's memory. There's so much screaming that my ears give up on trying to hear it, turning it into one long ringing tone. I take Lia's hand as we dodge through panicking Gazidans, carefully holding the sword so it doesn't hit any innocents.

We reach the massive wooden doors of the Halls of Virtue, which were held open as is customary, but the judicial guards on either side of it are quickly closing them to shut out the fighting. We can't lead the soldiers in here, and they won't let me in with a bloodied sword in my hand.

I push Lia away through the doors. "Go! Get inside. I'll stay here."

She hesitates, "But…"

"Go now!" I yell, sounding harsher than I've ever sounded. She grimaces and once again looks past me to the fighting that's quickly approaching.

"You can't do anything for them here."

She nods. "I know."

Then she runs through the doors, and they close behind her, keeping me outside.

Lia

The doors to the Halls of Virtue slam shut behind me, blocking out much of the noise outside. The contrast is palpable, and while I know I'm safe here, the difference makes my blood pulse in my ears. My life is no longer in immediate danger, but I have no allies. My only consolation is that here, the emperor shouldn't have any allies either.

The muffled sounds of fighting continue outside. I should get away from the door. It would take much gall to storm the Halls of Virtue, but I wouldn't be surprised if the emperor did it. After all, he is the only man in history to attack the palace and succeed.

The beat of my sandals resounds on the stone floor, echoing through the hallways in a halting pattern. My leg aches from running, but I keep moving. I have to. A breeze blows through the building from somewhere. But the chamber where the judges hold court is straight ahead.

My heart pounds in my ears, and my knees threaten to buckle as I walk. The hallway seems to extend. But I compel myself forward. Enra and all the men outside are counting on me. I can't fail them. I can't fail my family again. I can't fail all the slaves hoping for freedom.

The doors to the judges' chamber are now in front of me. I need to knock. My hand trembles, but I ball it into a fist and rap on the door three times. I barely have time to knock the third time before the door swings open in front of me.

The room is bright, much brighter than the hallway, and I can't make out who's inside, but a deep male voice calls out, "Enter."

I take one ragged breath and will my feet forward. I have to do this. There's no other way.

I take the courtroom—courtyard, really—in as my eyes adjust. I'm outside. What's left of the sunlight illuminates a short, beaten dirt path flanked by trees. Low bushes, grasses, and flowers fill in the spaces between them. I can hear the sounds of shouting faintly in the distance, but birdsong obscures it here. Ahead of me, a circular stone patio fills the center of the space, and seven men sit on stools facing me. The man in the center beckons to me.

"Come forward, Nahan's heir."

This is the first time anyone has ever referred to me as my birth father's heir, I realize. The thought that Duin is alive pricks the back of my mind, but the judges don't factor hope into their judgment. Until Duin is before them, I am the only living descendant of my father.

One foot at a time, I tell myself as I walk. I come to the place where the path meets the patio and stop short. There are two figures seated on stools to my right, sitting in a place where they were obscured by the bushes and trees. My heart drops into my stomach, and my vision blurs a bit, but I know who they are. I could never mistake them.

Emperor Pakel and Shaha Saretha are here. But why? They sent all those soldiers to stop me just to be here themselves?

Of course they did. In case I made it, they wouldn't want me to present my cause to the judges without them being here. And if I died along the way, all the better for them.

Emperor Pakel gives me a withering glare, but Shaha Saretha purses her lips into an amused smile. Somehow she's always amused. I don't know which of their expressions is worse.

The judges sit arrayed in the same way they were when they tested me. Nothing about them has changed, not even their clothing. It's like they've been waiting, frozen in time until I had to see them again.

"Have a seat," Bird-Mask says to me. He gestures to a stool on my left. Somehow I make it over there and sit down, though it feels like I can't move and like my body is moving on its own all at once.

"Welcome," Bird-Mask says. He is once again the spokesman, but that makes sense.

"What case would you present to us?" he asks.

My mind empties, and for a moment, I panic, unable to remember what to say. But when I open my mouth, words start spilling out.

"There's fighting outside right now."

"We hear it," Bird-Mask says.

"And you aren't going to do anything about it?"

Bird-Mask stares at me in silence, and my face warms.

"Show proper respect, slave girl," Emperor Pakel seethes. He turns to the judges. "I apologize. This girl is why I had to insist on the extra security outside the Halls of Virtue."

"This girl is?" Bird-Mask repeats, though he knows who I am. He called me Nahan's heir. He knows who the emperor is to me. But they're sitting there talking about me like I'm not here while they insist I show respect. Where were the judges when my birth parents were killed? Where were they when I lay burning on the pile of rubble that used to be my home?

Everywhere in Gazidah, from the palace to the slave quarters, they treat me like I have no voice. And I've believed them. My hands ball into fists. I'm better than this. And I'm tired of being used.

The emperor continues his platitudes to the judges, and the so-called impartial animal-masked men listen intently to his words. I don't even know what he's saying, but he ends his statement with, "We will end this quickly and let you return to your peace."

His voice clicks something into place in my mind. I turn sharply to Pakel, and I snap, "Yes, we will end this quickly."

I turn back to the judges, whose eyes refocus on me from behind their masks. "You should have received my records from the archives."

Bird-Mask nods. "We have."

"Then you know I'm here to make my claim for my mother's estate. So why ask me why I'm here?"

This time, another man, Horse-Mask, answers. "It is a formality."

"People are dying outside, and you're concerned with formality." It isn't a question. Aba is right. This empire is broken.

Emperor Pakel balks, and Shaha Saretha chuckles.

"You've underestimated the girl," she says under her breath.

The emperor doesn't respond to her. Instead, he addresses the judges. "I am here to contest her claim." He gestures to me. "As you can see, she does not have the decorum or upbringing appropriate for the station she pretends to."

The judges' masks obscure any reaction they may have had to that, but my face warms, and I tremble with rage.

"It is your fault I don't have the 'decorum', and as for my upbringing, I will not allow you to insult my parents here."

"Your parents are dead," Emperor Pakel scoffs.

I meet his glare, for once unwilling to back down. "My birth parents were murdered. My parents live, and I'm here to free them."

I turn back to the judges, who have been watching this exchange impassively.

Bird-Mask speaks to me. "State your case, Nahan's heir."

I swallow. The argument I rehearsed with Enra and Osman in the archive is entirely gone. The only things I have are the thoughts in my mind. Every time I've been in a forum like this, at Aba's secret meetings, in the palace court, and now here, someone has told me what to say, and I've said it. Now I can't do that even if I wanted to. But I don't want to. I don't know how this will turn out, but at least this time, I will speak freely.

"I may be Datu Nahan's heir, but my claim is not for him. Today, I'm not his heir but Meti's. It is her I speak for. I have few memories of my birth mother, and most of them—"

I glance at the emperor.

"Are heartbreaking. But I chose to remember her for her voice, her beauty, her happiness, and her love for my brother and for me. She is the one who left me her land and title, her life from before she became the diyan. And who knows, maybe if she had never married the datu, she'd still be alive right now. But she isn't, and I'm here in her place.

"I'm also here in the place of my mother and father, of my sister and my brothers. Here on behalf of thousands unable to live freely, despite the Ajudakai Akori's promises. I want to make good on that promise, the one made by my ancestors— not the emperor's—so that I can hold my head high and face the people with honor. And maybe I don't deserve to. But even if I don't, I couldn't live with myself if I didn't try."

The words spill out of me, and when I'm done, I take a deep breath as if I'd been running.

There is a deafening silence as the judges nod to one another. "We will confer. Wait here until we return with our judgment."

They exit the courtyard, and four guards enter, presumably to keep us safe. Emperor Pakel glowers at me. I wouldn't be surprised if he pulled a knife from his robes and killed me right now. At least the guards can prevent that.

The courtyard is quiet. The sounds of fighting have died down, and all I hear is the occasional bird chirping and the wind rustling the leaves of the trees.

But a familiar laugh breaks through the quiet as Shaha Saretha stands. "This has been most entertaining. I will return to the palace."

"What? We aren't finished!" Emperor Pakel insists.

"Yes we are," Shaha Saretha answers.

Some unspoken conversation happens between them, but unlike the ones I've witnessed between Aba and Ima or even Obipae Kula and Enipae Gowan, there is no sign of agreement or even care in this one. Emperor Pakel reaches out and grabs Empress Saretha's arm, but she wrenches it away as though someone had burned her.

"You can't go far without me," he says to her.

The room becomes oppressively hot as Empress Saretha levels a glare at Emperor Pakel. "I don't need to."

The emperor lets her go, and she walks around him to go back down the dirt walk way between us.

As she passes, I muster all the courage I have left to ask her, "Where did you get your tattoos?"

She turns to me sharply and clicks her tongue. "I wondered if you'd ever ask. They are older than yours. Much older."

And with that non-answer, she leaves the courtyard.

CHAPTER 41

I'm not sure how much time passes with Emperor Pakel and I and four guards in the courtyard. The emperor refuses to face me, but it's just as well. We have nothing to say to one another.

But my heart pounds and my mouth dries as we wait for the judges. They could reach any verdict. Considering my absurd speech, it wouldn't be shocking if they reject me and give my birth mother's estate back to the palace. How could I have said all that?

After a few minutes, Emperor Pakel turns to me. But instead of leveling curses at me, he says, "You are a fool."

I nod. "I probably am."

"This will change nothing."

At that, I shake my head. Even if it does nothing else, it's changed me. I hope that counts for something.

The emperor is quiet for a moment, and then he asks, "What about your brother?"

Duin. But Emperor Pakel doesn't know where he is either. So there's a chance I can find him first.

"I will protect him," I say, sounding more confident than I

feel. But I know it's true. I will do everything in my power to find Duin and make sure he and the rest of my family are safe.

After what feels like hours, the masked judges return to the courtyard.

They file in and sit on the same stools they'd sat on before.

I wrap my arms around myself to keep from shaking.

"We have come to a consensus," Bird-Mask says.

There is a long, painful pause.

Emperor Pakel taps his foot impatiently, and I remind myself to breathe.

"The claim of Meti's heir is sound. She has been granted the title of Sali Liani, Lady of Eutu in the Min Kingdom as the rightful owner of the land of Onide. All contestations must be brought to the high court of Gazidah. You are dismissed."

Emperor Pakel gapes, then he stands and whirls at me. But instead of saying anything, he gives me a look that could kill before storming out of the courtyard. He will make my life difficult. But then, I plan to do the same for him.

I stand and turn to leave, but before I do, I remember my manners for once today and bow to the judges. "Thank you."

Bird-Mask nods to me. "We will see you again, Sali Liani."

They know I'll be back, hopefully with a major change to the law in tow.

I exit the courtyard and walk back down the long hallway. The sounds of fighting outside have stopped, but I still pause in front of the door. I reach for it, but there's a loud creak as it swings open before I can touch it. I have to take several steps back as Enra comes barreling in.

It takes a moment for him to realize I'm standing right there, and he comes to an abrupt stop.

"Lia!"

I feel suddenly awkward. "Hello Enra."

He's wounded. There are deep cuts on his face and arms,

and I notice an unsettling amount of blood on the front of his tunic. I reach out despite myself, but his voice stops me.

"What happened?"

His eyes are wide, and he hasn't quite caught his breath from running—or fighting, I'm not sure which.

"The emperor and empress just left," I say.

"I saw them," Enra answers. "They took many of their soldiers with them. The fighting kind of died down once you were inside and some citizens took up arms to help us. But what did the judges say?"

"I'm now the Sali of Onide," I tell him, and Enra breaks into a grin.

"You did it."

"I… I did."

I'm tempted to disbelieve it, to think that I was wounded in the fighting and this is some kind of dream right now. But with Enra here, I know that's not true. I really succeeded.

The truth hits me like a bolt of lightning, and I break down into tears. Enra wraps an arm around me as I weep.

It's not over, but I've finally made a step in the right direction.

When all my tears are spent, Enra pats my shoulders. "We need to get back to the palace. There's something you need to see."

THE JOURNEY to the palace is unsettlingly peaceful. The sun has completely set, but the buildings in the city still have a bit of an orange halo to them. Candlelight flickers in windows as we pass them. You'd never know there was fighting in the streets just hours ago. This city is quite resilient.

When we reach the palace, Enra takes my hand and leads me through its halls. I let him guide me, and after several quick turns and many curious glances, we arrive at a location I recognize—the courtyard where Shaha Saretha "debuted" me. It's once again full of people milling around in the lamplight, and once again, they all turn to me when I enter, their voices quieting to whispers.

I search the crowd for familiar faces and notice one. Lady Zemuri is here, closest to the front. She gives a small bow of greeting. Behind her are some nobles I recognize from a few of the functions I've attended. I have to keep myself from gaping when I realize that Satrap Paykhan is here with his brothers, including Malik Tusun. Obipae Kula and Enipae Gowan aren't far, and the rest of the courtyard is filled with people I don't know.

I turn to Enra, who smiles. "They want to hear what you have to say."

"I brought a few sympathetic colleagues," Lady Zemuri adds, "as well as some who are more...open minded."

Tears spring to my eyes, but I blink them back. I can't believe so many would defy Emperor Pakel, but then maybe they've just been waiting for a chance. After all, his coup upended their lives too.

Everyone watches me, expecting me to say something. The only speeches I'm used to giving are the ones I gave to groups of slaves, convincing them I could free them. But I don't think the same thing would work here.

What would convince them? I don't know. The only thing I can think of to do is tell the truth and hope for the best. As soon as I've decided, Obipae Kula smiles, as if she's read my mind. If she has, this time I find it encouraging.

"I'm sure you all know who I am," I start, my voice shaky. "And you certainly know what I want to do. You wouldn't be here if you didn't. I want to finish what my grandfather started, and I could tell you it's for his legacy, and maybe you'd respect that. But to be honest, that isn't exactly true.

"I want this for my family, the ones who saved me, so they can live freely like I now can. And for all the families who'll have a future they never could have imagined. I want it so that no one has to live in fear of someone else controlling their lives because of who birthed them."

I pause and take a deep breath. They're still watching me. They're still listening. So I barrel forward.

"I know things will change, and it'll be difficult. To make it easier, I could tell you that your place in history will be secured, and you will be remembered as heroes, and that's probably true. But what's truer is that even if no one remembers it, you will have done the right thing."

When I finish, it's quiet, and my heart pounds in my ears, but after a moment, a man, one of Satrap Paykhan's brothers, asks, "How do you expect to make the transition easier, Sali?"

Before I can answer, a man in the back suggests, "Why wouldn't we make the process similar to indentured servitude?"

That gets several responses. I glance at Enra again, who grins and extends a hand to help me into the group. Now, the negotiation begins.

CHAPTER 42

"Are you sure about this?" Enra asks.

We're once again sitting in the archive at a wooden table. The conversation with the nobles was a few days ago, and it went well, better than I expected. We actually reached a preliminary agreement before midnight. It's being completed here by scholars and the senior members of the court with the proper language necessary to change the law. Then it will be ratified, and the institution that's plagued my family and so many others will end. I still can't quite believe it's happening, but it is. But that's not what Enra and I are here to work on.

This time, instead of stacks of parchment and stone, only two scrolls lay on the table in front of us. It's a sunny day, and rays of light beam in through the tall windows, creating a crown of daylight on Enra's head. Normally, that would make him more princely, but right now, it just highlights his concern.

I nod. "We've already talked it through. And I'm sure."

"But—" he starts, but I cut him off.

"I finally have the authority to make this decision myself, and I have decided what to do."

"But, I will release—"

"Do you really want to?" I ask him.

Enra taps a finger on the table. "I… no." He turns to me, a sheepish half-smile on his face. "No, I don't want to."

We've spent days dancing around the subject, but yesterday, Enra came to me and said he would dissolve our betrothal.

I don't know why it shocked me. Perhaps I was surprised he'd actually do it, and—a part of me admits—perhaps I didn't want him to..

My heart flutters, and my words get lost, but Osman clears his throat, drawing our attention back to him.

"If a decision has been made…"

It's my turn to smile sheepishly. "I'm sorry. We've decided."

"Then sign whenever you're ready."

The original marriage contract between Enra and I sits in front of us, signed by his father and mine. Next to it is my own addendum to protect myself, my family, and Duin, should… no, when I find him. When I marry, my property will be divided up between my siblings, and my title will go to Duin, so the rule of Eutu will stay in my family.

I'm still frustrated that Enra never told me about this contract, but it was my father's wish, and I… well… I could certainly do worse than to marry the man who has stood by my side through the worst time of my life. Besides, he is handsome.

So I sign my name to the addendum and hand the quill to Enra, and he does the same.

We exchange a glance as the archivist waves a hand over the parchment to dry the ink. I fight back a blush.

Osman bows. "Thank you. We will have the appropriate copies drawn up."

"That's done," Enra says.

"Yes," I agree.

"Now…" his voice trails off, but I know what he means.

We still have work to do. I nod, and together, we turn toward the section of the archives where the abolition agreement is being written.

I RAISE my palm into the air blowing around my open carriage, closing my eyes and enjoying the warmth.

The breeze cools my face as I turn my closed eyes to the sun. I can smell the sea on the wind, but I know it's my imagination. We've still got a distance to travel.

"Are we almost there?" Atar asks.

I open my eyes to see him on a horse—his own horse.

I laugh. "No. We're still days away."

Atar groans. "Every time I ask, we're still days away."

"Then stop asking every day."

Atar rolls his eyes. "I'm riding forward."

He spurs his horse faster as I call after him. "Don't go too far."

Aba rides up and calls. "Listen to your sister!"

He gives me a long-suffering glance and shakes his head. "He will be the death of me."

I laugh again. "Not so, Aba. He'd have to do a lot worse than that."

Aba laughs too, but then his expression turns serious. "You've done so much, Lia, and you still have a long journey ahead."

I glance beside me at Jorra and Ima. Jorra leans against Ima's shoulder, fast asleep, but Ima nods.

"I know," I say to Aba. "But I wanted you all to be free. And Onide is mine now."

I bought my family's freedom as soon as I got access to my birth mother's funds, and now I'm taking them home. It's not a home on the coast of Uze, but the coast of Min will have to do. After all, it is actually ours. The court will ratify the new law soon, but I didn't want them to have to wait.

Aba nods. "It's for the best that I remain far from you."

That hurts my heart. "Aba—"

He stops me. "No, it is. My foolishness will be a stain on you going forward. The less visible it is, the more you will accomplish."

I frown at my hands, not knowing what to say. My hastiness started all this in the first place, but I think I've finally turned my mistake into something good.

"You will accomplish so much," Aba continues. "I am proud of you, my daughter."

I look back up at him, and he repeats himself. "I'm proud of you, Lia."

Smiling, I resist the urge to cry. "Thank you, Aba."

I turn back to the road, trying to see how far Atar has gone. He's several hundred yards ahead, but we'll catch up to him soon.

We all will.

The End

ABOUT THE AUTHOR

Wendelyn Vega is an author, poet, and international woman of timidity. She's also a language-enthusiast, fledgling artist, and constant daydreamer. When she's not writing, she enjoys reading, trying out new recipes, spending time with her husband, and playing with the three mini tigers she keeps in her house.

ALSO BY WENDELYN VEGA

Kulebra

My Head Bowed: A Chapbook on Depression, Anxiety, and Faith

My Eyes Closed: A Chapbook on Identity, Grief, and Hope

www.ingramcontent.com/pod-product-compliance
Lightning Source LLC
Chambersburg PA
CBHW061752190726
48289CB00007B/1925